SWELTER

What Reviewers Say About
D. Jackson Leigh's Work

"*Call Me Softly* is a thrilling and enthralling novel of love, lies, intrigue and Southern charm."—*Bibliophilic Book Blog*

"D. Jackson Leigh understands the value of branding and delivers more of the familiar and welcome story elements that set her novels apart from other authors in the romance genre."—*The Rainbow Reader*

"Her prose is clean, lean, and mean—elegantly descriptive..." —*Out in Print*

"Leigh writes with an emotion that she in turn gives to the characters, allowing us insight into their personalities and their very souls. Filled with fantastic imagery and the down-to-earth flaws that are sometimes the characters' greatest strengths, this first Dragon Horse War is a story not to be missed. The writing is flawless, the story, breath-taking."—*Lambda Literary Society*

By the Author

Cherokee Falls series:

Bareback

Longshot

Every Second Counts

Romance:

Call Me Softly

Touch Me Gently

Hold Me Forever

Riding Passion

Swelter

Dragon Horse War series:

The Calling

Tracker and the Spy

SWELTER

by

D. Jackson Leigh

2016

ISBN 13: 978-1-62639-795-8

This Trade Paperback Original Is Published By
Bold Strokes Books, Inc.
P.O. Box 249
Valley Falls, NY 12185

First Edition: December 2016

CREDITS
EDITOR: SHELLEY THRASHER
PRODUCTION DESIGN: SUSAN RAMUNDO
COVER DESIGN BY SHERI (GRAPHICARTIST2020@HOTMAIL.COM)

Acknowledgments

Thanks always to my incredible editor, Dr. Shelley Thrasher. I always approach the editing process with a light heart because of my trust in her expert hand. A special thanks to my fellow writer VK Powell for an excellent beta read, but mostly for letting me crash her place on the weekend so she can talk me through my writer's block and brainstorm ideas for the plot in this book. She is really, really awesome. I can't express how much her friendship means to me.

CHAPTER ONE

A droplet of perspiration tickled its way along Teal "TJ" Giovanni's temple to her neck and traced across her collarbone. She stared down, eyes half-hooded, at the woman whose torso she straddled—the very powerful, stunningly gorgeous, and absolutely naked Senator Lauren Abbott.

"You're so beautiful, TJ, so very beautiful." Lauren's sultry alto was as tangible as the stroke of her long fingers that penetrated TJ with each rocking motion. Her touch sent tingles of electricity racing across TJ's skin. Lauren's subtle sweet musk perfume filled her every breath. TJ was a tuning fork vibrating to a higher pitch with each whispered encouragement and moan of pleasure. Lauren's two fingers withdrew and three returned, stretching her as Lauren slid back inside and gently rubbed her thumb against TJ's straining clit.

"Good. It feels so good." TJ shifted more upright, arms braced for leverage, and strained to reach that elusive peak. She'd already come three times in the past hour, but Lauren was insatiable.

"Come for me, baby. I want you to come in my hand." It seemed that each time they were together, she was trying to beat her previous record of how many times she could make TJ climax in one session of sex.

She closed her eyes and rocked faster. "Close. So close. I want to. Don't know if I can, again." The droplet of perspiration clinging to her collarbone fattened from her exertions and shook loose to roll a determined path between her breasts. With her eyes closed, she concentrated on the stroke of Lauren's fingers and willed her orgasm to gather like that droplet of sweat now meandering down the flat plane of her belly.

"Yes, you can. You can do anything I ask you to."

That was true, wasn't it? TJ always managed to do whatever Lauren asked. That's why she'd leap-frogged over a line of more experienced congressional aides to become the senator's right hand. Screw 'em if they wanted to say it was because she'd slept her way into the job. This wasn't about the job.

"Look at me, darling."

TJ obeyed, staring down into eyes as blue as the sky, eyes that gazed back at her with such hunger, and her clit incredibly swelled more and throbbed harder.

"I love being inside you." Lauren's hand that gripped TJ's hip to guide her motion moved to TJ's breast and pinched her nipple. The jolt made her jerk.

"You like that." Lauren hummed and smiled at TJ's whimper, then pinched the tender nipple again. "Now you're going to come for me." She curled her fingers inside, added pressure with her thumb, and thrust hard in counterpoint to TJ's now frantic up-and-down pumping.

"Oh, Lauren...I—" TJ sucked in a breath as the diffused pleasure coalesced into a roiling sphere deep in her belly. Without exhaling, she sucked in a second breath and held it as the sphere exploded and her body bowed in the grip of the most exquisite few seconds of pleasure a woman can experience. Her heart missed a few beats. She didn't see stars, but she was sure she heard bells ringing.

Then she was instantly pushed onto her back, and Lauren... wait, where did she—"Lauren?" Dazed by her climax and abrupt loss of Lauren's body heat, TJ struggled to make her arms and legs move, then settled for turning her head toward Lauren's voice. Lauren was in motion, her cell phone held to her ear. That must have been the ringing she'd heard.

"Fuck. Everything's in place to get me out of here, right?" Gone was sultry Lauren. This was the tough-talking Senator Lauren Abbott who chaired congressional hearing panels and filibustered until her party got the votes they needed for whatever piece of legislation they were trying to push through. She used the bed sheet to wipe TJ from her hand, then dry between her own legs. "Have you contacted Paul?" She stepped into her panties as she listened to the caller, then pulled on her slacks. "Hold on a minute."

Lauren dropped the phone onto the bed and picked up her blouse and bra from the floor. She stuffed the bra into her purse and shrugged into the blouse, buttoning it as she walked to a door that led to an adjoining hotel room and unlocked it.

"Lauren?" TJ sat up, her hormone-fogged brain starting to clear. She was beginning to feel very exposed and self-conscious since she was the only one still naked. She looked for the sheet Lauren had left bunched on the king-sized bed after she used it as a towel. "What's going on?"

TJ reached for the sheet, and Lauren was picking up her phone again when the door she'd unlocked swung open and her number-two congressional aide, Jeff Johansen, stepped into the room. TJ forgot the sheet and lunged for the blanket at her feet, pulling it up to cover her nakedness. "What the hell, Jeff? Get out!"

Jeff ignored her, and Lauren didn't even glance her way as she searched around the room for her shoes and sat to put them on.

"We're lucky that Congress is in recess for the long Memorial Day holiday," Jeff said.

Lauren rose and strode into the bathroom.

Jeff raised his voice to be heard over the water and Lauren brushing her teeth. "Paul's at the house getting some things together. He said he'd ask your housekeeper to pack for you. I've booked you in a private, secluded house on the South Carolina coast."

Lauren's voice sounded from the open bathroom door. "God, you know how I hate the beach, Jeff."

"The mountain alternative we had on retainer wasn't available. As it was, we had to pay extra to buy off the people who had the beach place booked."

"I'm sure I'll hear about that from Paul." She pointed to her suitcase that was sitting on the floor next to TJ's, and Jeff picked it up. "He loves to act like I'm spending his money rather than mine."

TJ's heart sank. Whatever the crisis, it was clear that their plans were not going to happen. After tonight here in Boston, they were planning to drive to the Cape to spend the weekend with a couple of friends Lauren trusted.

Jeff shouldered Lauren's bag. "We'll issue a statement that you and Paul are on a second honeymoon and left orders not to be disturbed unless there's a world crisis. That should give us a few days for the media frenzy to die down. Maybe something more catastrophic will happen, and you'll be relegated to the back pages. If not, it will give us time to find out exactly what they have and which scenario we need to deploy to handle this situation."

"What situation?" TJ scooted to the edge of the bed and stood, the blanket and her anger wrapped tightly around her. Teal Juliette Giovanni had worked her way to the senator's side by being hard-nosed and indispensable before she'd ever slept with Lauren. She wasn't going to start being a pushover now. "Tell me what the hell is going on."

They both turned to her with blank expressions, then to each other. The look that passed between them said a million things, none of which TJ could interpret. The muscle in Lauren's jaw worked and she drew in a deep breath, then waved Jeff toward the door that led to the other room.

"Go ahead, Jeff. Give us a minute."

"We don't have much time, Senator. The media's been tipped off that you're here. It's only a matter of time before they start prowling the place floor by floor or hack into the hotel's system to get your room number. Nothing's safe anymore."

"Two minutes."

He nodded and left, pulling the door closed. Lauren turned to her.

"What the hell, Lauren?" TJ was used to rolling with schedule changes. She had accepted many interrupted dates they'd arranged over the two years they'd been lovers. But, damn it, she didn't like being ignored.

Lauren stepped close, cupping TJ's face in her hands. Her eyes that burned bright with desire only moments before were blue steel now. Her lips were soft but quick. The kiss held no apology. It was more like a handshake on a deal completed.

TJ's stomach lurched with the sudden realization that something was way off kilter. "Where are you going?" She was Lauren's right hand. Why did Jeff know about these apparently secret arrangements and she didn't? Second honeymoon? That was ludicrous. Lauren had told her that Paul didn't mind her lesbian lovers because he had a stable of male and female lovers. They were careful, and their pseudo marriage benefitted both of their careers.

Lauren dropped her hands to TJ's shoulders and met her gaze without flinching. "TJ, I want you to listen to me closely. Don't say anything because I don't have time to argue or repeat what I'm going to say." She drew a deep breath. "We've been found out. It doesn't matter how or when. What does matter is that a lesbian lover will undermine everything I've worked for my entire career. So, this is where we end." She smiled ruefully. "You know I always have a back-up plan, and a back-up if that plan fails, too. Jeff knows about the plan because I didn't want you to know. It would have always been hanging over our heads and ruined our fun because you'd always be waiting for the ax to drop."

TJ stared at Lauren's mask of stoic resolve, eyes completely absent of the affection and desire they'd held only moments before. She was stunned. "I don't understand."

Lauren released her and stepped back, glancing at the clock on the bedside table. "I know you don't. Take a shower and get dressed. Jeff will be back with instructions for you. Don't leave until he returns." She hesitated. "Please. I tried to be generous with the arrangements."

TJ's brain began to thaw and put the pieces together at the super speed that had rocketed her career in the political world. She hadn't worked this hard to give up so easily. "Are you telling me that you're not only dumping me, but that I'm also out of a job? What if I don't want to go quietly?"

Lauren went still, her eyes narrowing. "If you try to make trouble, I'll make sure you never work in politics again. Not even to get a chicken farmer elected to Podunk City Council. Do what Jeff tells you, disappear for a while, and you'll still have a future." She walked away but paused with her hand on the door. She spoke without turning back to face TJ. Her voice was soft now, the hard edge of her threat gone. "Some things are more important than us, TJ. Duty to our country is greater than the pleasure we've enjoyed with each other."

"Enjoyed with each other?"

Lauren had never made promises, but she'd talked many times of whimsical things like finding a wrinkle in time and disappearing together for long periods to be alone without anyone noticing. Lauren often left small, surprise gifts in TJ's desk or in her messenger bag or had them sent to her apartment. She rarely said "I love you" in the context that a lover would say it, but she'd said it. The first time had been when TJ had convinced Senator Noe to change his position and give Lauren the swing vote she needed to get her education bill approved. Lauren had hugged her in the office, right in front of everybody, and declared, "That's why I love you."

Lauren lowered her head, her face shadowed as she stared at her hand where it rested on the door's handle.

"Look at me, Lauren."

Lauren straightened and turned to her. Not Lauren, her lover. Senator Lauren Abbott, with her trademark raised eyebrow and penetrating stare.

"I cared for you. I thought…I thought you cared for me." TJ cursed the break in her voice, but she didn't cry. She was glad she didn't cry.

Senator Abbott held her gaze. "Good-bye, TJ."

The door closed behind her with a loud click.

❖

August Reese rubbed her fingers in a circular motion against the throbbing in her temple and tried to focus once again on the client's case folder spread across her desk.

Christine hadn't come home from her business dinner until nearly three in the morning, then refused to even acknowledge her demand for an explanation. She'd simply gathered some clothes from their bedroom and locked herself in the guest suite. Again.

August had barely slept at all. She'd given up trying shortly before dawn and came into the office early. Then she'd stimulated her sluggish brain with too much caffeine and acquiesced to her queasy stomach's refusal of food. No wonder her head was pounding.

A light knock sounded on her open office door. Her favorite paralegal stood in the doorway.

"Susan, come in."

"I'm sorry to interrupt. You look busy." Only a few weeks past her twenty-eighth birthday, Susan dressed and carried herself in a much more mature, professional manner than most of her peers. August attributed that to everything the young woman had survived. Susan's Army Ranger husband had been killed in an ambush during his second tour in Afghanistan. Only a month before his death, she'd found out she was pregnant. The military survivor benefits were a great supplement to her paralegal salary, but August figured raising twins alone had helped hone Susan's superior organizational skills.

"I've got time if you need something. What's up?"

Susan glanced quickly down the hallway, then stepped into August's office and closed the door behind her. She sat in one of the two wingback chairs in front of August's desk and fingered a decorative upholstery stud that had worked loose. August had bought the two chairs at a yard sale when she and Christine first opened their practice, and she'd reupholstered them herself with a fake leather material. Christine had threatened to throw them out many times since, but August liked keeping a reminder of those early days when they answered their own phones and had one part-time paralegal. They hadn't had much money, but they were happier.

"I just wanted to tell you that I'm turning in my resignation." She half rose to lay an envelope on August's desk, then sank into the chair again. "I'm sorry. I know you have a lot of cases pending, but today is my last day."

"Is everything okay? I mean—" August rubbed her temple and started over. "You leaving will be a big loss to this firm, Susan. Can I do anything to change your mind?"

Susan's brow furrowed as she avoided August's gaze.

"Did someone offer you more money or a more flexible schedule? Give me a chance to match or better whatever they've offered." August opened her desk drawer and dug out her bottle of one hundred aspirins to shake three into her hand. She grabbed the bottle of water sitting on her desk and washed them down before turning her attention back to Susan.

Susan stared down at her lap. "Nothing like that. You've been great, August."

"I can't believe another firm wouldn't allow you to give—" She stopped. "The twins are okay, aren't they? I don't want to pry into your personal life, but we've worked together since they were babies."

Susan smiled briefly. "The girls are fine." She shook her head. "Different as night and day. One's all frills and the other a tomboy." Susan glanced up at August, then back toward the closed door. August sat forward in her chair. Something *was* wrong. The pounding in her head ratcheted up a notch and she massaged her forehead.

"Are you okay?" Susan sat forward, her expression worried.

August pinched the bridge of her nose, as if that could shut off the pain. "I woke up with a headache that I can't seem to shake." She gestured to the drawer where she kept her pills. "That was my third dose of aspirin. They don't seem to be helping."

"Did you eat breakfast?"

"No. My stomach is sort of queasy, too."

"Let's go to that new coffee shop down the street. You need some bread in your stomach, some chocolate, and extra caffeine."

"I don't think I can drink any more coffee right now."

"They have bagels, croissants, and the best hot chocolate I've tasted. They also sell those chocolate-covered espresso beans you like." Susan nodded toward the door and mouthed, *We'll talk there.*

"Okay. It can't make me feel any worse."

Mid-morning translated into few customers at The Infusion, but the staff was busy reloading after the breakfast rush and preparing the few sandwiches they offered for lunch. So, their order was filled quickly, and they sat at a small table in the back corner for privacy and to get August away from the bright sun coming through the windows at the front.

August watched most of the whipped cream melt into her hot chocolate before she took a sip. She could almost feel her sinuses open and the pain lessen as she held the cup close and breathed in the steamy aroma. She stared down at the huge cinnamon roll Susan had insisted she buy, and her stomach growled its approval. She put her cup down, pulled off a small section, and popped it into her mouth. Another sip of cocoa. August felt Susan watching her, so she looked up and smiled. "Thanks. This is making me feel better."

Susan's smile was tentative. Then she glanced nervously about the shop.

"I hope you know you can talk to me," August said gently. "Whatever we discuss in here will be handled with the utmost discretion."

Susan took a sip of her sparkling water, then looked up at August. "I don't have another job, but I can't work there anymore."

August sat back in surprise at Susan's blurted words, then took a slow sip from her mug to give her racing mind a chance to digest the implication.

"I know Christine can be a bitch sometimes, but you always seem to handle her. Is one of the other employees bothering you? I can straighten that out pretty quick."

Susan edged forward, her voice low. "Shady things are going on. I've tried to ignore it because I work mainly for you, and your name hasn't been on any of their paperwork. I told myself that you didn't know anything about what Christine's doing, and I've held my tongue because that Delgado guy scares the hell out of me."

August was stunned. Then she was instantly angry. Raphael Delgado, a freshly minted junior attorney Christine had taken under her wing as a law student, was the son of their biggest client, Luis Reyes. Was he using their office for something illegal? "What kind of shady things?" She put her mug down. "I need you to be specific, Susan."

"I'm talking about making witnesses disappear or go silent, and purposely letting a man go to prison to keep the real culprit on the streets."

"Those are pretty serious accusations." They weren't the kind of things Susan could have read in a case file.

"Did you know that when they put in the new central air, the duct to my office connects right to Christine's? When the compressor fan clicks off and she's working in her sitting area rather than at her desk, I can hear every word she and Raphael are saying."

August stared at her. "Why didn't you come to me before?"

Susan waved her hand dismissively. "It was nothing I could prove." She folded her hands in her lap and studied them. "And she's your lover. I couldn't expect you to believe me without proof." She looked up again and met August's gaze. "But I think I've found written proof that she's been setting up sham businesses and nonprofits to funnel money into offshore bank accounts."

"To dodge taxes?"

"I think it's to launder drug money. You know most of the criminal cases she handles for Reyes are drug cases that involve his employees or relatives." Susan dropped her gaze, and her next words were hesitant. "I've heard you guys argue about it."

August stood and paced toward the condiment table and back to Susan. Reyes was at the core of most of her domestic turmoil. The minor assault or drug possession cases he'd asked them to handle had been a blessing when their practice was new and they were broke, but August had grown uneasy when the incidents grew in number and cases were suddenly major felonies. It seemed clear to her they were representing a major crime lord, and this wasn't the reputation she wanted for their firm.

Christine disagreed. She thrived on the money and power earned as Reyes's legal eagle.

They'd argued over the nature of the cases—assaults evolved into murder cases and possession into trafficking—so Christine shifted all Reyes's work to her caseload.

Then they'd argued about Raphael. His position wasn't budgeted when Christine hired him without consulting her. A few months later, August had wanted to fire him after several women staffers complained that he'd made inappropriate comments to them. But Christine stepped in, promising he'd be assigned only to her cases and she'd keep a tight rein on him.

Lately, they'd argued mostly over Christine's increasing late-night meetings with Reyes.

August sighed. The last thing she needed was another fight with Christine, but she couldn't let this go. She rubbed her temple again. Hot chocolate and a cinnamon roll weren't going to make this headache go away.

"I have so much respect for you, August. You and Christine gave me a chance and helped me through a really bad time when Matt was killed." Susan's eyes filled with tears. "But Christine has changed. And, when I found out what they're doing now...I have to get out. I have to get my babies away from this."

August stared at her. "What more are they doing?"

Susan wiped at her eyes, then lifted her chin and met August's gaze. "They're putting your name on some of the nonprofit documents so it looks like you're involved. If they implicate you, then I'll be sucked in by association. They want leverage, I suppose, when things finally blow up between you and Christine." Susan abruptly stood and edged toward the door. "I mean, you know, over the Reyes stuff."

August had learned long ago to read the body language of a witness under questioning. Susan's sudden need to escape screamed that she had more to tell, something she hadn't intended to reveal. She stood, too, and rounded the small table to block Susan's path to the door. "What else, Susan? I want to know."

Susan's shoulders slumped and she stared at the floor. "I don't want to hurt you, August."

"Keeping me in the dark isn't helping me. I need to know if I'm going to defend myself."

Susan chewed on her lower lip, then looked up to meet August's gaze. "You're right." She put a steadying hand on her chair as though she needed support. "I came back late one Friday night after being out to a movie with friends because I'd left my cell phone at work. The light was on in Christine's office down the hall, but I figured she was just working late. My phone must have dropped out of my coat pocket, because it was on the floor next to the air vent, and when I bent to pick it up...oh, God." Susan's face reddened. "I wish I could erase it from my memory." She covered her face with her hands.

"Just tell me."

Susan lowered her hands but didn't raise her eyes. "Christine wasn't alone. I could hear Luis Reyes, too. They were…there was no mistaking what they were doing on the sofa in her office."

August felt the blood drain from her, and she slumped back into her chair. She was the one who needed support now. Sure, it'd been months since she and Christine had made love. Actually, longer than that because it'd been more than a year since their couplings felt like more than a simple physical release. But she'd never made the leap to suspect that Christine was actually cheating with another lover, especially a man. Christine had never mentioned being bi-oriented or having male lovers in her past. Her brain pounded painfully in her ears, her stomach twisted, and bile burned the back of her throat. A cool glass bottle—Susan's sparkling water—was pressed into her hand.

"Drink," Susan said. "Just a little."

August sipped at the liquid, if only to soothe the acid in her throat and wash the vile taste from her mouth. Then she closed her eyes and held the glass to her temple for a moment. "I'm okay." She opened her eyes and wearily met Susan's worried gaze. "Christine came home around three a.m. last night, and we had another fight. I didn't sleep at all." She rubbed her forehead again. "That's why I have a headache."

Susan sat again and waited as August held the cold bottle to her temple and gathered her thoughts. The news wasn't really such a surprise. In the back of August's mind and deep in her soul, she knew she and Christine were done, but she had refused to acknowledge it or do anything to change it. It was time to get her head out of the sand. Her heart walled off and her lawyer brain kicked in. "Put that resignation letter back in your purse, then go write us down on the schedule as out of the office for the rest of the afternoon to take depositions on a farm-machinery accident."

"You don't do those kinds of cases."

"Christine has been pestering me to branch out and accept cases that generate more money. Ambulance-chasing brings in lots of money."

Susan frowned. "I really am resigning."

August looked up at her. "I know. But we both need to make sure our exits from this practice don't look like we're leaving because we're guilty of something." She grasped Susan's hand. "Trust me, okay? I want to make sure you and the twins are protected. If Reyes decides to go after somebody when this explodes, I want it to be me." She stood. "Let's go back so you can sign us out. I want to grab some things from my office. Then I'm going to follow you to your home to make sure you're safe. Stay there until I call you. I need to think and set up a meeting with my attorney."

CHAPTER TWO

TJ eyed the temperature gauge on her old Honda Civic.
Not TJ. Teal. She'd left the whip-smart Ivy-league graduate TJ Giovanni behind in the Washington, DC, apartment Lauren had rented for her. She was once again Teal Crawley, the farm girl she'd buried when she'd taken her mother's maiden name and escaped her ultra-conservative father's Pennsylvania dairy farm. TJ needed to disappear for a while, so she'd serve a second sentence as that farm girl until she'd paid for her failure in the fast lane.

She watched the gauge's needle climb as steadily as the record-breaking temperatures currently cooking the Southern states. Was that a wisp of white steam curling from under the hood or just the heat shimmering up from the two-lane blacktop highway that had seemed to go on forever? Damn. She'd refilled the coolant in Missouri. That was several hundred miles ago, but she'd hoped to make it to her cousin's small ranch in New Mexico without stopping for an expensive repair. The way her luck was running, the problem would be a leaky ten-dollar hose that required removing the entire engine to replace.

Congressional aides didn't make much money when you deducted the cost of living in DC. She'd never had to worry about money because Lauren paid for everything—hotels, dinners, even a credit card that she insisted TJ use to buy expensive clothes for the events they'd attended. And, while other aides had multiple roommates to defray the excessive rent charged for basic apartments in downtown DC, Teal had lived in an apartment that Lauren's campaign leased where the building's owner made his private elevator available for a certain powerful senator's late-night visits to her most trusted aide.

So, Lauren had sent more than half of her earnings to her sisters. When their time came, she wanted them to have a chance to escape the farm, too. Then, after paying her living expenses like groceries and utilities, she invested the rest of her meager salary. Her nest egg wasn't huge, but most of it was locked up in short-term, high-yield investments that had two more months to mature. So, her current cash flow was down to a meager few thousand dollars.

Lauren had Jeff deposit a significant "pay-off" in Teal's account, but Teal had withdrawn it all in cash, put it in a plain brown bag, and donated it anonymously to the Human Rights Commission's fight to extend the federal law protecting the workers' rights to all workers, no matter what their sexual or gender orientation. She would have felt like a whore if she kept it.

She debated whether to stop and let the engine cool. The needle appeared to vibrate in the red zone. Hot. Hot. Very hot. Crap. She needed to do something. She should've brought a few jugs of water with her. If she stopped and shut off the engine, it might not crank again. Then what would she do?

A loud pop followed by a few clunks under the hood made the decision for her. The engine died, and Teal wrestled the car off the roadway without power steering. She let it roll as far as momentum would carry it. As if a few feet would make a difference.

Fu—No. She hated Washington's most common curse word. Her granny had said cursing was a sign of coarseness. If America only knew the real personalities of the people they sent to Congress. The majority of those who came from money were scavengers living off the backs of the middle class and poor, and the bootstrap crowd was just a bunch of pigs wearing lipstick. They were the guys you had to avoid standing next to in the elevator or you'd have a hand on your ass for the entire ride. But she'd willingly wallowed in the same political sty. She wouldn't hesitate to use that hand on the ass as political blackmail down the road. Yet she never indulged in their habit of foul language, afraid of slipping up in front of a media camera if she grew accustomed to speaking those words in private conversation.

Perspiration beaded along her forearm, and she pressed the window button. Nothing happened. She checked the ignition. She hadn't switched it off when the engine died. She turned the ignition off and on again, then tried the window. No power. Crap. Whatever happened must have shorted the electrical system, too.

Okay. TJ Giovanni had been a problem solver. She solved problems for very high-powered people. Need a reservation at a restaurant that's been booked for months? She'd take care of it. Need more backers to get your bill out of committee? She'd line them up. Need an evening dress and date for the visiting senator's teen daughter who decided to fly in at the last minute? No problem.

So, Teal Crawley should at least be able to handle a little engine trouble.

The car's interior was quickly becoming an oven, and Teal felt a little queasy. She wished she hadn't eaten that greasy cheeseburger two hours ago. TJ, but not Teal, would have remembered to restock her small cooler with bottled water. Stop it.

One step at a time. She pulled the hood release—thank God it was manually operated—and got out to raise the hood. She was no mechanic, but she'd learned a few basic things while growing up on that dairy farm.

"Shit." So much for her resolve to avoid profanity, but crap, that hood was hot. She could almost feel her skin bubble into a blister. Although she'd shipped most of her belongings ahead, her small car was packed almost to the top. She found a T-shirt in the basket of dirty laundry and used it to protect her hand as she grabbed the release latch again. She groped for the rod to prop up the hood and coughed as steam poured out. Only this wasn't just steam. Smoke.

Sparks flew at the telltale sound of wires shorting. Wet hoses sizzled when flame erupted near the fuel line. "Holy crap!"

Teal scrambled back to the trunk, hastily dumping her belongings on the ground to dig out the fire extinguisher stored in the spare-tire well, praying it would work and she could extinguish the flame before the car exploded. She'd shipped her Washington life—suits and heels to her cousin's ranch, but this car held the real Teal—all of her jeans, T-shirts, running shoes, and boots.

She skidded around the front fender, spraying the engine until the small extinguisher sputtered and spit the last of its chemicals. Her heart thumped a loud counterpoint to the soft tick of the subdued engine as she waited a long moment. When no explosion erupted, she sucked in a huge breath and let it out slowly. Then she lurched to the passenger side of the car and vomited the contents of her stomach onto the dirt. She kicked dirt over the masticated pieces of cheeseburger as she spit bile and saliva on top of the mess, then swiped a shaky hand over her mouth. She really wished she had a bottle of water.

The car crisis could have prompted her reaction, but the heat and dehydration more likely caused it. She hadn't been able to keep much on her nervous stomach since Lauren had walked out of their hotel room and the media scavengers began circling. The legitimate news media lost interest after the initial reporting, but the entertainment and social media bloggers were relentless as long as the public kept lapping it up.

She stumbled back to the trunk and rummaged through her bag for mouthwash. Ah, frosted mint. Better than water. She swigged a mouthful, gargled, swished, and spit. She turned too quickly and braced herself half in, half out of the trunk until a wave of dizziness passed.

"Whoa. Got to watch that." She closed her eyes until the world stopped spinning around her, then slowly withdrew from the trunk and stood. Her head felt like it was stuffed with cotton.

Okay. Deep breath. List the facts of the problem. Brainstorm options. Evaluate and rank possible solutions.

Option number one: find the problem and fix it. Teal walked back to the front of the car and stared down at the now-white hunk of metal and melted hoses. Not a viable solution. Option two: call Triple A. She was so glad she hadn't given in to the temptation to let her membership lapse or opt for the cheaper plan when it had come up for renewal last month. She'd call for a tow. If absolutely necessary, she'd sell the Honda for junk and rent a car. The next town couldn't be that far away, and her GPS had estimated she was a little more than an hour from her destination.

She ducked into the car and retrieved her cell phone from the front passenger seat. Geez. The faux leather seat was already so hot, she'd have to cover it if she wanted to sit while she waited for a tow truck to arrive. Heat seeped through her cut-off jeans where she propped a hip against the Honda. Teal gathered her long, dark hair and held it off her shoulders, silently praying for a breeze—no matter how hot. She punched in the 800 number and listened... to nothing. She checked the phone. Christ almighty. "What? No signal? How can there be no signal?" As if to answer, a message flashed across the phone in red letters. LOW BATTERY. "Great. Just great. There's no signal because I don't have enough power to pick up one."

She unbuttoned the lower half of her sleeveless blouse and tied the tail ends together to leave her lower back and stomach exposed just in case a whisper of breeze happened. Mama would say she looked like a trailer-park hooker, but when the alternative was heat stroke, who would care? Her father would.

"You can't come here, Teal. Those television people are pestering us night and day. Your father has put up No Trespassing *signs, and he even held two of them at gunpoint until the sheriff could come arrest them. Good Lord. When I took the trash to the dump center yesterday, some fellow jumped in the dumpster and pulled the bags out before I had time to leave. He was going through our trash! I don't know what he expected to find in it."*

"I'm so sorry, Mama."

"Give me that phone, woman. You stay away from here, girl."
"Daddy, I never wanted this to involve you and Mama."
"You've not only disgraced yourself, you've disgraced us. We can't hold our heads up in church. You always wanted to be one of those fancy people. Well, get one of them to help you. We're just simple, God-fearing people. You're not one of us anymore. Lose this phone number."

She didn't blame them, really. She'd been pretty full of herself as she climbed higher among the inside ranks in Washington. She hadn't had time to remember birthdays or go home on holidays. When she did visit, it was mostly to see her sisters. Still, she didn't go often because her visits usually devolved into a political argument with her right-wing father, which made everybody's holiday miserable.

Trouble was, her "fancy friends" had all disappeared, too—ducking for political cover. Driving to Canada and getting a waitress job some place where nobody knew her face was starting to look like her only option when her phone had rung one evening. Wade, a second cousin she'd met maybe once, was calling. He said Mama had given him her phone number. He had a small ranch in New Mexico and could use some help in the house and around the barn. Yep, he knew about her problem. As long as she didn't lead the media dogs to his doorstep, they wouldn't likely be able to find her in the remote area where he lived. If you don't like it, you don't have to stay, he'd said. So, she'd agreed. It wasn't like she had a better offer.

He'd hesitated. *You'll be welcome here, Teal.* Then he hung up.

She wasn't sure how to interpret his parting remark. She knew nothing about this guy, but he didn't sound all that old. Geez. Surely Mama wasn't trying to match her up with a second cousin. If that was the case, she'd have to set him straight, so to speak, right away. She sighed. Suck it up, Giovanni. Okay, she might not be the TJ who'd taken Washington by storm, but she was a Giovanni. She hated the Crawley side of her family, and using the name now was a bitter pill to swallow. But she still had some identification under that name, so it was convenient.

She stared at the reddish-brown dust covering her expensive running shoes, her mind suddenly blank. What had she been doing? She shook her head to clear the confusion. Her split second of panic evaporated when the Honda's raised hood came into her peripheral vision. Oh, yeah. She rubbed at the pain that had begun pounding her temple and gathered her thoughts.

Option number three: abandon ship.

She looked north, then south. Tufts of long, coarse grass, an occasional cactus or stubborn scrub of a tree dotted the red, sun-baked earth. The distant, jagged outline of mountains shimmered in the east. Not even a coyote in sight, much less a gas station. When was the last time she passed another car? There was that eighteen-wheeler about an hour ago. She'd spent the past six weeks with hordes of media following her every move and prayed for a moment of solitude. Now, when she actually needed another person—preferably one with transportation or a working phone—she seemed to be the only person on the planet.

She drew a shaky breath. She was so screwed.

August lifted the brown Stetson with one hand and glanced into her rearview mirror to adjust it on her head as she steered down the old state highway. She hadn't worn one of these since she was a kid, showing her grandfather's calves in the junior livestock show at the county fair each summer. She'd even started French-braiding her hair again, rather than leaving it down to soften her angular face. It was more practical in this heat, and if she wanted to hide in plain sight, she needed to blend in with the rest of the ranchers in the area.

"What do you think, Rio?"

The solid-black border collie watching her from the passenger seat yipped her approval.

"Eh, you're biased."

She checked the mirror again. The slight smile that reflected back at her was grim. Under different circumstances, the hat would have been a good look for her. A real chick magnet. Her own hard stare admonished her. Fool. Don't think about her. Just remember that she's the reason your law degree and everything else you've worked for since you passed the bar might as well be compost now.

She jerked the steering wheel when her right tires kicked up a cloud of dust as the truck drifted off the edge of the roadway. Shit. She checked her mirror again—this time for vehicles behind her, just in case someone saw her driving like a drunk because she was busy lecturing herself.

August relaxed at the sight of empty highway behind her, then tensed when she spotted the car pulled off the road ahead. The driver's door was open, and two bare legs with sneaker-covered feet extended out to rest on the pavement. She didn't see any other vehicles ahead or behind her on the long, flat ribbon of highway, which wasn't unusual. Most traffic had shifted to the newer four-lane bypass that opened up about five years before. Was it a trap? Had Reyes already found her? Was she being stupidly paranoid? Maybe. But being paranoid is better than dead.

She slowed the battered ranch pickup to a crawl as she approached. DC plates. Anyone sent by Reyes should be smart enough to use a vehicle with a local license plate. August pulled her truck over about five yards before reaching the car. She left the engine running, ready to throw the truck in reverse, then execute a three-point turn and burn rubber in the opposite direction.

Rio stood in her seat, ears canted forward to catch any sound.

A dark head popped out of the doorway, and then a woman sprang from the car. If Reyes was setting a trap, this would be the bait August would expect him to use. Right now, most guys would be adjusting their pants and warming up a thousand-kilowatt smile at the sight in front of her.

The woman's long, dark hair shone in the afternoon sun, and sweat glistened on the long, smooth slope of her exposed belly. Jean shorts hung low on her slim hips and were cut off a little too short for the shapely legs that seemed to go on for days. She was dressed like any of the small-town local girls looking to hook up with somebody holding a one-way ticket to some place more exciting.

But August wasn't a guy and she saw a different picture.

The DC plate on her car wasn't the only thing screaming that the woman didn't belong here. Her teeth were too perfectly straight and a brilliant white. Her hair, which fell just below the top of her shoulders, was professionally cut in the uneven lengths of a full, flowing style. August would put money on those cut-off jeans being a designer brand. They didn't look like the usual Wrangler or Carhartt clothing brands common in these parts. Also, those weren't outlet-store sneakers. August recognized the Adizero Adios as a favorite among marathon-race enthusiasts, which explained the shapely legs.

August reached under her seat to grab her 9mm Colt Defender, tucking it in the waistband of her jeans at the small of her back as she opened the door and stepped out. "Stay," she said. Rio whined and sat but didn't take her eyes off the stranger.

The woman's quick smile wavered when August remained standing behind her open door. August watched her duck briefly back into the car. When she reappeared, her shirt was untied and straightened to modestly cover her previously exposed belly, and her right hand was tucked casually into the pocket of her shorts. The woman shaded her eyes with her left hand and squinted against the sun's glare. She remained next to her open car door and raised her voice to be heard when August didn't approach either.

"Hi. I'm sort of stranded and my cell phone is dead. Do you have a phone that gets a signal out here so I can call for a tow? I have Triple A."

August dismissed the idea that the woman also had a gun. There was barely enough room in those shorts for her ass, much less a weapon. She stepped out from behind the truck's open door. The woman shifted nervously, withdrawing her hand from her pocket. She was palming a small canister. Probably pepper spray.

August relaxed. She'd read the body language of a lot of witnesses, and this woman was afraid of her. She realized then how she must appear. At a bit over six feet tall and with her hair pulled back, August would appear to be a tall, square-jawed person in dusty jeans and a hat pulled low over the eyes—someone the woman surely interpreted as a man. She was all alone with a disabled car, and August's cautious approach wasn't exactly friendly. August dropped her hands to her sides, turning them so the woman could see they were empty. Then she pushed her hat back on her head and smiled. "I've got a phone, but if you want to go through Triple A, you'll probably have to wait for a tow truck to come out from Tulia. It could be a while."

The woman's posture relaxed, and August swept her hat off for good measure, then started toward her. She held out her hand when the woman met her halfway. "I'm August."

"Teal."

August cocked her head. "As in the color teal?"

Teal crossed her arms over her chest. "Yeah. My mother fancies herself an interior decorator and viewed children as marriage accessories."

Ouch. August tried to read the guarded brown eyes. "I hesitated when I stopped because you were acting sort of suspicious, like someone else might be in your car. Then I realized that if you're from DC like your license plate says, you probably weren't used to seeing a woman wearing a Stetson. You were sticking close to your car because you probably thought I was a guy."

Teal shaded her eyes again and licked her dry lips as she peered at August. "I have to admit that being out here alone… well, every crime story I've ever seen on television was running through my head."

August chuckled. "I can't blame you." She moved around Teal and pointed toward the Honda as she walked. "Like I said, it will take a while for you to get a tow truck way out here. Maybe there's a simple fix that can at least get you to the next town."

"Thanks, but I've already checked. If I could just use your phone for a moment, I'll make the call."

August waved off her protest and rounded the front fender of the Honda. "It's no problem. I know a little bit about engines." She looked down. A small fire extinguisher rested on top of the charred motor. "Well, hell." She grabbed the fire extinguisher and held it up as she stepped around the car to confront Teal. "You didn't say the engine was burned to a crisp."

Teal still stood where they'd met halfway between the vehicles, her hands on her hips and glaring at August. "You didn't give me a chance. I'm not an idiot. I might have DC plates, but I grew up in rural Pennsylvania, thank you very much. I've repaired a tractor engine with nothing but baling wire—" Her face suddenly contorted into a grimace, and she crumpled to the ground.

August raced to her, sliding to a kneeling stop next to her. "What's wrong?"

"Cramp." Teal groaned as she frantically massaged her right calf, then whimpered and clutched at her left thigh. "Oh, oh, crap. Oh, man, that hurts."

August grabbed Teal's right foot and gently extended her leg while pushing the toes upward toward the knee. "You work on the Charlie horse in your thigh. I'll focus on your calf." Teal's jaw was clamped tight, and her nostrils flared as she breathed through the pain in short, rapid puffs. August massaged the rock-hard muscle for several minutes, flexing the foot more as the calf muscle slowly relaxed and softened. She tried not to think about the smooth, tanned skin of the shapely leg slowly becoming more pliant under her touch. Teal's hand stopped hers mid-stroke.

"I'm good now. Thanks."

August looked up into eyes the color of rich chocolate. She realized Teal's face didn't match the tan on her legs. She was pale and her skin was clammy. August hoped the overreaction to her checking the engine was out of character, too. It would be a shame for a woman so beautiful to be a total bitch. "Headache?"

Teal blinked at her. "What?"

"Does your head hurt? And are you nauseous?"

Teal visibly swallowed, then nodded. "I might be a little dehydrated."

August stood. "More than a little. You're probably suffering from heat exhaustion." She picked up her new hat and shook the dust from it.

"I'm not having a heat stroke." Teal tried to stand but cursed when she misjudged the residual soreness from the cramps, lost her balance, and landed on her rear again after August failed in a belated attempt to catch her.

"I said exhaustion, not stroke. But it can be as bad if you don't take care of it. I have air-conditioning in the truck." August picked up her hat she'd dropped again and dusted it a second time, then looked at her watch. BJ needed the pump part she'd gone into town to buy. Without it, eighty-five heifers still nursing babies in the west pasture would go thirsty. Their milk wouldn't dry up in just one day, though. She could go out and fix it at dawn. "I'll drive you to a clinic in the next town. When you're better, you can get someone to come out and tow your car."

"How about while you drive, I'll call Triple A and find out who they contract. You can drop me there. I promise to buy a huge bottle of water and drink all of it. But no clinic."

"You should see a doctor." August extended a hand.

Teal accepted the help and got to her feet, more slowly this time. She avoided August's gaze. "I don't have insurance. No clinic. I'll be okay."

August pursed her lips. "I can't just drop you off at some garage. What if you're not okay?"

Teal straightened her shoulders and raised her chin to look directly into August's eyes. "I'll be fine. I managed on my own in Washington for eight years, so I can certainly survive the rural

Southwest. My GPS said I was close to Caprock anyway. I can call my cousin who lives there to come get me."

"Why didn't you say so? I'm headed that way. My ranch is next to Caprock Canyon. Is your cousin a park ranger?"

"What? No. He's a rancher. Wade Crawley." She frowned. "Why did you ask if he was a park ranger?"

"Because Caprock is a state park," August said.

"Caprock, New Mexico?"

August shook her head, failing in her attempt to hold back a chuckle. "I think your GPS was confused. You're still in the Texas Panhandle."

Teal stared at the ground, her shoulders slumping. For the first time since August had stopped, Teal seemed genuinely shaken, and August instantly regretted laughing.

Teal raised a shaky hand to rub her temple again. "How... how far am I from Caprock, New Mexico?" Her face had gone from pale to ghost white.

"I'm not sure, but probably about two hundred and fifty miles."

Teal closed her eyes. "I don't feel so good." Her words were faint, and when her eyes began to roll back in her head, August instinctively squatted to fold Teal over her shoulder as she collapsed. Teal had the trim body of an avid runner but was only a few inches shorter than August and nothing but lean muscle. August grunted under her weight and moved as quickly as she could toward the truck.

Teal groaned from her upside-down position. "Put me down. I'm going to be sick."

"Almost there." Just a few more feet. August reached for the door handle on the passenger side. "We're here."

Teal struggled weakly. "Down now."

August tightened her grip on Teal's long legs. "One more second. I'm opening the door." She pulled the handle and stepped back to swing the door open when an awful retching sound preceded something warm and wet soaking the back of her jeans.

"And, I'm guessing I'm just a little too late." She gestured for Rio to hop over into the backseat, then bent her knees to quickly but gently deposit Teal where the dog had been. She took a big step back as the poor woman braced against the door's frame to lean out and finish vomiting what little was left in her stomach onto the ground.

August trotted around to the driver's side and rummaged behind the seat. BJ kept the jump seat in the extended cab filled with tools and old rags for fixing things he might come upon when patrolling the eight-hundred-acre ranch. She grabbed a couple of rags and cleaned off her backside as best she could. Ugh. She'd just have to ignore the dampness and puke smell until she could get back to the ranch to change. She laid a few more rags on the seat, not that the dirty upholstery would suffer much from her sitting on it. Then she grabbed her melting fountain drink from the cup holder and rounded the truck again.

Teal was no longer gagging but still sat doubled over with her head between her spread knees.

"Hey. I don't have water, but I have what's left of the Coke I was drinking. It's pretty watered down because the ice has melted, but you could at least wash your mouth out." August took the top off and held out the large cup.

Teal sat up slowly, her eyes bloodshot and watery from retching. She took a mouthful of the diluted soda, swished it around, and spit it on the ground. "I'm so embarrassed," she said, refusing to look at August. Her hand trembled, and she took hold of the cup with both hands to keep from spilling it.

"Are you ready to go to the clinic now?" August put her hand on the door and motioned for Teal to swing her legs into the truck.

"No clinic. Promise me." Teal's protest was barely more than a whisper. She shifted her legs slowly into the truck as though weights were tied to her feet, and August closed the door.

"Lots of people with no insurance go to emergency rooms," August said as she climbed in on the driver's side and started the engine. She adjusted the air-conditioning.

"No." Teal winced at her loud protest. She closed her eyes and covered them with one hand as if too much sunlight were bleeding through her eyelids. "I can't go to a clinic." Less emphatic, but still firm. "Can you...get my purse and the blue duffel from the backseat and lock the car? Then just drop me at a motel. Nothing seedy, but something inexpensive. I'll be fine once I cool off. I'll worry about the car tomorrow when I'm feeling better."

August weighed the efficiency of continuing their debate. "Keys?"

Teal's brow furrowed. Then she dropped the hand covering her eyes and squinted at her car. "Still in the ignition, I think."

August retrieved the requested items, stowed the boxes Teal had hastily unloaded to retrieve the fire extinguisher, and locked the Honda securely. Not that it would matter. If anyone really wanted anything, they could strip the tires and inside of the car easily before any other motorists came along. Judging from the things stuffed in the backseat, Teal appeared to be relocating. The beat-up, over-packed car and no insurance felt like a recent college graduate...maybe a grad student since Teal appeared a little older than the usual undergrad. But her designer clothing and something else August couldn't put her finger on didn't match up with that scenario...or with the junker car, for that matter.

Teal was slumped against the door and appeared to be asleep when she returned. August studied her for a few moments.

She was beautiful—feminine, but not girlish. She had a fine brow, full lips, and long, thick lashes that lay against her smooth cheeks. Even pale from nausea, her complexion hinted of a Mediterranean or Hispanic heritage.

August argued with herself as she nosed the old truck onto the blacktop. Even if she was Hispanic, that didn't mean Teal was tied to Reyes. Her refusal to go to a clinic, though, was suspicious. Maybe she was wanted for something. Maybe she was in the country illegally. Hell, maybe August had just spent too many years defending criminals and was too suspicious of everyone. Still, she probably should've snuck a look in her purse. No way.

That went against every moral code ingrained in her. She should just stay alert and ditch her at the first decent motel. But what if she got sicker? Nobody could fake the symptoms she was displaying. She'd be fine. Maybe. Shit. This was a very bad idea.

"Don't do this. Pierce Walker will piss his pants," August said softly. She didn't want to wake Teal, but if she said it aloud, maybe she'd listen and take her own advice for once. Fat chance.

CHAPTER THREE

BJ was pacing the wide porch of the house when August rounded the last bend of the long driveway of The White Paw ranch. This couldn't be good. The ranch's foreman should still be with the hands checking fences and counting new calves. She slowed the truck to a gentle stop and turned to check her passenger slumped against the door. Teal didn't stir, even when August gently touched her forearm. Chilled now by the truck's air-conditioning, her skin was too dry, and it worried August that she didn't wake. They needed to hydrate her soon.

BJ yanked her door open. "We've got trouble. That law fellow—" BJ's eyebrows shot up, his blue eyes traveling to Teal's slumped figure, slowing over her bare legs. "Damn, August."

She held her finger to her lips and slid out of the truck, closing the door quietly behind her.

BJ shook his head. His face was an expressive road map weathered by years in the sun and wind, the deep creases rearranged into a half grin. "You always did bring home the pretty ones." His smile transformed into a scowl. "But since Julio and your grandpa ain't here to advise you, I reckon that falls to me. Chasing girls ain't what you need to be doing right now."

"I ain't—" August almost laughed at her immediate step back into her teen years. "I'm not a kid anymore, BJ, and I'm not chasing girls. Her car engine caught fire out on the highway. Her cell phone was dead, and I'm guessing she was sitting out there in the heat for a couple of hours before I came along. She has heat exhaustion. I couldn't leave her there."

"Should've taken her into town and dropped her at the ER then."

"She refused. Said she didn't have insurance."

"Half the people around here don't have insurance."

"I know that, but she absolutely refused. Then she threw up on me and passed out."

BJ made a show of sniffing the air. "Well, I wasn't going to mention how you smell."

August gave him a gentle shove. "Let's get her in the house." She circled the truck and carefully opened the passenger door. Teal blinked and struggled weakly when the door gave way and she fell into August's arms. "I've got you." August shouldered under Teal's right arm and wrapped an arm around her waist to pull Teal snuggly against her side. "Can you walk a little?"

Teal clumsily moved her feet as August propelled them toward the porch. "Where are we?"

"We're at my ranch. You can stay here tonight."

August tightened her hold when Teal stumbled on the two steps up to the porch. "BJ, can you get—" She paused when Rio appeared next to them with Teal's purse in her mouth. "Can you give Rio a hand and get that duffel out of the back?"

"Damn dog is too smart…hold up and I'll get the front door for you first."

"I don't want to be any trouble," Teal said softly as they waited for BJ to open the door.

"It's not a problem. We have a couple of empty guest rooms. Coming here was a lot closer than going all the way back into town." August maneuvered them through the door BJ held open and turned into the first guest suite on the left, across from her bedroom. "When you're feeling better tomorrow, you can call someone about your car and we'll get you into town so you can take care of things."

August continued through the bedroom to the attached bathroom and lowered Teal to sit on the closed commode. "You should soak in a cool bath for a while. Towels on the rack are clean." She hesitated. Maybe that wasn't a good idea. What if she fell asleep and slid down into the water?

BJ appeared with Teal's duffel and a couple of cold sports drinks. "Here's your bag and something better than plain water. Drink one of 'em before you get in the tub."

August stared at him.

He stared back. "What?"

"I didn't know we had any of that."

He shrugged. "It's my private stash. I don't take the heat as well as I used to. It helps." He glared at her. "But I ain't buying it for all them young guys in the bunkhouse. They drink it up like candy water. They'd break our food budget in less than a month."

She shook her head. Sure, she'd been here only a few weeks, but she'd been so wrapped up in her own problems she hadn't paid much attention to the things that were different since she'd last been to this ranch as a teen. That was going to change. This was her ranch now. Her new life. She smiled at BJ. "Thanks for sharing."

He nodded curtly. "Couple more on the table by the bed. She ought to drink 'em all." He turned to leave, then hesitated. "You get that part for the pump?"

"It's in the truck."

He nodded and was gone.

Teal had downed half the first bottle of sports drink when August turned back to her. She was sitting more erect and her eyes appeared more focused. "Feeling better?"

A hoarse croak was her first attempt to answer, so Teal cleared her throat. "Yes, I am." Clear and fairly strong now. "I think that's actually going to stay down." Her face reddened. "Sorry about throwing up on you."

"Forget it. It's not nearly as bad as sliding down in a pile of cow poop." August turned the faucets to start filling the tub. "If you show me you can stand on your own and aren't too dizzy, I'll leave you to undress and get in the tub without my assistance."

Teal's eyebrows shot up. "And if I can't?"

August's brain stuttered at the timbre of Teal's response—a challenge, yet tinged with a hint of tease. She straightened, and the spark of chemistry was undeniable as they studied each other for a long moment. Teal's gaze was focused but still undeniably weary. August hooked her thumbs in her jean pockets and shrugged, sheepishly. "If you nearly pass out when you stand, I'm staying." She crossed her arms over her chest. "The last thing I need is for you to lose consciousness in the tub and drown because you're in here alone." Naked Teal wasn't a picture she wanted in her head but—damn. Her face heated at the image. Still, she refused to look away as Teal's eyes held hers.

Teal nodded. After another big swallow of the drink, she took a deep breath, placed a bracing hand against the wall, and slowly stood. When she'd straightened to her full height, she dropped her hand from the wall and smiled tentatively at August. "All good. Legs are a little weak and my head's still throbbing, but no dizziness or nausea."

August studied her. Teal wasn't as pale as earlier and even more beautiful now that her natural olive complexion was returning. "Okay then. Make yourself at home. Dinner won't be for a couple more hours. You should relax and drink as many of those sports drinks as you can. BJ will pester me to death if you don't." She stepped backward toward the door. She couldn't seem to take her eyes from her visitor. "I have some paperwork to do, so I'll be in my office that's…well, it's a pretty big house." She slapped the side of her leg and Rio appeared in the doorway. "This is Rio. If you need something, just send her to get me." She pointed, and Rio settled on the rug by the sink.

Teal sat on the side of the large tub and trailed her long fingers in the water, then adjusted the faucets to modify the temperature. "Is she going to watch me the whole time?"

"Rio, turn your head while the lady undresses," August said, flicking her fingers in a quick signal. Rio lowered her head and covered her eyes with a paw. August liked Teal's low, throaty chuckle. She smiled. "You let me know if she's anything but a gentlewoman."

Teal returned her smile. "Thank you again. I'll be fine."

"Right. Okay." August reluctantly stepped out and closed the bathroom door. She crossed the hall to her own suite and searched the bathroom's medicine cabinet. Aspirin. The woman had a terrible headache. She was getting her some aspirin. That's all. So, why was her heart pounding? "Shit." She scowled at herself in the bathroom mirror and willed her heart to slow, then marched back across the hall and placed the bottle on Teal's bedside table. She stared at it. She shouldn't be playing Florence Nightingale. Geez. It was just aspirin. She wheeled and strode out of the room before she talked herself into taking it back.

Still, she shouldn't be bringing strangers to the ranch. The measures she'd taken after Susan's revealing visit had put her at the top of both the DEA's and Luis Reyes's most-wanted list. So, she'd fled Dallas to the one place they'd never think to look for her. She was being irresponsible to bring this woman here because she could get caught in the crossfire if they found August.

"Hold up there, Grasshopper."

Immersed in her self-lecture, August was halfway through the spacious den when BJ's stern command brought her up short. She instinctively responded to his nickname for the active child she'd been. "You don't have to say it. I was stupid to bring her here." She slowly turned to face him. "I don't know what I was thinking."

BJ's drawl was low and firm. "You were thinking that girl needed help and that's what Gus raised you to do—offer assistance to a stranded traveler."

This was true, but she wasn't that kid dogging her grandfather's heels any longer. She wasn't in the mood to reminisce. "I'll give her a ride into town tomorrow."

BJ shook his head. "Not sure that's a good idea."

"What?"

"Anybody recognize you when you picked up the pump part?"

August stiffened. "I saw Tank Hansen."

"Anybody else?"

"Nobody I saw or talked to. Why?"

"Tommy ripped a glove on some barbed wire and radioed in for me to throw his extra pair in the Jeep when I made the rounds with lunch for everybody. Wouldn't you know that when I went to the bunkhouse to get 'em, Tommy had left the TV on...again. If I've told him once, I've told him a hundred times—"

"I thought we were talking about why I shouldn't go back into town tomorrow." August pushed down her irritation and added a hint of tease to her interruption. She rubbed her face. BJ hadn't changed. The man could take two hours to answer a yes-or-no question. Ownership of the ranch made her BJ's boss, but he'd been an uncle figure to her since she was a kid and deserved her respect.

BJ scowled. "That's what I'm telling you if you'll just listen." He squinted one eye and pointed a finger at her. "Big-city living's made you impatient. Details are important, Grasshopper. Didn't I teach you anything?"

She pressed her hands together as though praying and bowed slightly. "So sorry, Sensei."

"Miss Smarty-pants." He grabbed her hands, his blue gaze boring into her. "Listen to me, August. That TV was tuned to a news program out of Dallas, and they were talking about you."

This was bad. "What'd they say?"

"Some girlie was reporting about Christine being locked up and you being AWOL, so a judge was complaining that the court schedule was in a huge mess. Then she interviewed that FBI guy—"

"DEA."

"Don't matter. He's says you're a key witness in a big case and possibly kidnapped. He says they're going to have a press conference in the morning about you going missing."

"Shit. I don't need my face all over the television. I'd better call him." She felt around her pockets until she located the one that held the simple flip phone and pulled it out. "Do you know how hard it is to find a basic phone these days? Everything is a smart phone, but those are too easy to trace." She dug her wallet out of a back pocket and was thumbing through credit cards to find the scrap of paper with Pierce Walker's phone number on it when she felt him watching her.

"What?"

His expression was pensive, but he held out the pump part for her take. "After you make that call, you can go fix the pump for me."

"Where are you going?"

"I'm going to put that girl's car onto our flatbed trailer and haul it over to Tank's garage. While he takes a look, I'll have a talk with him to make sure he don't spread it around that you're back in town."

August sighed. "Yeah. Okay. That'd be a good idea. Tank's solid. If you ask, he'll keep an eye out for anybody asking about me around town, too."

"I remember him being a little sweet on you when you were teenagers."

"And I was infatuated with Karen Simpson."

BJ chuckled. "Joke was on you. She's married and got three young'uns now."

She shook her head, smiling a little. "Better her than me."

He rested a large hand on her shoulder. "I know Gus and Julio aren't around anymore, but old BJ has your back, Grasshopper."

August's throat tightened. In the achingly lonely nights since she'd fled Dallas and taken refuge at the ranch, she felt the absence of her grandfather and his partner, who had been a second grandparent to her. She was like an orphan cast adrift into the cold world. BJ jerked when she surged forward and wrapped her arms around him in a tight embrace. Then he returned her hug, awkwardly patting her back. She wasn't adrift. BJ was here. The White Paw Ranch was hers. They were a familiar ship and crew.

His wiry frame was a little bent and gimpy now, and the ranch sorely needed an infusion of cash and sprucing up. But she'd get past this trial and put Dallas, her law practice, and Christine behind her. She'd find her true north. She was meant to be a rancher. She'd known that since she'd thrown a leg over her first pony and chased her first calf. "Thanks, BJ. I miss both of them so much."

"Me, too, kid. But I'm sure they're up there looking out for us." He pushed her back and moved away, clearing his throat. "Go on and call that guy. You only got a few hours of daylight to get out to that pump. You can take the Gator. The tools are already loaded in the back of it."

"Sure you can get that car by yourself?"

"No problem. Julio had an automatic winch put on the front of the trailer some years ago so one person could load the tractor if it broke down. I'll need her keys, though, so I can get inside and put the gearshift in neutral."

"I'll get 'em." August strode back through the spacious ranch house to Teal's room and knocked lightly on the partially open door. As she expected, Teal was still in the bath. Her duffel of clothes was in the bathroom, too, but her shoulder purse and keys were on the bed. August grabbed the keys and hesitated, glancing at the bathroom door. This would be a perfect opportunity to check Teal's identification, just to make sure she was who she said she was. Of course, there was no reason to suspect she wasn't. But then she hadn't really given out anything more than her first name and her destination, had she?

"August?" BJ stood in the hallway.

"Got 'em right here," she said quietly, turning away from the purse and leaving the bedroom door ajar for Rio as she exited the room.

❖

Teal jerked awake. Confused for a split second by the slosh of water, she instantly stilled when her memory flooded back. She wasn't drowning. Intent brown eyes stared at her from little more than a foot away. She'd dozed off and the dog must have nosed her to wake her up before she slipped under the water. Her heart—the less logical of her organs—still beat wildly in sync with the throb in her head. Not as bad as before, but the headache hurt enough to make her squint against the glare of the bathroom's light. She felt as weak as a newborn calf.

She opened the drain and cautiously levered up to sit on the edge of the tub. The towel August had set out for her was thick and soft. Her legs were shaky, so she dragged her duffel over to the tub and plundered through it until she found underwear, the bottoms of a nylon warm-up suit, and a T-shirt.

"Oh, thank God." Teal held up her toothbrush and mint paste. She braced against the sink and gave her teeth and tongue a good scrubbing. Her hair was damp, but she didn't think she could stay upright to dry it. She was struggling just to hold her eyes open long enough to brush out the tangles.

She put down the brush and stared into the mirror. She'd done a good job picking out an over-the-counter hair dye very close to her naturally very dark brunette. You had to be blond to get anywhere in Washington, so Lauren had paid an outrageous amount to have her hairdresser streak Teal's beautiful dark hair with reddish-blond highlights, then touch up the roots every few weeks.

She narrowed her eyes and growled at the woman in the mirror. She was glad to see the real Teal reflected back at her for a change. She didn't like Senator Lauren Abbott's TJ Giovanni anymore. Her shoulders sagged. But who was the woman in the mirror? She didn't know her either. She could never be that mousy farm girl again. And the chances of her being a player in the political arena now were slim to none. She hadn't donated that money in Lauren's name, but the sizable anonymous donation had been widely reported. Lauren had surely figured it out, and Teal could never work in DC again.

She trudged into the bedroom and crawled onto the four-post bed. She tugged one pillow under her head and hugged the other to her chest. She missed her sisters. They'd had to sleep three in one bed when they were girls and complained about it bitterly as they grew older. Their father had grudgingly built triple bunks when Teal hit puberty and her mother whispered that she deserved a bed of her own for a little privacy. But now, sleeping in a stranger's house with no idea what tomorrow would bring, Teal would have given anything to see the only two people in the world she knew would still love her.

She choked back a sob. Crying was making her head hurt worse. She sat up. A box of tissues sat next to a digital clock on the bedside table. Blowing her nose, she spotted the small bottle of aspirin next to the sports drink BJ had left for her. She shook three capsules out of the bottle and chugged half the drink, then blew her nose again. Her head was beginning to clear with her change of position. She lay on her back this time but hugged the pillow to her chest again and closed her eyes. Damn it. As much as she wanted to hate Lauren, Teal still missed falling asleep with the weight of Lauren's head on her shoulder and Lauren's breath warm on her neck.

She was so tired she barely registered the bed's slight dip and the warm, furry weight that settled against her side.

❖

"Special Agent Walker."

"It's August Reese."

"Where the hell are you?"

"I'm safe."

"I didn't ask you that, God damn it. Where are you?"

"There's a leak in your department, so all you need to know is that I'm safe."

"Son of a bi—" Pierce Walker stopped and lowered his voice. "Why do you think there's a leak in the DEA?"

August figured his yelling must have turned the heads of several lesser agents sitting at cubicles outside his office. She sank into the tall back of the thickly padded leather office chair and swung her boots up onto the huge desk. She checked her watch. Thirty seconds. "Because when I visited Christine at the jail, she told me Reyes had a contact in the DEA who was feeding him information."

"Ah, that would be the Christine who lied and cheated on you, then helped her boyfriend try to frame you for money laundering?"

His barb sank deep into her still-raw wound, and August focused on her watch to ignore the stab of pain. He was angrier than she'd anticipated. "She warned me that he knows I have copies of the computer hard drives your people took from our law offices and wiped clean so there was no evidence on them."

"We didn't wipe them, damn it. They somehow had them set up to self-destruct when they were disconnected from your office network. If you don't turn those copies over to us, I can charge you with impeding an investigation."

Ninety seconds.

"Are your IT people amateurs? They should have been prepared for booby traps."

"Word on the street is that Reyes is looking for you. Come in with the copies so we can protect you."

"You're too late. I drove home from the jail to find my security system bypassed, the house ransacked, the safe torn out of the wall, and my dog missing. Makes you wonder what would have happened if I hadn't been under your protection."

"You're saying they didn't get the copies?"

So, the son of a bitch already knew about her house. She wondered what else he knew that he wasn't sharing with her.

"I did find my dog, thanks for asking. She's a border collie, not a pit bull, and managed to escape before they could hurt her." If they had harmed Rio, Reyes wouldn't have had to look for her any longer because she would have found him and beat him within an inch of his life.

"Damn the dog, Reese. What about the computer records? Right now, that's the only hard evidence we have on him."

Two minutes.

"They weren't at the house. They're in a safe place." August put her feet back on the floor. "The evidence stays where I put it until the trial."

"I can have you arrested."

"You'll have to find me first." She sighed. "I'm not trying to be difficult, Pierce. I'm just afraid you'll decide you don't really need my testimony and get sloppy. If you know where I am, then Reyes's contact in your office could find out."

He cursed under his breath. "How can I get in touch with you?"

"You can't. I'll be in touch with you every three days."

"This is my cell phone. It isn't secure."

"Neither is your office."

"God damn it, Reese."

Two minutes, thirty seconds.

"Gotta go, Walker. Just know that I'm safe. Say that when you hold the news conference tomorrow morning. Better yet, cancel it. Because if you start showing my face all over television, I won't be safe any longer."

"Reese, damn it. I can't protect you if I don't—"

She flicked the phone closed, ending the call. She smiled. She enjoyed hanging up fifteen seconds short of the three minutes he needed to lock a trace on her. She pictured him throwing things around his office and screaming at a couple of junior agents right now. He really was wound just a little too tight.

CHAPTER FOUR

Teal woke to semi-darkness and silence. She was so utterly comfortable, she lazily snuggled deeper into her warm nest to take stock of her situation. She sighed in relief. Her pounding headache and nausea were gone. So was her furry sleeping companion. She was still in her warm-up pants and T-shirt, lying on top of the bed covers, but someone had tucked a soft blanket around her while she slept.

While the wall before her was a soothing shade of dark green, it wasn't adding much to her information-gathering. She reluctantly rolled over but held tight to the pillow hugged against her chest and tugged the quilt up to her chin. Weak sunlight filtered between the slats of the window blinds. The door to the hallway was closed. She wished it could stay closed and keep out the rest of the world, along with all her troubles. She'd just stay under her blanket where it was comfortable and quiet. Her gaze wandered to the open door of the bathroom, and as if on cue, her bladder reminded her of the three bottles of fluid she'd consumed before she slept. Ugh. She'd have to abandon her haven. Just a few more minutes.

She relaxed again as she replayed the events of the day, then drifted off course and into a slow-motion review of a tall, blond woman wrangler. A rooster crowed and her eyes drifted to the digital clock on the bedside table. Five thirty. Mmm. What was her name? August, like the month. That's right. August had said dinner in a few hours. It was late afternoon. Dinner should be soon. Teal's stomach growled at the thought, and her bladder issued another plea for relief. The rooster crowed again.

"Crap." Teal shot up to look at the clock. Five thirty AM. In the morning. She'd slept through the afternoon and all night. *Stop. Evaluate. Make a plan.* "Okay. It's a little embarrassing but not a problem. There wasn't much I could do until today anyway. This is a ranch. People will be up early." She stood slowly. Still good. No dizziness.

She pulled on a worn pair of jeans and a fresh T-shirt, then quickly plaited her hair into a simple, single braid. She brushed her teeth and checked her reflection in the bathroom mirror. No makeup, but she didn't really need it. She silently thanked her mother's Italian genes for her even complexion and thick, dark eyelashes.

She'd left the wholesome but simple farm girl in Pennsylvania when she headed north for college. She'd never be naive again, but reverting to her farm-girl look would keep her from being recognized. And she was more comfortable in these clothes than the business suits and panty hose she'd been wearing for the past eight years. Maybe leaving that fashionable politico behind in DC wouldn't be so bad. She could find a new career that rewarded smart but allowed casual.

"Sloppy is the new savvy," she quipped. "Maybe I should write advertising slogans." She shrugged. "Nah. Sloppy isn't new. The computer nerds started that fad fifteen years ago." She gave her reflection a stern stare. "You'll figure this out, Giovanni. You're not going to give up like your mother. Suck it up, and get moving. You can do this."

Her cell phone and purse were still on the bed next to where she'd been sleeping. Crap, crap, crap. She'd forgotten to plug it in. Deep breath. It was the latest iPhone and equipped with a fast charger. It would be a couple of hours before any garage opened anyway for her to arrange a tow, and Wade would surely have voice mail if he didn't answer. Next order of business.

She gave her quiet haven one last look and opened the door to re-enter the world.

The smell of bacon frying made Teal's mouth water and her stomach rumble noisily, so she followed the enticing scent to a modern kitchen cheered by the sunlight that poured through large bare windows over the triple sink and prep counter. She was surprised, however, to find a huge skillet sizzling unattended. She grabbed the fork on the counter and flipped the bacon slices before turning down the flame. Where was everybody?

A folded newspaper lay on the kitchen's island, and with one eye on the bacon, she began to thumb through it. The item was small and on an inside page, but the headline read: PROBE SOUGHT INTO ABBOTT'S CAMPAIGN FINANCES. Shit.

WASHINGTON, DC A conservative watchdog group is calling for an investigation into the campaign finances of Sen. Lauren Abbott.

The right-leaning lobby says they have uncovered information that Abbott's campaign manager authorized more than two hundred thousand dollars to pay expenses charged on two credit cards for first-class plane tickets to and hotel stays at secluded, and sometimes exotic, luxury destinations. Expenses charged to those cards also included restaurant bills averaging several hundred dollars, clothing from designer boutiques, and rent on two downtown DC apartments.

The authorizations were listed on campaign expenditure forms simply as a credit-card number, but Americans for America said they'd received information that those cards were issued to two fictitious campaign staffers.

Abbott's campaign manager, Russ Zukowski, said the senator's personal staff, not the campaign staff, set up the accounts. He said, however, that using fictitious names on some credit cards was a common practice utilized to give high-profile candidates some relief from the crowds of trailing media, especially when they were meeting with big donors who might be publicity shy. Donations made by anyone Sen. Abbott met with privately were properly reported on campaign finance records, he added.

Federal Election Commission officials said that, while they have no evidence of criminal malfeasance at this point, they are interviewing the senator and her entire staff. They also are seeking to locate and interview Abbott's former chief aide, TJ Giovanni, who resigned and has dropped out of the public eye since reports surfaced earlier that she and the senator were involved in a romantic relationship. Sen. Abbott, married to financier Paul Abbott, says those rumors were manufactured by the opposing party seeking to unseat her in the upcoming election.

Two credit cards? Sure, she knew about one card. Lauren had given it to her even before they became lovers. And Lauren had insisted she use it to buy expensive gowns or business suits when she accompanied her to formal functions or important meetings, to charge living expenses on it, and to book their clandestine weekends together. Two apartments? Was Lauren screwing somebody else at the same time they were seeing each other? God, she couldn't even think about it. Maybe it was for one of her husband's flings. Yeah. That had to be it. She'd have known if Lauren was seeing someone else.

She turned the bacon again. Where was everybody?

The room was an open concept that looked into a spacious den. Nobody there either. A sliver of light shone from a door left ajar on the left, and she could hear the indistinguishable murmur of voices. Must be the absent-minded cook. She turned down the flame under the pan and started for the door, then stopped cold when the conversation grew louder.

"You should have left her belongings in her car, BJ."

"Come on, August. Tank had me dump the car out back of his shop. Kids have broken out the windows of half the vehicles behind there. Everything in her car would have been gone in two days. It ain't all that much."

"She isn't staying past breakfast, so her stuff isn't our problem."

"You've sure had a change of attitude. I'm glad you still remember some of what Gus taught you and didn't leave that girl stranded on the highway yesterday. But today you're acting like your daddy, durn his sorry hide."

"That was low, BJ. I've got too much going on to be playing Good Samaritan."

"Your granddaddy was never too busy or too poor to lend a helping hand when somebody needed it, Grasshopper. And, even though you're acting like your ass of a father this morning, we both know you've got your granddaddy Gus's soft heart." A low chuckle rumbled from the room. "And when you drag home a stray, dang if it's not the pick of the litter."

"You're awful, old man."

"I don't hear you denying it."

"Doesn't matter. It's bad enough I might be exposing you and the rest of the guys to my problem. She can't stay here another night, so no need to unload her things from the truck."

"You call that Walker fellow?"

"Yeah. I picked up a pay-as-you-go phone from ShopMart. I don't want him tracking my cell and coming here to drag me back to Dallas. Now tell me what the crew and I need to do today so you can drive her into town after we eat."

Teal hurried back to the kitchen. So much for her safe haven and good mood. She transferred the bacon onto the napkin-covered plate left on the counter and sulked as she turned off the flame. If she hadn't been there, smoke alarms would be blaring by now.

She shook her head and adjusted her attitude. She still owed August for rescuing her and BJ for towing her car for free, even if August did want her gone as soon as possible. She went to the big stainless-steel refrigerator and perused the contents.

❖

August wrote down BJ's instructions for preparing lunch. Geez, these six guys ate a lot. A dozen ham sandwiches, two bags of chips, two gallons of sweet tea. Dessert? Really? Were they ranch hands or vacationers on a dude ranch? She turned the dude-ranch idea over in her mind. Nah. More trouble than she wanted.

She frowned at the list. "Why don't we have a cook to handle all this?"

BJ scratched at the stubble on his chin. "We did. Josie. Handled everything here at the house. The chickens and the pigs, too."

"We don't have pigs."

"We did until Josie made a pet of one. After that, she wouldn't hear of us getting our bacon from anywhere but the grocery store." His eyes widened. "Oh, Lordy. The bacon." He jumped up from the chair where he sprawled and bulleted toward the kitchen.

August dropped her paperwork and hurried after him. That old man was faster than a jackrabbit when he needed to be. They both pulled up short at the sight of Teal sliding a second plate of food in place on the eat-in bar.

She gestured to the place settings. "Sit, eat. I hope you like Spanish omelets."

BJ grinned and plopped onto a tall stool beside one plate. "Well, I'll be. Thanks for saving my bacon."

Teal smiled at him, settling her own plate on the end of the bar and dragging over a stool.

August hesitated, then went to the coffeepot to refill her cup. She couldn't look at Teal. The woman took her breath away. Her thick, dark lashes framed rich brown eyes. August had thought her attractive before, but her hair braided back accented her sculpted cheekbones. A small scar bisected one perfectly arched brow. August stirred another spoonful of sugar into her coffee to distract herself. "Anybody else need a refill?"

"Hit me," BJ said.

"I'm staying away from caffeine for a while longer," Teal said softly.

"Good idea," BJ said. "You need to stay good and hydrated for a couple of days until you've fully recovered. Can't be too careful."

August slid onto her stool and dug into her food. The sooner she finished and headed for the barn, the better. She shoveled in a mouthful of omelet, then paused when the combination of cheeses and fresh peppers exploded on her palate. Damn, it was good. She swallowed and glanced at Teal. "Thanks for making breakfast."

BJ was a bit more enthusiastic. "Woo-wee. Now that's what I call an omelet. I don't believe I've tasted anything that good since I courted that woman in San Antonio."

"You're welcome," Teal said to August before turning to BJ. "What happened to the woman?"

"I liked her cooking more than I liked her." He took another bite and closed his eyes in a dramatic display of appreciation as he chewed. "We could use a cook around here."

"But we're not hiring right now." August winced inwardly as she cut him off a little too quickly, a little too loudly.

Teal shrugged one shoulder. "My cousin is counting on me, so I need to be on my way."

They ate in uncomfortable silence until BJ put his fork down and slurped his coffee loudly. August winced and glanced over to see Teal hiding a smile behind her own cup. Her eyes gave her away though, and August caught herself returning the amused look. August dropped her gaze to her plate and frowned. *Stop it.* BJ would never stop pushing for her to stay if he thought she liked the woman.

"That's durn good coffee." He held up his cup and looked at Teal. "Did you make this?"

Teal lowered her cup. "I hope you don't mind. I have a friend who owns a coffee-bean company. She imports and blends her own brand. I always carry some with me."

"Don't mind at all. You'll have to tell us how we can get some of this." BJ slurped noisily again. "Right, August?"

"Didn't know you were a connoisseur. Coffee is coffee, as far as I'm concerned." She refused to encourage him or look up from her plate, even though Teal's gaze felt as though she was actually touching her.

"I wouldn't mind a breakfast like this every morning. August here can't even burn toast. After Julio passed on, I mostly just ate in the bunkhouse with the boys until she showed up. Pops used to be the ranch chuck wagon, but his mind is about gone, and he's started leaving out this and that when he cooks. We never know what dinner's going to taste like. He's also nearly burnt down the bunkhouse a few times—"

"Like you almost burned down the house this morning."

"What?" BJ paused, then dismissed her growled accusation with a wave of his fork.

His friendly rambling was grating on August's nerves. Teal didn't need the history of the ranch. She wasn't staying.

But BJ continued his story as though August hadn't interrupted. "So, anyway, the boys mostly chow on cereal or pre-packaged crap they can microwave since Josie—that was our last cook—up and ran off with that lady wrangler I hired last summer. Whew, now she was a hot one."

August nearly spilled her coffee as Rio bumped August's thigh with her nose. She looked down. "Stop that. Since when do you beg?"

Without pausing his rambling, BJ tossed a scrap of bacon on the floor. "Yes, sir. Josie was a big woman. Not fat, but tall as Grasshopper here and twice as stocky."

Teal raised both eyebrows and Rio snatched up the bacon. August would swear the dog was grinning when Rio looked her way before turning her attention back to BJ. August scolded BJ this time. "No wonder her manners have gotten so bad. You shouldn't feed her from the table."

Nobody was listening to her complaint.

"So, Josie did the cooking because she was a woman?" Teal's challenge held a teasing tone.

"Heck, no. She could wrestle a steer with the best man out there, but Josie had a gentle, laid-back nature and a bad back that bothered her if she had to do much wrangling. That worked out just fine for us when she volunteered for ranch duty. She did all the cooking and house cleaning, and kept up the barnyard stock. She also could fix the roof or tend a sick cow if needed and was a whiz with paperwork."

"You said she left with another woman who was a wrangler." Teal rested her chin in her hand, fixing her gaze on BJ.

He preened under her full attention. "Yep. Amy was a pistol, sure enough. She weren't but about one-thirty soaking wet, but she was quick as a rattlesnake and tough as the cow dog that was always at her heels. She'd won a bunch of roping and barrel-racing trophies on the rodeo circuit, but said she was tired of traveling and wanted to put down roots. She'd been working her way across Texas, looking for the right spot to spend her winnings on a place of her own."

The morning sun that shone through the windows warmed Teal's profile, and August was startled by a sudden déjà vu moment. It was as if Teal belonged there in the kitchen with her and BJ. She scowled.

"So, Amy caught Josie's eye?"

"More like Josie caught Amy's eye. She'd been here about two weeks before she was bossing every man in the bunkhouse. But Josie, well…Amy sweet-talked her, just like she talked to the horses."

Teal's slow smile gripped August low in the belly. This was ridiculous. She was just missing Christine. Not Christine, but what they'd had together. August closed her eyes. That wasn't a box she really wanted to open and examine at this very moment. Teal needed to go. August stood and began clearing their empty plates. Maybe that would shut BJ up and get the two of them on their way into town.

BJ ignored August's efforts, holding on to his coffee cup when she nudged him sharply to take his plate away. "By the end of the summer, Amy bought old man Johnson's 200-acre spread about twenty miles from here and lured Josie and her pet pig away from us. I hear they're running some cattle and Amy is breeding and training some high-dollar horses."

Teal did take notice of August's prodding and stood.

BJ, coming to the end of his story, finally gave up his cup and rose from his stool, too. "I sure miss Josie, but can't say I miss that pig much. She'd let that durn animal in the den, and it'd lie over there on a dog bed and watch TV, I kid you not."

August put the last plate in the dishwasher and started it half full. "Sun's getting high." She glanced at Teal. "BJ has to take Pops into town for a doctor's appointment, so he'll drop you off at the garage that has your car." She turned to BJ. "Before you head into town, why don't you get our visitor to help you put together the lunch I'll need for the crew later. You can tell her all about the pig while you're doing it." She'd heard enough about Josie and her pig. "I'm heading out to check the west fence. I'll come back and pick up the food." The back door banged shut behind her.

❖

Teal stared after August. "I think I've overstayed my welcome."

"It ain't nothing personal, Miss Teal," BJ said softly. "August's got a weight on her shoulders and a lot tangled up inside her right now." He took a large ham and a jar of mayonnaise from the refrigerator, then a long loaf of bread from the cabinet. "How about you go get your things together while I make these sandwiches?"

"I can help."

"Won't take me no time. I've got a system. Been doing it ever since Josie left. Go on, now."

Teal smiled her thanks and headed to her room. She thought she'd developed a thick skin while working in DC. You learned quickly how to let things go and move on when you couldn't change them. Who you stepped on and what you traded to reach your goals wasn't personal. But she wasn't in Washington any longer, and August's apparent rejection bothered her. What had happened to the sweetly gallant woman who'd blushed ten shades of red when she insisted she'd have to keep watch if Teal was still woozy as she soaked naked in the tub? She didn't like the grumpy, distant woman who'd shown up for breakfast.

She packed her things away in her duffel, neatly making the bed. She gathered her towel and washcloth to take to the laundry room as soon as she asked BJ where that was located. Then she checked her phone. It was fully charged but still no signal. She'd been afraid of that. Lauren had asked all of her staff to switch their phone contracts to a company that made substantial contributions to her campaign. There was never a problem getting a signal from their cell towers in the city or most of the East Coast, but the mountains or rural areas were another issue. She needed to switch her phone contract to a company with better range. For now, she hoped she could get a signal when they drove into town.

Teal slipped the phone into her purse and shouldered her bag. She surveyed the cozy bedroom. There'd been no mention of a woman of the house, other than the lesbian cook, so she wasn't surprised that the decor was predominantly masculine and of a Southwestern theme. The forest-green and khaki tones of the bed's patchwork quilt perfectly complemented the pine furniture and desert reds in a Navajo tapestry that hung on the opposite wall. She was surprised, however, at how quiet the world felt when she was in this room. Reluctantly, she picked up her duffel and closed the door on what she decided must be really good feng shui.

❖

"Hawk and Tommy, head out to finish repairs on that fence break in the northwest pasture." The men had been waiting in the bunkhouse's kitchen for August or BJ to set the agenda for the day and rose from their seats around the long picnic-style table to empty the dregs of their coffee cups into the sink. "Manny and

Brick, you guys split up to do the morning sweep for any new calves."

"How 'bout me?" Pops squinted at her. Years of hard riding hadn't been kind to the seventy-eight-year-old man. Arthritis knotted his hands, and cardiac disease weakened his heart. He'd been Julio's first hire and dug the hole for the first fence post at The White Paw. It was an unspoken understanding that he would live out his years on the ranch, even when he could no longer complete even the smallest chore. "Chickens and horses already fed."

"BJ says you're going into town with him this morning."

"Ain't going into town. I'm going with Manny and Brick."

"BJ says you've got an appointment—"

"Now, Pops," Manny said. "You know BJ will lollygag all day in town if you don't go and make him get on back here." He waggled his eyebrows at the old man. "Besides, I heard he has a really pretty lady riding with him. You know what a dog he is. You need to go along and protect that young woman's virtue."

Pops scowled. "What lady?"

Manny had everyone's attention now. "Don't know, but Tommy saw August carrying her into the house yesterday afternoon. Why don't you ask her?"

All eyes turned to her. She narrowed her eyes at them, but the men didn't appear intimidated. She opened her mouth to tell them it wasn't any of their business, but the truth was sure to be a lot less interesting than what their imaginations were likely to conjure.

"I wasn't carrying her. Her car broke down, and she'd been stranded out on the highway for hours in the sun. She was suffering from heat exhaustion, so I was helping her into the house, where she spent the night in one of our guest rooms while she recovered. BJ is driving her into town this morning to get her car repaired so she can continue on her way."

"So, she isn't staying?" Tommy, twenty-three years old, was the youngest of the crew.

August shook her head. "She's headed to her cousin's ranch in New Mexico."

"Damn." He slapped his hat against his leg. "We never get any new women around here."

Brick laughed and threw a muscled arm over the young man's shoulders as he guided him out of the bunkhouse. "You've got to go hang out around one of those college campuses on your days off. Those coeds love cowboys. Meet you one and drag her back here."

"Don't work that way anymore," Tommy grumbled. "All they want is a good ride, and then they leave you in the dust wondering when the hell you came out of the saddle."

August watched them go. "I know exactly what you mean, buddy," she said under her breath. She turned back to urge Pops toward the house but came face to face with Hawk.

"If you want to come with us, we can unload the fencing we need and you can have the truck."

"Thanks, but I think I'll saddle up and check out the southwest fence this morning. I can be back in time to bring lunch around on one of the ATVs."

Hawk nodded. "I like to ride the fence when I need to think. It clears my head."

"I don't need to think about anything. I'm just looking for fence breaks."

"Didn't say you did." He gripped Pops's shoulder. "Come on, Pops. How about I walk you up to the house so I can get a gander at this visitor Tommy's drooling over before you and BJ drive her into town."

August selected a tall bay gelding with a wide blaze and black mane and tail from the horses that came up out of the paddock when she banged one of the feed buckets against a post. She brushed and saddled him with the quick, efficient movements that had become second nature in her summers here and was unclipping him from the crossties when Teal appeared at the entrance of the barn.

"I thought you'd be gone by now," August said, stopping a few feet away.

"BJ got a business call. It sounded like someone was inquiring about one of your bulls, so we're waiting for him to finish." She drew a fold of money from her pocket. "I tried to pay BJ for towing my car into town, but he wouldn't take it. He said you give the orders and take the money around here." She held the money out. "So, please take this, along with my thanks."

August shook her head. "That's not necessary."

Teal stiffened, one hand defiantly propped on her hip while she insistently held out the money in her other hand. "Really. I'm not as poor as I appear. It's just that I've had to relocate unexpectedly and my savings are mostly tied up in short-term investments and I'm still driving my old junker from college because I didn't need a car where I've been living and—" Teal stopped mid-explanation, as though she realized her volume had grown to near shouting. "Just take the money," she said softly.

She knew she shouldn't, but Teal's flashing eyes and passionate defense stirred something in August. She stepped closer and closed her hand around Teal's and the money, pressing both against Teal's chest. "You keep it and pay it forward next time you see someone who needs a helping hand."

Teal's lips parted, surprise flickering in her eyes. They were inches apart, and for a second, August had a ridiculous impulse to close the distance and cover those full lips with hers, to run her tongue against those straight, white teeth. Her horse snorted, his bridle jangling as he impatiently bobbed his head and mouthed his bit.

"If that's what you really want," Teal said, her eyes still holding August's as she stepped backward, out of the barn's cool interior and into the harsh sunlight.

August nodded and whirled to swing smoothly onto the saddle. She tugged her Stetson low on her brow, allowed herself one last long look at one of the most attractive women she'd ever met, then steered the gelding out the other side of the barn entrance and kneed him into an easy canter toward the wide-open pasture, where she hoped to catch her breath.

CHAPTER FIVE

A ugust tugged off her sunglasses and squinted under the bright near-noon sun that denied every shadow, exposed every place possible to hide from its glare.

Fence posts stretched toward the horizon in a wavy line like mile-markers, bisected by strands of rusting wire that twisted into barbs every five inches. She shook her head. The wood posts and minimum three strands of wire were outdated methods, as was Julio's lack of efficient pasture management. He was old school.

The only thing she could see that had changed on the ranch was the bunkhouse. Instead of an open room lined with bunks and a table in the middle for chow, the long building had been sectioned off to give each wrangler a small, private dorm-style room. They prepared and ate meals in a shared kitchen and dining area that joined a large room with a pool table, well-worn sofas, and a big-screen television. Or, they could retreat to their individual rooms for some quiet, private time to watch a smaller television of their own, read a book, or sleep. The main house—bathrooms and kitchen—had been updated, too.

The business part of the ranch, however, needed to be brought up to speed. She already had started with the fence in the northwest pasture. After consulting with the local agriculture agent, she ordered new supplies, and the men were repairing the damaged fence with modern metal posts and stringing four strands of new galvanized barbed wire.

She reined the bay to a walk and then halted next to a post that jutted outward, stretching the wire attached to it. Some heifer had probably used it for a scratching post. She dismounted, dropping the bay's reins to the ground, and untied the duffel of tools from behind the saddle. She grabbed the top of the post and planted her feet to jerk it upright, then dropped to her knees and used a cut-off shovel handle from her tool bag to tamp down tight the dirt that should hold it upright.

Sweat dripped from her chin.

The physical labor felt good. Better than sitting behind a desk and shuffling paper. Sure, there were things she'd enjoyed about being an attorney, such as the drama of courtroom arguments. Not all her clients were guilty, and some had made stupid, one-time mistakes. Helping them was personally rewarding.

But ranching felt more like honest work. Everything was black or white, good or bad. It rained or it didn't. Calves lived or they died. Beef prices rose or they dropped. Each year was a gamble, but the rules were clear.

She couldn't say the same about being an attorney. Between the black typed lines of the recorded laws were a lot of gray shadows. Guilt or innocence could hinge on evidence undiscovered by investigators or disallowed by a judge. It could depend on the demographics of a jury or the cleverness of an attorney's closing arguments. A smart criminal could play the legal system and its guardians to his advantage. An innocent person could just as easily be declared guilty.

August jabbed at the dirt. Reyes had played them all. She had stood by while he lured Christine into his sordid schemes. She'd been running around with her do-gooder cape on, patting herself on the back for taking pro-bono cases, while he courted Christine with fancy business dinners and flattered her by recommending her to influential people. She'd stuck her head in the sand while he was putting his hands all over her lover. Ugh. Ugh. Ugh. She grunted angrily with each vicious stab at the now tightly packed soil, then stood and flung the tool away. The bay skittered a few feet even though he was trained to never move when ground tied.

She stood and panted in the oppressive heat, unable to hold the memories at bay.

August worked quickly to protect Susan and then herself.

A private-detective friend she trusted recommended a computer geek, Steve, who specialized in security issues, and they went to his office to make arrangements. Then she called an old college friend, who was an FBI agent in Atlanta and married to a DEA agent. They put her in touch with Pierce Walker, who met them at the home of a retired military officer Susan trusted. Pierce nearly drooled. He'd been trying to nail Reyes for a long time.

August returned late in the day, closing the door to her office and working long after everyone else had left. When she finally gave in to fatigue and went home, Christine was in the kitchen.

"You can have the bedroom tonight," August said as she walked past her without stopping, gathered some clean clothes from her closet, and locked herself in the guest suite for the night. Christine was gone when she woke the next morning, but she'd stayed the night. The coffee carafe was half full and still warm.

Steve, the security geek, visited the office the next day, posing as a pest-control worker after Susan made a show of complaining loudly about roaches in the break room. He confirmed the offices were bugged with cameras and listening devices. They were probably transmitting to a remote recording device, he said, because Reyes wouldn't likely waste the manpower for live monitoring unless he had reason to suspect they were on to him.

August's gut told her their time was short. Her rift with Christine would make Reyes cautious.

She had court most of the day but returned to the office afterward with take-out food and very watered-down whiskey. When the cleaning crew was gone and the bottle near empty, she pretended to turn out her office light, stagger to the couch, and pass out. Her phone buzzed in her pocket at one a.m. and she cautiously checked it. The text read: YOU'VE GOT ONE HOUR.

August copied the hard drives of Christine's and Raphael Delgado's computers as her security guy scrambled the signal the planted cameras were sending to Reyes. While they were downloading onto thumb drives, she poked around in Raphael's desk. The idiot had all his passwords on an index card stuck in his top desk drawer. She hadn't thought about the phone system. She typed in the password to retrieve his messages. He had eighteen archived conversations in which Christine was instructing him what to tell his father to do to manufacture or alter evidence to implicate someone other than the person he had hired her to defend for felony crimes. Raphael must have been keeping them for blackmail in case Christine ever turned against them. August didn't know how to download the messages, so she forwarded them straight to Pierce Walker's cell phone.

Ten minutes before her hour was up, she tucked the thumb drives into the gym bag that she kept under her desk. She couldn't remember the last time she'd actually gone to the gym. Then she texted her friend an ALL CLEAR, splashed the remaining whiskey onto her shirt, and resumed her place on the sofa.

August set the fence mender on the bottom strand and wrapped a short shank of new wire around the old to repair where it had stretched out of shape. Each twist of the new wire forced the old strand to tighten.

She'd stared at the ceiling with her gut churning most of the night but finally drifted into sleep. She was startled when Christine woke her with a gentle shake the next morning.

"You look like hell." Christine's hair and business suit were perfect, as always, but her eyes were red, as though she hadn't slept either.

"Yeah, well, I feel like hell." She sat up and rubbed her hands over her face.

"We need to talk." Christine gave August's forearm a gentle squeeze. "But you should go home and get a shower and some real sleep first."

August looked down at Christine's hand on her arm. The familiar gesture had always been their personal signal of affirmation and affection when they were in public. But all she could see was the new Rolex watch on Christine's wrist. She couldn't stop herself. "Reyes give that to you?" Christine didn't answer, and August stood, jerking her arm away from Christine's grasp. "I'll be back after lunch. I've got a deposition scheduled at three."

She called Pierce on the way home. He was ecstatic. The forwarded messages were enough to get warrants. He didn't think Raphael would turn on his father, but he felt sure Christine would roll over on Reyes once she found herself in a jail cell, facing a prison sentence. He promised to have warrants by that afternoon so they could arrest the two of them and confiscate all the files and computers in the office.

There was much more to do. She showered quickly and fed Rio. She searched their home for any files Christine might have kept there—or planted there to implicate August—while her security guy scanned the house for illegal surveillance, examined their home-computer network, and copied the hard drives.

Then she drove Susan and the twins to the airport. Until the trial, they'd be living on a secure military base, under the protection of her late husband's old army ranger commanding officer.

August moved the mender to the second strand. She swore when a rusted barb bit into her flesh and jerked her work glove off to suck at the blood seeping from her thumb. She couldn't seem to do anything without hurting herself in the process.

She returned around one p.m., barely settling in her office when Pierce Walker burst into their reception area, followed by a handful of agents and the US Attorney. Not an assistant from his office, but the big man himself. She sat in her office while Christine fired angry questions at the attorney to buy time as she scanned the search warrants. Then she was shouting those questions at Raphael while he read them. An act to deflect any blame from herself? She might as well save the effort. The phone messages alone were enough to indict her. Several agents began packing up files and computers, while another agent herded the rest of the staff into the break room.

When the attorney announced that he had arrest warrants for Christine and Raphael, August finally got up and walked to the door of her office.

Christine turned to her, her face white. "August, what have you done?"

"Bitch." Raphael sneered at August as an agent handcuffed him. "You will regret this day and wish prison had been your punishment instead of what's coming."

Pierce stepped forward, his phone held up as though he was recording the exchange. "Did I just hear you threaten a federal witness, Raphael Reyes Delgado?"

Christine gave her one last desperate look as she was led out in handcuffs.

August sat in her office for another thirty minutes, then grabbed her gym bag and slipped out the back door.

She was halfway home when her phone buzzed. Pierce Walker.

"Where are you?"

"On my way home. I haven't eaten or hardly slept in the past twenty-four hours."

"We'll have everything set up tomorrow to stash you somewhere until we can bring this to trial. Until then, I'm putting a tail on you and an agent outside your house."

"Are you kidding? This will take months, maybe years to come to trial. I'm not the criminal. You can't just steal my life from me."

"I'm not going to let my prime witness disappear like all the other witnesses in cases against Reyes's organization. So pack a bag, and then get a good night's sleep. We'll be there first thing in

the morning with search warrants for your house and to move you some place safer."

"I have a dog, and I'm not leaving her behind."

"Call a friend or family member to come get the dog. It'd be a dead giveaway to have her with you. I'll move this along as fast as we can, and once Reyes is in jail, we might reconsider whether we need to keep you tucked away. We should have an indictment tight enough to arrest him tomorrow and hold him without bail. Your law partner was crying like a baby before we turned her over for the deputies to process her into the jail. She'll lawyer up, but she'll deal. I'm sure of it."

August ended the call. As a criminal-defense attorney, she was well acquainted with the degrading process of fingerprinting, photographing, and strip-searching anyone unlucky enough to be arrested. She was furious with Christine for screwing up both their lives but felt sick at the thought of her going through that in front of jailers who knew her as an attorney.

She swung into the drive, jumped out of her car, and hurried to unlock the back door of the home they'd shared before sprinting to the bathroom to throw up.

August worked the top, final strand of wire, twisting it tighter and tighter. The wire twanged and she eased up. Another turn and it'd break, like she almost did. She'd barely finished heaving up her guts that night before another phone call landed her at the jail. Not Pierce this time. It was Christine, asking for a face-to-face. That visit had twisted August to the point of snapping, and then her phone had buzzed a third and final time as she drove away from the jail.

She steered into the parking lot of a convenience store to answer it. It'd been years since that caller contact had flashed on her screen. Maybe the universe was looking out for her. Her childhood safe haven was calling at just the right moment.

"Julio. You don't know how glad I am to hear from you."

The caller cleared his throat. "August? It's BJ."

Dread filled her. "No. Tell me Julio's fine. I've been meaning to visit. I just…you know, with the practice taking up all my time. It's not like when I was a student and had summers off."

"He understood," BJ said softly. "But I've got bad news, Grasshopper. Old Julio's heart gave out day before yesterday. I reckon your granddaddy's been waitin' on him and those two are riding the big trail together now."

Could this day get any worse?

"I got somebody here who needs to talk to you, August. Okay?"

She sighed. "Yeah, okay."

"Ms. Reese?"

"Yes?"

"This is John Stutts. I've got a will here that deeds The White Paw to you lock, stock, and barrel."

"To me? Julio didn't have any relatives? Why didn't he leave it to BJ? He runs the place."

"There is a stipulation that you have to keep the ranch in operation until Mr. Billy Jack Johnson and Beauregard Davis White are deceased and no longer need the ranch as their residence."

"Who is Beauregard Davis White?"

"BJ says that's Pops."

"Oh. I never knew his real name."

"So, shall I send the paperwork for you to sign in Dallas?"

"When's the funeral?"

He hesitated. "I'm real sorry, Ms. Reese. Julio asked to be cremated immediately and his ashes scattered at Caprock Canyon, though I know nothing about that since such scattering on federal property would be illegal."

August laughed, in spite of everything. "He always did cut his own path." Hadn't Julio and Gus taught her to do the same? This call was a beacon lighting the way before her. "Don't mail that paperwork, Mr. Stutts. I'll see you in day or two to sign it in person."

She closed her phone and checked her rearview mirror. The agent in a dark sedan was parked behind her. She waved to him. No suspicious vans nearby, so she doubted they were listening in on her phone calls. Things had moved too fast for that, especially since she was a witness, not a suspect. She closed her eyes and took a deep breath. Gus and Julio were still looking out for her. God, she loved those two old men. She drove slowly to allow the agent time to follow, calculating scenarios for giving him the slip before Pierce Walker and crew showed up in the morning.

CHAPTER SIX

Y ou might as well let her go for scrap metal and put a down payment on a new car." Tank shifted the toothpick to the other side of his mouth. "Well, not necessarily a new car. You'll find lots of good used cars for sale around here."

Behind his repair business stretched a graveyard of rusting auto husks mired in a tangle of unchecked weeds pushing stubbornly up through the cracks in the brick-hard soil. Despite the sun that beat down on the shadeless lot, an occasional curled fender or upturned hubcap hid in shadows and harbored pools of brackish rainwater— breeding havens for mosquitoes. Teal swatted another of the little bloodsuckers as she, Tank, BJ, and Pops stood around the raised hood of her car. She lifted the neck of her T-shirt and wiped at the spot on her neck where it'd been feeding. Couldn't they talk about this inside?

"You can't drop a new engine in it?" BJ asked.

"It's not as simple as replacing the engine. That fire warped both front tires, melted the entire electrical system, every hose, the brake system, hell, even the headlights and every other plastic part they put in these things." Tank shifted the toothpick again. "Even if it was a classic car, I doubt it'd be worth the cost to restore it." He made a condescending sound. "And this here is a twelve-year-old Honda Civic. Scrap-metal yards are the only ones who collect these things."

"That's what you get for buying one of those foreign cars," Pops said, hitching his jeans up over his modest belly.

Tank's and BJ's expressions indicated they clearly agreed, and that just pissed her off. That same backward, uninformed herd mentality had driven Teal to flee her small-town roots. She could point out the three hundred thousand miles on the odometer, which you'd rarely see on an American car that had the original engine. In fact, she could quote impressive statistics that she'd compiled for Lauren when the Senate was mulling over the US car-industry bailout during the Bush-triggered recession. But it'd be wasted on this audience.

"You can blame my daddy. I wanted a Ford truck, but he said only boys can drive trucks to college. He wasn't from around here." Her mimic of their Texas drawl and jab at the local culture of pickup trucks flew right over their heads. Instead of taking offense at her sarcasm, the men nodded sympathetically. Originating from some place other than Texas was an acceptable explanation for almost any irrational behavior.

"I can get you a good price for the scrap metal pretty quick," Tank said. "And BJ could probably get you a good deal over at Eddie's car lot."

The three men looked at her expectantly.

Teal instantly regretted her behavior. Sure, she'd already perspired enough to need another shower, and—damn, these mosquitoes—she was being eaten alive. But she'd been in Washington too long and was acting like a snob. She studied the men. Good fellows, all of them, and she was going to need a bit more of their time and assistance to find a train station, or—she groaned inwardly at the thought—a bus station where she could by a ticket to Caprock, New Mexico.

She smiled at Tank. "I'd appreciate it if you could arrange to sell it for me, but I'm going to hold off on buying another car." She turned to BJ. "Is there a UPS or other store around here that packs and ships? I can catch an Amtrak or a bus, but I'll need to ship the things that were packed in my car."

BJ checked his wristwatch and scratched his cheek. "There's one of those stores over by ShopMart, but we need to take Pops to his doctor's appointment first."

"Don't need to go to no doctor." Pops glared at BJ. "I told you I feel fine."

"Do we have to go through this every time?" BJ met Pops's stare. "I told you that you have to get checked regularly to make sure your medicine don't need adjusting, or they won't give you any more. Now just suck it up and let's do what you have to do to keep that old ticker of yours going."

"It's a lot of trouble for nothing. I'll call Rita and get her to tell the doc I feel fine. He can just call the drugstore to refill my medicine."

"Rita already told you Doc wasn't going to do that again."

Pops kicked the dirt like an angry child. "I ain't going."

Although the old curmudgeon's little rebellion was kind of cute, Teal decided it was time to mediate. "Actually, it could be a lot more trouble if you don't go and your ticker stops on us."

"Sometimes I wonder." BJ's grumbled remark drew an obscene gesture from Pops.

Teal continued as if BJ hadn't spoken. "There's all the arrangements for a funeral, not to mention the cost. Then the whole crew would want time off for the visitation, and the funeral. Probably lose two, three days of work. Of course, BJ could just get a backhoe and bury you up on a hill, like the Old West days, and be done with it in a few hours—that is if you don't want a preacher and flowers and all that."

BJ and Tank stared at her, mouths open, then burst into hoots of laughter.

Pops squinted one eye at her. "I reckon I haven't weighed all that out." He threw up his hands in surrender. "I'll just have to go to the damn doctor until I've had time to think it over."

"Good." She looped her arm around Pops's and tugged him gently toward the front of the shop where the ranch truck was parked. "Because going to the doctor first is not a problem. It's not like I've got a schedule to meet."

❖

The doctor's office, a former residence with a wide wrap-around porch, was two blocks away from an emergency-room facility affiliated with the hospital in the nearest city and from the town's original downtown Main Street. BJ checked in at the desk, but a handful of others were ahead of them, quietly thumbing through a variety of magazines or catching up on local gossip. Before they settled in the comfortable chairs to wait Pops's turn, he held the truck keys out to Teal.

"If you take a right, then a left onto Main Street, you'll see the ShopMart on the left when you hit the outskirts of town. The shipping store's in that shopping center. We might be here a little while. I have to go back with Pops because I don't trust him to tell me everything the doctor says."

Pops made a disgusted noise but didn't deny the accusation.

She hesitated. "Are you sure? Is there any errand I can run for you while you're here with Pops?"

"I'm out of my candies," Pops said, digging in his pocket. He held out a five-dollar bill.

"He likes those butterscotch hard candies." BJ took a twenty from his wallet and added it to Pops's fiver. "And I need me some almonds and a can of walnuts—as much as this will cover. Helps my cholesterol, you know."

"Are you sure?" BJ's truck wasn't like the beat-up farm vehicle August had been driving the day before. It was an expensive crew-cab limited edition with a locking, lift-up hard cover over the bed. "I'll hurry so that I don't keep you waiting."

"Take all the time you need. If we're not in here reading six-month-old magazines, it means we're still back seeing the doctor." BJ waved her toward the door. "Passenger trains don't come through here, but you'll see the bus station on your way to ShopMart. Can't miss it."

❖

Main Street emptied onto the six-lane highway, lined with fast-food restaurants and other businesses, which had sucked traffic and commerce from the community's once-thriving downtown. The familiar logo and the two buses loading passengers on the side of the building were easy to spot, but Teal decided it would be easier to access if she turned into the ShopMart shopping plaza to find the shipping store first, then hit the bus station on her way back downtown.

She parked and climbed out to survey her possessions BJ had transferred from her car to the bed of the big truck. A set of matching luggage held clothing as well as health and beauty products, the patchwork quilt her grandmother had given her for high school graduation was zipped into a heavy plastic bag, and the rest was camping gear she'd used at one overnight stop to avoid the chance of being recognized at a hotel while her face was still on national newscasts. The news reporters had probably already moved past the scandal when it was clear she'd left Washington, but the entertainment shows and Internet bloggers were still milking the story with constant speculation and false sightings. She might as well pay to have the store pack the items for her to save time before they shipped them. First, she should call Wade to see if there was a certain carrier she should designate or time of day for delivery.

Teal rummaged in her shoulder purse for her phone. She was about to touch her cousin's contact icon, when a bit of information she'd tucked away for later investigation popped up like a red flag. What had August said about some guy tracing her phone and dragging her back to Dallas? Only law enforcement would have the authority to trace a phone call, but that didn't mean some paparazzi reporters didn't have contacts who could confirm an originating cell-tower location if she used her phone. August had said she'd bought a burner phone to use. Teal's eyes went to the ShopMart sign. Good idea. She had butterscotch candy and nuts to buy anyway. She locked the lid covering the truck's bed to safeguard her possessions and pocketed her wallet. If she hurried, maybe she could find a restaurant or Starbucks along the highway that had Internet service so she could initiate a search on August Reese and find out who wanted to "drag her back to Dallas" and why.

❖

"Teal. I've been trying to call you. Are you okay? Where are you?" Wade sounded worried.

"I wasn't specific enough for my GPS, and it led me to some small town near Caprock Canyon, Texas. I didn't realize the mistake, though, before my car engine decided to catch fire and sacrifice itself to the scrap-metal gods."

"Well, that's got to suck."

She laughed, despite the bad situation. She was starting to like this guy, even if she was worried that her mother was trying to play matchmaker. "Yeah. Fortunately, a Good Samaritan rescued me from languishing in the Texas desert and brought me into town. The car's a loss, so I'm about to ship the boxes I had packed in it to you. Then I'll text you when to expect me after I buy a bus ticket to Caprock, New Mexico."

"You might want to hold up on that."

Oh, no. Was he withdrawing his offer? She drew in a deep breath. "Have you changed your mind about having me at the farm?" If Wade refused her, she didn't know where she'd go. Canada?

"No." His answer was quick and adamant. Then he chuckled. "You need to start thinking like a tough cowgirl, not a dairy maid. This is a ranch, not a farm."

She relaxed a bit. "Ha. You don't know tough until you've worked a dairy farm." She hesitated. "So, what's the problem?"

"You should sue the shipping company after all this blows over. One of their employees must have seen your name on the paperwork for the things you shipped from DC and sold my address to some sleazy blogger who's stalking you."

"Tell me a murder of media crows aren't flocking to your farm...I mean ranch."

"I'm afraid so, but they won't come up to the house. We normally use the front pasture that the driveway runs through as turnout for horses. But at the first sign those media dogs had tracked you here, Boone put old BB out there."

"BB?" Boone must be his foreman.

"One of the biggest Brahma bulls you've ever seen. His horns are more than three feet long. And he's cranky about people being in his pasture."

She laughed again, picturing the bull chasing the paparazzi from his field. "I'm so sorry to involve you in this. I can go—"

"Absolutely not. My offer stands."

She was relieved, but she still needed to clear the air. "Wade, if my mother gave you the impression that I was single and available—"

"Teal." He cut her off gently. "You don't have to worry about that. I'm in a committed relationship. I'm just offering to help out a family member."

"Oh, nobody told me. Sorry." She was embarrassed to have brought it up. "It's just. Well, if you knew my mother, you'd know why I had to say that."

"It's okay, but you can relax."

She could hear a muffled voice, then Wade answering. "I'll be right there. I'm talking to Teal."

"Problem?"

"No, just Mr. Impatient. It'll do him good to wait."

Teal could hear him opening and closing cabinets. "So, is there a way to sneak in the back of the property where the media won't see me?"

"Afraid not. Can you hang where you are for a while?"

She mentally counted her dwindling cash. "How long?"

"I figure to wait a week or two and ship a pair of boots up to my friend in Canada that he's been wanting. If I act secretive enough, that busybody at ExPress will jump to the conclusion that I'm shipping something to you and sell the information to the paparazzi."

"Thanks, Wade, but then your friend will have them camping at his door."

"Honey, he's in theater. He'll love the drama. I'll email him about what I'm doing and wouldn't put it past him to disguise himself as you and have them chasing him all over Toronto. So, you'll probably need to lay low there for three or four weeks at the most."

"Maybe I can find an extended-stay hotel." If she was careful with her money, she probably could get by without tapping into any of her accounts.

"When you get settled, set up a new email account with a fake name and message me. We'll stay in touch through email. Cell phones can be risky."

"Okay. I'll email you when I've found a place."

"Teal? It's all going to be okay. We just need to throw the hounds off your scent. Meanwhile, you take care of yourself."

"Thanks. I will." She ended the call. Crap. Well, she couldn't ship her stuff now. It would have her "shipped from" location for the ExPress busybody to give out to the highest payer.

She stopped by the bus station and checked on the price of a ticket to Caprock, New Mexico, then separated that amount from her stash and tucked the cash into her back pocket.

Teal drummed her fingers on the steering wheel. What was she going to tell BJ when she returned with all her stuff still in the truck? She needed to spin this. She snorted. That was Washington-speak. She needed a plausible lie.

When she drove up to the doctor's office, BJ and Pops were waiting in two of the white rocking chairs lined up on the broad front porch. She'd never, even in her rural Pennsylvania hometown, seen a doctor's office with a wrap-around porch and rockers.

Pops was all smiles and insisted she take the front passenger seat. "Doc says my ticker is thumping along like a marching band.

Said me being tired didn't have nothing to do with my heart. He said BJ was working me too hard."

BJ bristled. "That is not what he said, and you know it. He said you need more rest. That means going to bed at a reasonable hour instead of staying up late to watch movies."

Teal only half listened to their banter as she stared out the window, serious and silent. BJ glanced at her briefly but kept quiet while Pops continued to gloat over his good news.

"Don't matter. You lost the bet, so you've got to buy us all lunch at Sophie's. I want a cheeseburger, fries, and one of them big banana-split sundaes for dessert."

"You will have a heart attack after eating that," BJ said.

Pops was undaunted. "Man's gotta die sometime."

"You got time for lunch?" BJ asked Teal.

She stared down at her hands. "It appears that I do." She gave him a weak smile. "A cheeseburger and ice cream sounds perfect."

It was hard not to wolf down the best cheeseburger she'd ever eaten, but she did truly feel a bit sick to her stomach at the lie she was about to tell these two very nice men. They'd nearly fallen over each other in their competition to open the door for her and pull out her chair to seat her at the Formica-topped, single-leg table. They sat on either side, which was fine with her, because without someone sitting on the fourth side directly across from her, she had a clear view of the door. After her call to Wade, she couldn't shake the feeling that someone might recognize her at any moment and alert the local media.

Pops was digging into his ice cream already, and Teal was swabbing a warm fry through the dollop of ketchup on her plate when she jerked her head up as the door chimed to alert the waitresses another person had entered. BJ followed her gaze, then returned his attention to his cheeseburger. "Expecting somebody?" he asked quietly.

This was her cue. She took a deep breath. "I hope not."

"Want to tell me about it?"

Pops slowed his attack on the banana split, his gaze bouncing between her and BJ.

"My stuff is still in the truck." She put her French fry down and picked up her burger. "I can't go to my cousin's right now. Is there an extended-stay hotel around here? Out on the highway, maybe?"

"Maybe."

"I know you've already towed my car in and hauled me all over creation, but could you take me by Tank's garage so I can see if the junk guy has picked up my car yet and left some money for me? Then you can put me and my stuff out at the hotel and I'll be out of your hair."

"How long you reckon you'll be staying?"

She shrugged. "Not sure. A couple of weeks, a month maybe."

Pops opened his mouth to say something, but BJ held up a hand, so he shoveled in another spoonful of ice cream instead.

"Well, sir. The way I see it, I can drop you off and you can pay out money to stay in that hotel, or you can come with us and I'll put you to work for the few weeks you're here. I can offer you room and board, plus twelve dollars an hour."

Teal chewed her lip and studied him. The ranch was secluded and a better place to hide for a few weeks. An out-of-towner holing up in a hotel day and night could arouse enough suspicion that somebody might actually try to figure out who she was. But then there was August. She didn't want her at the ranch. Why? Who was August hiding from? "I'd have to be stupid to choose a hotel over having a job while I'm stuck here."

"There's only one thing." BJ wiped his mouth and tossed his wadded napkin onto his plate. "You gotta tell me what's got you spooked. You're not in trouble with the law, are you?"

She shook her head and dropped the last bit of her burger onto her plate before shoving it away. She was hoping she wouldn't have to do this. "I can't go to my cousin's because my ex showed up there first. The fact that we're not dating any longer doesn't seem to matter. Getting thrown in jail twice for assaulting me hasn't made a difference either. And the restraining order I got isn't worth the paper it's printed on. If I'd stayed in DC, I'd probably be dead by now."

"You get you a gun and shoot him next time he shows up and tries something." Pops gave her a righteous glare. "Men like that don't stop just because the judge signed a paper."

"I could go to jail," Teal said.

"I'll shoot him if he comes around here. I'll tell 'em my eyesight is so bad, I thought he was a bear."

"There are no bears around here," BJ said, dismissing Pops.

Teal patted Pops's arm. "I don't think I could actually shoot somebody."

"All the more reason that you should come with us."

"I would feel safer, but I don't think August wants me there."

BJ picked up the check the waitress had left on the table. "You leave August to me. She might own the ranch, but I've known her since she was knee-high to a grasshopper."

"Oh. So that's why you called her 'Grasshopper' this morning?"

"Nope." BJ headed for the cash register without further explanation.

Teal looked to Pops.

"Ain't my story to tell," he said, shoveling in the last of his ice cream and standing to follow BJ.

After checking in at Tank's garage—the junkyard man hadn't come by for the car yet—BJ headed for the ranch. Teal was nervous about August's reaction to her return, but she didn't doubt the old cowboy held considerable sway over the grumpy ranch owner. So, if it meant free room and board in a place where the media wouldn't find her for a few more weeks, she'd keep her head down, clean toilets if that's what BJ assigned her, and try to stay clear of August as much as possible.

CHAPTER SEVEN

"The answer is still no, BJ, and you know why."

"Keep your voice down. She's right outside the door." BJ pointed in a silent command for her to sit back down. August held his eyes in a hard stare and put her hands on her hips, refusing his instruction. He continued to point to the chair. It was a stand-off of wills.

August's grandfather and Julio had taught her most of what she knew about ranching, but BJ had been her patient instructor in many things beyond cattle. She'd learned the Native American "spirit" rituals, the art of being one with nature, and—most importantly when she realized her sexual orientation was toward her own sex—how to be comfortable with herself even when others weren't. She finally dropped her gaze and sat because of her respect for him.

BJ acknowledged her act with a slight bow, accepting the responsibility of her trust in him. "She needs our protection, August. There's no way that guy can track her to this ranch, so it's the perfect place for her to lay low for a few weeks."

This was a bad idea on so many levels. She wasn't worried about some jealous boyfriend. She was worried about Reyes and who might get caught in the crossfire if he showed up. Now BJ was asking her to add one more person. She sighed. But what if she turned Teal away and the boyfriend did track her to this area and hurt her? She'd feel even worse.

"Why does her cousin think she'll be safe in New Mexico a month from now?"

"He's got a plan to make the ex-boyfriend think she's gone to Canada, but he needs a few weeks to make it look good and then maybe a couple more to be sure the guy took the bait and headed up there."

August drummed her fingers on the arm of the chair, then met his gaze. She didn't have to say it. His eyes told her that he'd known from the beginning she'd make the right choice. "Okay. Put her on the payroll for a month. Then she's on the first bus to New Mexico."

BJ laid his hand on her shoulder and squeezed. "I'll take care of it."

August stood and opened the office door. Teal was in the middle of the den, her butt propped against the high back of the sofa, cargo shorts riding up on her long, perfect legs. She was staring at her feet, apparently lost in thought, so August cleared her throat. Teal's head lifted and thick black lashes slowly shuttered, then exposed rich brown eyes as she focused. August's belly tightened. This was such a bad idea. She gestured to the office door. "BJ will give you a list of duties." She grabbed her hat from the coat tree next to the office door as Teal walked toward her. A warm hand on her forearm stopped her exit.

"Thank you, August," Teal said softly.

August shifted uneasily and stared at the door leading outside that would be her escape. "You'll have to do more than cook, and I doubt you'll be thanking me after BJ has you clean out the chicken coop. That's a really nasty job."

Teal's hand briefly tightened before she released August's arm. "Nothing's worse than shoveling manure during milking time. I grew up on a dairy farm."

August tucked that small bit of information away in her mental "figure this woman out" folder as she combed her hair back with her fingers and settled her Stetson into place. Maybe Teal *was* just an innocent farm girl who'd followed a bad boyfriend to DC before she found out about his aggressive side. Now she could get caught in the crossfire of the crud that was trying to follow August from Dallas. "I don't know. I personally think the politics of the urban jungle craps a bigger, smellier shit pile than anything an ark full of animals could produce."

She glanced over in time to see a flicker of pain in Teal's eyes as she went still for a split second. Then her shoulders slumped and she seemed...sad...before her face tightened into an unreadable mask. "A good reason not to go into politics." Odd. August had commented about urban life, not really about politics. And, though Teal's tone was benign, her body language was telling. There was more to Teal—hell, she'd never even asked the woman's last name—than she'd told them. But BJ would take care of that when he got her tax information. Now wasn't the time to ferret out the woman's background, if ever. She was only going to be here a few weeks.

"Would you tell BJ that I'm going for a ride? Don't hold supper if I'm not back."

❖

Teal silently cursed as she watched August leave with Rio close on her heels. August's remark had caught her off guard. Stupid, stupid, stupid. She'd almost given herself away by mentioning politics. Not that she thought August or BJ were the kind of people to sell her location to the paparazzi, but if August was hiding from someone, too, Teal's notoriety and the fact that she'd lied to them would surely get her thrown off the ranch. What would she do if that happened and she had to spend a month hiding in a hotel room? Ha. She could write a book about her affair with Senator Lauren Abbott. It probably would sell enough so her banishment from politics wouldn't be an issue. Nah. She'd probably spend all her royalties defending against the lawsuits the Abbott campaign would file to try to discredit her.

BJ was already writing out a work list when she entered the office. "August said she's going out for a ride and might not be back for supper."

He didn't seem surprised. "She gets like that sometimes. Her granddaddy, Gus, used to worry about her being too solitary. But it's just her way. Sometimes I think she'd be happy if that dog was the only other breathing thing in world. So, unless you need an advance beforehand, payday is end of the month."

"I'm good. Just tell me where to bunk and give me a list of what you need done. I can feed horses and chickens, muck stalls, clean chicken coops…whatever. I draw the line at slaughtering chickens, though. If you want one for dinner, you'll have to get one of the men to do that."

"Not a problem. We get most of our chicken meat from the grocery. If we do fry one up for dinner, Pops does the neck-wringing around here."

The image that formed in her head made Teal's stomach churn. "Sorry. I know most farm kids adjust early to putting the animals you raise on the table for dinner, but I never did."

BJ paused his writing and regarded her for a few seconds, then nodded as though confirming a decision. "You can bunk in the same room you slept in last night."

"I don't want to be any trouble."

"All my wranglers are gentlemen, but some have jealous girlfriends. It'll be better for you to stay in the house. I hope you're an early riser, though."

"I am." In DC, she rose at five a.m. to review the overnight news and was in the senator's office to begin work by seven a.m.

"Breakfast is at six in the summer. You'll need to collect eggs and feed the chickens beforehand, but you only have to cook breakfast and supper for me, August, and yourself. The men have their own kitchen and can take care of themselves. Monday through Friday, around noon, you'll put together lunch for everybody and take it out to wherever the guys are working." He peered at her. "How are you at office work?"

"Proficient. I can handle spreadsheets, general accounting, and correspondence…anything you need."

"Good. A lot of record-keeping goes with a ranch. We have to keep extensive records on each steer. We also keep a close inventory on all expenditures such as vaccines, feed, and fertilizer, and double-check deliveries and billing to make sure they match up. I'll be happy to let you do as much of that as you can handle. This time of year, I need to be out there with the herds to make sure everything is going well and our head count is consistent."

"What about house cleaning?"

"Nope. Brick's wife runs a cleaning and household shopper service. We contract with them to clean the ranch house and bunkhouse twice a week. They do our grocery shopping, too. I just give them a list of what we need. Since you'll be cooking, though, you can be responsible for giving them a list when the cleaning crew comes every Monday and Thursday."

"Okay."

"Let's see." He reviewed his list. "Oh, yeah." He began writing again. "We don't usually stable horses in the barn unless the weather is bad or one of them goes lame. If we do, you'll need to muck out their stall every day." He wrote one more thing down. "Last of all, you need to check on Pops at least twice a day and don't let him work too hard or long in that durn garden he insists on keeping."

"Right. Check on Pops."

"Any questions you can think of?"

"No. Wait, does the ranch have wireless Internet?"

He jotted down a short string of numbers and letters at the bottom of the list. "Yup. We get it and our television through satellite so it's not really reliable in bad weather, but this is the password."

He handed her the list. "Now, let's go unload your things and get you settled. Then I'll give you a quick tour of the rest of the place."

She took the list. "Thanks, BJ. You don't know how much I appreciate this."

He stood and wrapped a fatherly arm around her shoulders to guide her out of the office. "You don't know how much I appreciate you being here. Julio took care of all that paperwork. I hate doing it. I want to get back outdoors where I belong, and I have a feeling August needs some wide-open spaces right now, too."

She wanted to ask about August, but she didn't want to seem too nosy. She'd see what the Internet turned up and wait for a better chance to slip in a few discreet questions.

❖

The days were growing longer and the sun didn't set until almost nine o'clock, but it was dark and Teal had just enjoyed a luxurious soak, then slipped on a tank top and sleep shorts, when she heard someone quietly enter the front door and the thud of boots coming down the hall.

She'd seen August ride into the barn several hours earlier. Teal had been curled up in a butter-soft leather, oversized chair in the mostly unused living room, engrossed in a lesbian romance on her eReader because BJ was cursing loudly at a baseball game on the big-screen television in the den. The movement of horse and rider had caught her attention outside the front windows. But when dusk had begun to settle over the ranch and August still hadn't come into the house, Teal had decided to retire to her room to finish her novel.

She opened her bedroom door. "August?"

August stopped, her hand on the door of the bedroom across the hall. She smelled of sweat and horses, and a grass stain was bright against the back of her white, sleeveless cotton shirt. Teal let her gaze drift from the stain to the well-shaped denim-clad ass, then jerked it upward as August turned to face her.

"Sorry. Didn't mean to disturb you." August's eyes traveled slowly downward and locked on a spot in the carpet she was worrying with the toe of her boot—as though that had always been their intended destination.

"You didn't." Teal felt exposed in her skimpy sleeping attire, her nipples immediately hardening to push against the thin cotton material. She resisted the urge to cross her arms over her chest when August flushed at being caught checking her out. "I was about to climb into bed and read for a bit." She held up her eReader as exhibit one. "I just wanted to tell you that I left you a plate of spaghetti in the microwave. I didn't put it in the refrigerator because I saw you ride in a few hours ago and thought you'd come inside sooner."

August licked her lips. "I got caught up oiling an old saddle."

Teal realized something was missing…not something, but someone. "Where's your dog?"

"Rio? She's probably in the kitchen, checking her food bowl or looking for BJ."

"He's watching a baseball game in the den."

August's slow smile warmed Teal in unexpected places. "You're not a baseball fan?"

Teal smiled back and shook her head. "Not in the least."

"Me neither." They stared at each other for a moment.

"Well, the plate I fixed for you should warm right up if you're hungry. It's my mom's recipe, and being…I mean, it's pretty good if I say so myself." Crap. She'd almost revealed her last name because it was Italian.

"Thanks. I am hungry," August said.

"Well, then I hope BJ didn't make good on his threat to eat your dinner, too."

August's eyes narrowed. "He'd better not." She tossed the leather gloves she carried onto a table just inside her bedroom and headed for the kitchen.

Teal called after her. "If he did, there's more in the fridge. I hid it behind the gallon of lemonade."

She liked this nicer version of August. And she really enjoyed watching that perfect ass as it disappeared down the hallway. She closed her eyes, holding the image a bit longer. Then her hands were cupping those denim-clad cheeks, pulling those hips into hers as they stood and kissed...and she was on her back, digging her nails into firm muscle and soft skin as those bare hips flexed and thrust against hers. She opened her eyes and blinked at the empty hallway. Whew. She literally shook herself. This romance story she was reading was really winding up her imagination.

❖

August propped her shoulder against the porch support as she sipped from her coffee mug and watched Teal and Pops in the diffused light of the newly risen sun. Teal must have been up for a while because crisp bacon and a plate of fluffy biscuits were warming in the oven, and three clean mugs were lined up next to a fresh pot of coffee. Now, she was patiently following Pops and nodding as he pointed out different places where the hens sometimes laid wayward eggs outside the coop. Those eggs were few, and everybody but Pops just left them to the snakes or other scavenging vermin.

The morning was still cool, but an unbidden image of Teal standing in her bedroom doorway, dressed in a flimsy tank top and skimpy sleep shorts, spread heat up through August's belly and warmed her neck. She relaxed and let it happen. Christine had left her so raw and bleeding she wasn't sure she'd ever risk involvement again. She was relieved, though, that she wasn't so damaged her libido couldn't respond to a beautiful woman.

Teal was a farm girl who had a boyfriend—correction, ex-boyfriend. She probably didn't have a clue about lesbians. That created enough physical and emotional distance between them for her to relax and silently enjoy how delicious she found this stranger. Jesus, Mary, and Joseph. Talk about rebound. Well, that was one horse she definitely wasn't going to climb back on any time soon. She was just noticing. No harm in that. Even if Teal was bi-oriented, August had had enough drama in her life. She certainly wasn't interested in a woman with a stalker ex-boyfriend.

Teal glanced her way, and when August lifted her hand in a little wave, she patted Pops on the arm and jogged toward the ranch house with her basket of eggs swinging beside her.

"Sorry. I'll have breakfast ready as soon as I scramble up some of these eggs." She hesitated. "Unless you prefer them cooked some other way."

August pushed away from the post to hold the door open for Teal. "Scrambled is fine. You can add some diced jalapeños, though. I pretty much like anything that's hot and spicy."

Teal set the basket of eggs on the counter and raised her eyebrows at August.

"Food, I mean." August's neck and face heated, but this time in a different way. She scowled. "You know what I mean."

Teal laughed, washing off a half dozen eggs and grabbing a bowl from the cabinet. "I know. I couldn't help it. You left yourself wide open."

August rubbed her face and then smiled sheepishly. "Yeah. I guess I did."

BJ clomped into the kitchen, *The Dallas Morning News* under his arm. "Morning," he said, taking a seat at the kitchen bar next to the mug of coffee Teal set down for him. "Appreciate that." He looked over at August. "See how she treats me. You could learn a thing or two from her."

"In your dreams, old man," August said, her tone teasing. "Anyway, you should be pouring my coffee."

"Now you're dreaming, Grasshopper."

"Not worth arguing over since I'm here to pour for both of you," Teal said, combining eggs, jalapeños, and cheese in the heated skillet and scrambling everything into a spicy mix.

The conversation among the three of them was easy as they ate. BJ wanted to make sure Pops had shown Teal all of the early morning chores. Teal asked questions about the personalities of horses she'd fed that morning. August warned her about Pops's usual pranks—a fake snake in a feed bucket or a whitewashed horse turd placed in a hen's nest—to initiate a new hire. The old man had a silly side.

In fact, the ease at which Teal fit into their household bothered August. She suddenly felt the need to remind them all of Teal's status at the ranch. She rose to put her empty plate in the sink and refill her mug.

"I'll get those dishes," Teal said, grabbing BJ's mug to refill it, along with her own.

August returned to her seat and cleared her throat when Teal sat again. BJ shot her a wary glance as he buttered another biscuit.

"I know BJ talked with you, but I need to make sure we're crystal clear on a few things."

Teal glanced at BJ but nodded her agreement. "Okay."

"It's my understanding that you have to delay going to your cousin's ranch because you have an ex-boyfriend stalking you and he's already been there looking for you. Do you know how he found out you might be going there?"

Teal chewed her lip for a few seconds, and August wondered if she was deciding how much to disclose or whether she should lie. But she raised her eyes to August's.

"I don't know for sure, but he has friends in...government who would trace things for him. My apartment was furnished, but I had clothes, kitchenware, and stuff like that. Instead of renting a storage unit somewhere, I stupidly shipped most of my belongings to my cousin's ranch. I'm guessing he somehow found out where it was going and figured I was headed there, too."

That made sense. It could have been as easy as chatting up the movers as they carried the boxes out to load them on a truck. Teal still held August's gaze. She was either telling the truth or was a really great liar.

"Do you have a location app on your phone? Were you using it for your GPS?"

Teal was shaking her head before she finished the questions. "My GPS is an old Garmin. It's dumb, but I'm kind of attached to the voice on it, so I wasn't using my phone. I didn't have a signal out there, but I don't know for how long. The carrier doesn't seem to have a good signal in this area, so I picked up a cheap phone when we were in town yesterday to call my cousin." She pulled a flip phone like the burner August had bought from her pocket and held it up. "It's one of those buy-minutes-in-advance plans. After I talked to my cousin, I turned my other phone off because I've seen on crime shows that you can be tracked by your phone."

August drummed her fingers on the countertop to collect her thoughts. "Did you use a credit card to get the phone?"

"I'm only using cash. His name was on all my cards and my bank account, so I withdrew all the cash I could and left."

BJ swallowed the last bite of his biscuit and pushed his plate away. "Aren't you being a little paranoid, August? If this guy did show up, me and the boys—"

She silenced him with the stare she used to intimidate witnesses who were lying in court, then turned back to Teal. "While you're here, BJ will lock your smart phone, credit cards, and the laptop I saw on your bed in the office safe. I'm not saying I don't trust you, but you and Pops will be here alone when the rest of us are out on the range all day. You can be traced through any of those things, and I want the employees of this ranch to know that I'm doing everything in my power to keep them safe."

Teal's eyes narrowed. "I understand your concern, but I'm not as naive and poor as it might appear. I'm only cash short right now because I have money stashed in some short-term investments that have a few more months to mature—investments that my ex knows nothing about. I need Internet access to keep an eye on those and to keep in touch with a few friends so they don't think I've been kidnapped and ended up in a shallow grave somewhere."

"Feel free to use the computer in the office, but please wait to email any friends. I have a hacker friend who can set up an email account for you that won't lead back to my computer's IP address. I'll get in touch with him this evening if that's soon enough."

Teal's steady stare seemed to methodically dissect August and study each piece. Then she blinked and her chin dipped infinitesimally in consent. "Thank you."

August stood. "BJ and Pops got you all lined up for the day?"
Teal and BJ stood, too.

"Yes," Teal said.

Despite her intention to use distance to dampen the attraction she felt toward this woman, August regretted the tension her lecture had created. She wanted to see the flash of white teeth, hear that throaty chuckle again. She picked up her hat and swatted at BJ with it. "Don't let them take advantage of you. They're perfectly capable of doing their own laundry."

"Sez you." BJ grabbed his own hat, ignoring her tease, and left in a cloud of disapproval.

"I won't iron shirts, but I don't mind doing laundry if he's happy with them just pulled out of the dryer and folded or hung up," Teal said, staring after him.

"It's not the laundry. He's pissed at me for making a few rules." An angry heat crawled up her spine and burned her ears. That wire was twisting too tight again. Perspiration gathered along her hairline and trickled down her neck. BJ might think she was going overboard, but she was tired of being ignored and questioned by people who worked for her. August closed her eyes and counted silently to rein in her temper. "Damn, he's getting cranky in his old age," she said under her breath.

She opened her eyes and faced Teal, keeping her tone professional and precise. "The keys to the farm truck are on the table by the front door. Pops will ride out with you to show you where to find us when you have lunch ready and loaded." She slapped her hat onto her head and snugged it down over her brow. She'd taken only two steps when she stopped again. She didn't want to leave on a sour note, so she softened her tone. "And could you make sure he doesn't kill himself weeding that garden of his? He doesn't know how to pace himself in this heat."

"Sure," Teal said, her tone matching August's.

August nodded curtly and stepped toward the door again.

"Speaking of laundry—"

Her hand was on the door handle when Teal's voice stopped her one more time.

"The shirt you were wearing last night had a big grass stain right between your shoulder blades," Teal said.

"I guess my horse used me for a napkin."

"Just letting you know I'm going into your room to get *your* laundry and take care of that stain."

"You don't have to do that."

"That stain will set if it hasn't already, and the shirt will be ruined."

The low, full timbre of Teal's voice was like a soothing bath, and for a fleeting moment, August wondered what it would be like to drown in it, in Teal. Rio, waiting for her to open the door, sat and stared up at her. What were they doing? She blinked. They were going to the barn. Teal was waiting for her answer. "Well, it is one of my favorite shirts, so thank you." She opened the door but glanced back at Teal and nodded to confirm her permission. "See you at lunch."

Chapter Eight

Teal's first couple of days had been full as she learned her new duties, but after the hectic pace of Washington, her multitasking skills and natural inclination for efficiency left her four free hours until she needed to begin preparing dinner. She'd planned the meals and done the grocery list, also folded the laundry and returned it to its owners. Pops was napping since his garden was completely weed-free with two of them tending it. Even the chicken coop was newly clean. She fingered the bill of goods that she'd checked off when the items were delivered to the barn that morning. Maybe she'd see about logging it into the accounting records.

Surprisingly, the office computer was fairly new and powerful, the desktop neat, and the ranch's business software the same her older sister had installed for her father's farm. Gray was incredibly brainy but made it clear she didn't intend to fulfill her teachers' goals by accepting one of several Ivy League scholarship offerings or bow to her parents' ideal of marriage and children. But, because of her love for farming, she'd found some common ground with their father that Teal had never managed. She wished Gray were here now. She'd always been a rock they all leaned on as kids. Teal could almost feel her sister's strong arm wrapped around her shoulders…like August's arm had felt. She shook her head. "Don't even go there."

She opened the program and easily found where she needed to log the morning's invoice. Then, she poked around the software, familiarizing herself with the records the ranch kept. She'd talk to BJ at supper about helping him with the paperwork. If she stayed busy enough, she wouldn't have time to think about tall, blond, and, yeah, sexy.

She drummed her fingers on the desk, then opened the search engine. No, she shouldn't. She typed in Stetson, instead. She needed something more than her ball cap when she worked outside. Her ears and neck were feeling tender even though she'd applied sunscreen. Wait. She couldn't order online without using a credit card. Maybe next time BJ went into town, she could go with him.

She checked several websites, but the news media had moved on to a report of some survivalist kook claiming that Iran had a bio-weapon nearly ready to launch at the US. She watched a few cute animal and music videos just out of boredom and checked sports scores. Finally, she gave in to her curiosity and returned to the search engine to type in AUGUST REESE.

Her eye immediately went to "images of August Reese." She clicked and nearly drooled. August was hot enough in jeans and a dirty T-shirt. But in a business suit? She was smoking. Who was the woman in most of the photos with her? Ah. Law partner. But the woman seemed more than that in several of the photos. A bit of disappointment dampened her thrill. She was being silly. It wasn't like she expected anything from August, but truthfully, given a chance at a naked night with that tall, lean body, she'd probably jump at it. She smiled at the photo of August in an elegant, fitted black suit at a fund-raising event for a Dallas charity. "I am such a slut."

So, if August is a lawyer from a fairly prominent Dallas family, what's she doing running a cattle ranch in the Texas panhandle? BJ had mentioned she'd recently returned after being gone a number of years.

Teal peeled her gaze from the pictures and clicked back through her previous screens to the search results. A couple of Dallas news agencies made the top of the list. She clicked one and began to read. The articles were vague, but a few facts were clear. August's partner was in jail, and an associate was out on bail. The charges had something to do with evidence tampering or interfering with investigations, withholding discovery, and some other things she'd have to look up to understand. The district attorney said more charges were likely, and the reporter implied that the associate lawyer's father, a Dallas businessman, was being investigated by DEA. International drug trade? Was August hiding at the ranch? From the good guys or bad guys?

Maybe August was just disillusioned by her partner's cross over to the dark side and had thrown in the towel and decided to change careers. God knows, she should be thinking of doing the same thing instead of hoping to eventually work her way back to Washington. She glanced at the time noted in the bottom right of her screen. Holy crap, she needed to get supper started. She shut down her session and hurried to the kitchen.

❖

"I don't even know her last name."

BJ didn't acknowledge her implied question, and August had to grab the dash of the truck when it lurched through a particularly deep dip in the pasture.

"Damn it, BJ. If you want to get rid of me, let me get out so you can just run me over and be done with it."

He slammed the truck to a halt next to a stand of trees where a newborn calf peeked out from behind a first-time mama. He jerked the gear into park and growled. "If I wanted to be rid of you, I'd drag you over to Caprock and throw you in a rattlesnake den."

August let out a disgusted snort. "You're too scared of snakes, and you know it."

They glared at each other for a long minute, then both grinned.

BJ whisked off his hat and slapped at her with it. "You ain't never going to let me forget that, are you?"

She fended him off with her hands, laughing. "You screamed like a little girl. It wasn't even a real snake."

They each opened their door and climbed out. BJ lowered the tailgate of the old truck, and Rio jumped to the ground as he reached for the calving box. "You remember how to do this?"

"I remember throwing up when Gus made me castrate a calf the first time."

"Well, you ain't a kid any more. You're a rancher, and I ain't going to be around forever to handle it for you."

"I know."

He eyed her. "We can always band them at branding."

August took a deep breath. "No. I am going to be making some changes at The White Paw, but this isn't one of them. This is the least painful and the least stressful for the animals." She readied the yellow ear tag, the tattoo stamp, and the testosterone pellet injector, lining them up on the tailgate. Then she laid out the scalpel, iodine mixture, and a fly-repelling antibiotic paste for a castration if the baby was male. Reaching into her pocket, she added a pair of latex gloves and a couple of small syringes.

"What's that?" BJ eyed her suspiciously.

"A local anesthetic."

"Jesus, August. It don't hurt them much when they're this young. It's like clipping off puppy tails when they're newborn. You could have fifty steers born in one calving season. You know how much that would cut into profits?"

Rio whined.

"Rio and I don't hold with docking dog tails like that either."

BJ stared at Rio. "Does that dog understand every word anybody says?"

August shrugged. "Besides, I only need the ranch to break even after I take care of you guys. Even if Dad cuts me out of his will, Gus left me enough to live comfortably off investments." She settled the metal bracket that suspended the hanging scale into the stake pocket of the truck's fender and squared off with him. "This is one of those changes I mentioned, and it's not up for debate."

He dismissed her with a wave. "It's your money."

The anxious heifer bellowed at them as they approached. Humans usually meant food, but the new mother obviously wasn't sure about that dog and this new instinct to protect her baby.

"I'll try to keep her attention while you circle around behind her to grab the calf," BJ said, taking a slow but direct path toward the young cow. August signaled Rio to stay back while she cut a wide path around the heifer. The animal swung her head toward August, but Rio barked sharply to draw the heifer's attention. When BJ drew too close, the heifer turned away from him while keeping an eye on Rio and trotted right past August, who scooped up the baby.

"A female." She relaxed in relief. She knew castrating the young males was necessary, and it wasn't like she didn't have any experience. She'd emasculated the egos of several cocky young assistant district attorneys in the courtroom, but she wasn't looking forward to actual physical castration, anesthesia or not. The yuck factor didn't sit well on her stomach. That's why she'd gone to law school instead of becoming a doctor.

"I was hoping this one would throw a heifer," BJ said. "It's a good breeding line."

He kept a watchful eye on the young mama while August carried the baby over to the truck and loaded her into the canvas sling to weigh her. She recorded the weight in her small notebook, then clamped the handle of the toothbrush dipped in tattoo ink in her teeth and worked fast while the calf hung still helplessly suspended in the canvas sling. The mama bellowed when the baby bleated at the momentary pain of having its ear pierced by the tag, then swabbed with an inky toothbrush and pricked by the needles of the tattoo stamp. She was so busy bleating for her mama, she didn't even react to the punch of the medical gun that embedded the testosterone pellet. That would ensure proper growth during her first months. Boy calves would get a second dose at five months.

August recorded the ear tag and tattoo information in the notebook as well, then gently released the calf from the sling and herded her toward her worried mama.

"Good job." BJ squinted at her. "But you aren't likely to get so lucky next time. Next one might be a steer."

She wrinkled her nose. "I know."

He laughed and slapped her on the back. "Put a star or something by that entry. We might want to keep this calf for your herd."

Rio jumped back onto the truck's bed, and August began stowing the tools. "My herd. I like the sound of that." She felt him watching her, wondered again why Julio hadn't left the ranch to him. They climbed into the truck, and BJ flipped down the driver's visor where he'd stowed a pack of slim cigarillos. He drew one out and dangled it from his lips as he flipped open an old butane Zippo to light it.

August frowned and lowered her window. "I thought you quit smoking."

He lowered his window, too. "I did mostly." He scrunched up his face. "But this seat still smells a little like puke after being closed up in the heat."

August laughed. "Why do you think I was letting you drive?"

He puffed on the cigarillo and blew the smoke toward her as he put the truck in gear and guided it toward the ranch house. They were quiet for a while, each lost in their own thoughts when he answered the question she'd posed more than an hour before.

"Her last name is Crawley. Teal Crawley."

"So, your grandfather never remarried after your grandmother died?"

"No. He said she was the only woman he'd ever love."

Teal was pleasantly surprised by August's more relaxed mood tonight. She'd consulted Pops about the ranch owner's favorite meals when she was a teen, then whipped up mashed potatoes, black-eyed peas, and baked chicken for supper. She was hoping to soften August up to ask a favor, and it appeared to be working.

BJ chewed slowly, watching August as if he was waiting for her to say more. But August seemed to be contemplating the peas she was stirring into her mashed potatoes.

"Grace was one of a kind," BJ said quietly. "Julio and Gus had just got this ranch started when she moved into town and stole Gus's heart. It caused a big rift between them two when Gus said he was going to marry her. But then Julio went up into the canyons for a couple of weeks, and when he came down, him and Gus talked it out and the three of them made their peace." He smiled. "Grace found out Julio had a weakness for those little chocolate-covered cherries, so three or four times a year, that UPS guy would show up with a box of them things. She had different kinds shipped from all over the world for him, but his favorites were the ones that were brandy soaked."

August looked up from her plate. "My favorites, too."

BJ wagged his finger at her. "This one thought she'd outfox him by eating all his cherries and putting the empty wrappers in my bathroom trash."

August grinned at Teal. "It worked the first time. I learned a few new Spanish words when Julio discovered all his cherries gone."

Teal laughed. "But you eventually got caught?"

BJ answered. "Yep. I cut me a little foam strip and glued it to the inside of the bathroom door knob where it wasn't obvious. Then I soaked the foam in the ink we use to tattoo the calves. When she grabbed that knob, she had her fingers coated in ink that would take weeks to fully wear off. Caught her purple-handed."

August ducked her head and pushed the food around on her plate while Teal and BJ laughed at her expense, then looked up with a cocky grin and winked at Teal. "Wasn't the last time I got caught stealing cherries."

Teal's face—and other places—warmed at the double entendre. At least, that's how Teal interpreted it. Maybe she was projecting because she found August so attractive. Just because she was a strong, athletic woman didn't mean she was a lesbian. And she hadn't actually admitted her orientation to August either.

"So they all lived here?"

August shook her head. "Gus and Grace started up an operation closer to Dallas. Gus still had his partnership with Julio and spent weeks here during the peak of calving season every spring and fall. But when the heifers and steers were weaned, they were shipped down to the Double G to be fattened for slaughter or auctioned to other ranchers for their breeding herds."

"How old were you when your grandmother died?"

August shrugged. "Actually, she died before I was born. My father was at Duke, finishing up a master's degree in finance. He really had no interest in hands-on ranching. So Gus left the Double G in the hands of his foreman and moved back here with Julio."

"If your father was in his early twenties, then Gus must have still been fairly young. It's unusual for a man widowed that early to never remarry. He must have loved your grandmother very much." Even though she'd never found it, Teal still held to that romantic ideal of true love.

BJ abruptly stood and took his empty dishes to the sink. "That supper was fittin', Miss Teal." He patted his stomach. "You keep it up and I'm gonna have to buy some bigger pants." He gestured toward the door. "Need to talk to Hawk about a bull he's hot for me to see." He glanced at August and pointed to the kitchen's large windows. "Couple more hours of daylight."

"Yeah." Instead of rising to follow him out, August buttered the last two yeast rolls and popped them in the microwave for a few seconds, then returned to the kitchen island where they'd made a habit of eating their meals.

"Thank you." Teal tore off a piece of the warm roll August had plopped on her plate as she returned to her seat. She waited while August chewed a bite. BJ's sudden exit was not his usual after-dinner pattern. He either didn't want to talk about something, or he was giving August room to discuss it with her. Maybe it was both.

"Gus and Julio were…*special* friends." August's eyes searched Teal's, and Teal nodded to confirm her comprehension. No. She wanted to give August more than understanding. She hoped to maybe open the door for a discussion about what was going on between the two of them. "Do you think your grandmother knew about their relationship?"

August shrugged. "If she didn't before, I'm sure my father told her when he found out." She chewed and swallowed a bite of her roll and rubbed her face. "He apparently walked in on them when he was a teen, and Dad never forgave Gus for it."

"I'm sure he saw it as your grandfather cheating on your grandmother."

August shoved her plate away but didn't lift her eyes from it. Her words were bitter. "Judging from his own frequent affairs, he wouldn't have a problem with that. He just had a problem with his old man being queer."

Teal hesitated. He must have had a problem with his daughter being gay, too. But they hadn't really admitted that to each other, had they? "So, you and your father aren't close, I gather."

August ignored the opening to reveal her orientation. "No. We aren't." She stood and rinsed her dishes in the sink before placing them in the dishwasher. "Dinner was great."

Teal dumped her own dishes in the sink and hurried after her. "Are you going back out? Is there something I can help do?" She followed August out onto the wide front porch.

August stopped and finger-combed her blond hair back before settling her Stetson firmly in place, a gesture Teal was beginning to associate with August. Damn, she was sexy in that hat. Her slate-colored eyes studied Teal for a few seconds, as if she was deciding how to answer.

"I've been riding the big bay you've seen because I'm still working the green out of my new mount."

"Which one is yours? Wait. That was a dumb question. They all technically belong to you. Which have you chosen to be your main riding horse?"

"Some of the horses in the paddock do actually belong to the wranglers. But I'm working the Paint colt in the left paddock to be my personal ride."

Wow. The young stallion was a gorgeous piebald tobiano that Teal had seen August work in a round pen some evenings. She was surprised that she planned to work cattle with him. "I would have guessed he was just for breeding."

"I'll breed him some, too, but this ranch is about breeding and raising cattle, not horses." August squinted at the sun and strode off toward the barn.

Teal followed. "Do you mind if I watch you work him?"

"Actually, I'm going to ride him out to one of the herds, to get him used to being around cattle in an open environment."

"What if he spooks and throws you and leaves you out there? Wouldn't it be better if someone was riding with you?"

August glanced toward the bunkhouse. "The men have earned their evening of rest. Besides, I'm pretty hard to buck off and he's already trained to ground tie, so he'd probably just stop and wait for me once he got past his fright. If not, he'll come back to the barn and I'd just have to walk back."

"I could go with you."

August stopped and studied her. "You ride much?"

"We had a palomino mare on my dad's dairy farm. My brothers preferred to get around the farm on the four-wheelers, but I liked to ride Goldie instead." Teal smiled at the memory. "I wanted to be a cowgirl. The dairy cows, of course, seemed to have a clock in their heads. They'd stop grazing and trudge up to the milking barn at the same time morning and evening, but I liked to ride out on Goldie with one of the border collies trailing us and pretend we were rounding them up."

August smiled, too. "Gus said he caught me trying to herd the chickens on my Shetland pony when I was about five years old." August chuckled as she pointed to a well-oiled saddle several racks down from the saddle she was grabbing. "That'll fit the bay."

Teal almost wanted to squeal with excitement. The twelve-year-old girl she used to be was jumping up and down inside, but she forced herself to saunter over and casually shoulder the bridle draped over the saddle's horn before sliding it off the rack.

August looked relaxed in the saddle, but Teal was aware that almost imperceptible movements of her legs and hands constantly talked to the stallion as he danced next to her own calm mount. She felt like a sack of potatoes in the saddle riding next to her. "Did your grandfather teach you to ride?"

"Gus? No. Julio did."

They came to a gate, and August spent the next fifteen minutes patiently convincing the three-year-old colt that the metal contraption wouldn't bite him when it followed as he backed up to swing it closed. Once the gate was secured again, they walked for a bit to settle the skittish stallion, and August picked up their conversation again.

"Julio is...was originally from Spain. His formal training as an equestrian began when he was a child, before he came to America as a young man. He taught Gus a lot about horses, and Gus taught him about cows. So, Julio was my riding instructor. Gus was my teacher when it came to breeding and handling cows."

The heat had eased a bit, and a faint breeze wafted in from the west where the red cliffs of the Caprock cut a jagged pattern in the horizon.

"How far is it to ride to the state park? I'd love to see the canyons sometime," Teal said, enjoying how the sinking sun lit the mountains.

"It's about six or eight hours on horseback if you're not in a hurry. But if you want to go some weekend, we can trailer the horses over to the park and ride some of their trails. The best one, though, is on the north side of the park, and horses aren't allowed on it. You have to hike it."

"That would be fun, too." Teal thought about Julio and Gus. "Is that where Julio went when he found out Gus was going to marry Grace?"

"He went to the canyons north of the park. It's a maze of gorges and wider canyons. Gus said he almost went after him when Julio wasn't back after a few days."

"Why didn't he? I'm sure he was worried."

"BJ and Pops stopped him. They said Julio needed to be alone to see deep inside himself and…how did Gus say it…find a light in his storm."

"So I guess he did, if he came back and they all remained friends."

"BJ mentioned that you haven't been at the ranch long. Why'd you leave? Or maybe I should ask, why'd you come back?"

August didn't answer but gestured with her chin. "There's the herd. Canter a circle around them a few times. Start about twenty yards out, then make each circle tighter until you're about five yards away from them. I'm going to start on your outside, but I'll fall back behind you so he can see the cows at some point. You just keep a steady pace."

Their conversation over, Teal concentrated on August's request. The bay loped smoothly along, responding easily to her leg pressure. She, on the other hand, was growing tired. She was working muscles that running didn't exercise and would be sore tomorrow.

The cows were used to the horses and barely raised their heads. Now that the day was beginning to cool, this was their grazing time. The stallion's ears worked back and forth and he snorted at the heavy smell of the cows, but he seemed to settle as they drew closer. Then a young cow spooked and the herd began to shift. A few steers darted away and the stallion hopped sideways, then put his head down and bucked. August grabbed the saddle horn and rode through a series of crow-hops before she got his head up, slowed him to a walk, and pointed him straight for the herd. He balked a few times, and then Teal moved the bay next to him and they waded into the herd. Most were mature mama cows that calmly shifted to let the horses pass. Still, Teal relaxed when they left the herd and started for the barn.

In the barn, rubbing the horses down, she tried again. "So, are you going to tell me why you left the ranch?"

August bent to check the stallion's hooves as she spoke. "No mystery. I went off to college."

Teal waited, but when August didn't elaborate, she prodded her. "And you came back because…?"

"Julio passed away, and his attorney called to inform me that he'd left the ranch to me. I was tired of the city, so I came back."

"The city was Dallas?"

August gave her a sharp look. "Yeah." She unclipped the stallion's crossties and led him out of the barn to his paddock.

Teal had obviously asked her limit of questions. She turned the bay out in the opposite paddock, a little surprised that August was waiting to walk her back to the house. Dusk was settling around them, and the warm evening was heavy with the pleasant musky smell of horses and sweat. She didn't want their time together to end with August distant and silent. "Thanks for letting me go with you."

"No problem." Reaching to open the door, August paused when Teal laid a hand on her forearm. Her gray eyes were guarded, and her gaze shifted when Teal searched them.

"I don't mean to pry, August." She couldn't stop herself. Something deep inside told her this ranch, here with this woman, was where she was supposed to be right now—for whatever reason. It felt as if they had known each other in another time, another place. Two stars destined to cross. She'd never really believed in that sort of thing. She didn't believe in anything specific, really. But she felt this. Did August feel it, too? She traced her fingertips along August's cheek—so soft—and watched her gray eyes darken. "But sometimes you seem so sad. I'm a good listener if you ever want to talk." When August's gaze lifted and held hers, Teal flattened her palm against August's warm skin. August's eyes closed for a few brief seconds as she pressed into the caress, then gently moved back and held the door open for Teal.

"You can ride the bay any time you want."

"Thanks. I'll probably be sore tomorrow, but I'd forgotten how much I love being on horseback."

The flicker of a small smile drew Teal's attention to August's mouth. Before she realized what she was doing, she touched her fingertips to August's bottom lip. "Your lips are chapped. You should use sunscreen on them when you're working outside." She just couldn't stop touching her.

Teal held her breath when August stepped close again. She tucked a strand of hair behind Teal's ear. Her skin tingled along her neck and down her arm as August traced the curve of her ear. "And you should put sunscreen on your ears. They're already burned." August's eyes searched hers, then moved lower to her mouth.

"I will."

They were inches apart as August swayed toward her. But something told her they'd regret it tomorrow. August would, anyway.

"I'd better finish cleaning up those supper dishes." Teal turned, breaking the spell, and went through the door August still held open.

They both walked through the house to the kitchen, where Teal poured two glasses of iced tea. She loaded her dishes she'd dumped in the sink earlier into the dishwasher and started it, then prepared the coffeemaker and set the timer for the next morning.

"I think I'll take a long soak in the tub and go to bed early," she announced.

August nodded. "I'm sure I don't have to tell you since you're a runner, but it will help if you do some stretching before you go to bed tonight."

Teal cocked her head. "And how'd you know I was a runner?"

"I'm a trained observer. The day I found you wilting on the side of the highway, you had on a brand of running shoes I've only seen serious runners wear."

"So, that's where you've been since college."

August frowned. "What?"

Teal narrowed her eyes and tapped her chin in an exaggerated expression of concentration. "You must have been a military spy. No. CIA."

That seemed to amuse August. "Maybe I worked at the mall, selling athletic shoes at one of those sporting-goods stores."

"Nope. You said *trained* observer."

"True." August shrugged. "Okay, I confess. I was trained by the best gossip in the Dallas Junior League—my mother. Nothing gets past her."

"Ha, ha." Teal threw the dish towel she'd been using to wipe down the counter at August, who neatly caught it and tossed it back. "On that note, I'm headed to my room."

August pointed toward the office. "We had two new calves today, so I need to log their info in the records. Also, I meant to tell you that my buddy has fixed things so it's safe for you to access your email and any accounts you need, even from an iPad or a smart phone if you do it through the ranch Internet."

"Oh, thanks. You know, I really haven't minded being cut off from the rest of the world, but I guess I should email Wade for an update." She didn't want to think about leaving. Maybe if she made herself indispensable, August would let her stay. Maybe if she ever got to kiss her, August would beg her to stay. *That really worked out well in DC, didn't it?* Better stick to the job. "If you're going to log on, I have an order ready for Jeffers Brothers—fertilizer for the hay fields, cattle wormers, and such—ready for you or BJ to sign off on before I send it in."

"Thanks. I'll look it over. BJ's going to get lazy with you doing all his work for him," she said as she walked through the den to the office.

"Hmm. I figured all the paperwork would be the ranch owner's responsibility," Teal called after her. "I thought I was taking on that extra work for you."

August stopped and turned. Her smile was broad. "Did you now?"

Teal returned her smile. "Just sucking up to the boss. Don't let it go to your head."

Still smiling, August shook her head. "Good night, Teal."

"Good night, Boss."

August quickly logged the stats on the two newborns, then checked Teal's order. Damn, that woman was efficient. Some DC executive must really be missing his top administrative assistant right now. She hesitated only a second before opening the web browser and typing "Teal Crawley" in the search field. The results were scanty—a few scholarship announcements, attended University of Michigan but it didn't show her graduating. She checked for a criminal background, using her passwords from the law practice. Nothing other than one speeding ticket as a teen. In fact, there was nothing on Teal Crawley after she apparently left college. Not too suspicious. She could have married and changed her name for a while. Maybe she'd divorced and reverted to her maiden name. Maybe the supposed stalker boyfriend was actually an ex-husband.

Disappointment swelled in August's chest. She could have sworn Teal was about to kiss her earlier. Maybe she'd imagined it. Maybe she'd been about to kiss Teal. "Shit." She needed to get her head together and her hormones in check. Teal wasn't a bandage for the wound that undoubtedly would reopen when she had to face Christine in court—whether it was later this year or next year, depending on how the evidence-gathering against Reyes went.

Christine.

The woman she'd visited at the jail her last night in Dallas hadn't been the one she'd argued with the night before Susan came in her office to resign.

August showered again after she fled the office as the deputies took Christine away in handcuffs. The whole business made her feel dirty inside and out. She had to figure out what to do with Rio while Pierce whisked her off to God knows where. She hated to put her in a boarding kennel, but she didn't trust her parents to take care of her. She'd Google area hotels to see if any of the better ones were pet friendly. Yeah. Maybe she'd hide out in a nice hotel somewhere outside Dallas. Austin, maybe. Or Galveston. The beach would be nice.

She packed enough jeans and shirts for a week, and one business suit, then lay across the bed and closed her eyes. Their bed. She opened her eyes and stared at the ceiling fan. One of the four light fixtures was missing a bulb. She felt like the fixture, like part of her was missing.

Her phone buzzed in her pocket. It was the jail. She might have let it go to voice mail, but she was still a defense attorney and there could be a million reasons someone arrested would have her cell number—a fellow attorney charged with DWI or domestic violence or one of her less responsible friends who hadn't taken those speeding-ticket court dates seriously.

"August Reese."

"Please don't hang up. This is my one phone call." Christine's voice was choked with tears.

"Are you insane? I shouldn't be talking to you and you called my cell. They'll have a record of it. You should be calling an attorney who can represent you."

"I don't care if they do. I need to talk to you, August. Please. I know I don't deserve any favors from you. But I'm begging. This isn't about getting me out of this mess I've let myself get sucked into...that I've let destroy us and our law practice. This is about us."

August knew she should refuse, but months, maybe years, would go by before there would be a trial. She needed some answers now.

"Pierce Walker won't let me in to see you."

Christine spoke quickly. Her time on the phone was almost up. "Word is out that you're helping take down Reyes and you're royalty with the cops right now even though I'm dirt. Cleo's on duty. She said they'll let you come back to the visitors' room."

"Walker's got an agent tailing me so Reyes doesn't do anything stupid."

Christine's voice choked again. "It's okay. I'm glad they're keeping you safe. I'm sure the jail staff will tell him anyway."

"We won't have much time to talk once his agent phones in where I am."

"I know."

❖

Even with puffy, red eyes and dressed in an orange jumpsuit, Christine was beautiful. The guard brought her into the empty visitors' room and then stood just inside the door to keep watch. They faced off on opposite sides of a scarred wood table, Christine's hands unnecessarily cuffed in a waist restraint. She clasped her hands together, but they still trembled.

"They treating you okay?"

Christine nodded, tears welling. "If Walker thought putting me in a group holding cell overnight would scare me, he forgot what kind of attorney I am. Cops might not like us, but among inmates, defense attorneys are rock stars."

"Things will go better—"

"I'm going to tell them everything, August. I asked you here for two reasons. First, to apologize."

August's chest and neck flushed hot as her fury boiled up suddenly, scalding away any sympathy she'd felt when Christine first shuffled into the room. Did she want forgiveness? Absolution for ruining their lives?

"Were you fucking him while you were still sleeping with me, Christine? Do I need to get tested for STDs or HIV?" She felt sick. She stood and paced over to the wall where a floor vent

blew a cooling stream of air into the room. She breathed it in, then turned back to Christine, who sat with her head bowed, the tears finally overflowing and trailing down her cheeks. "I can't stop taking showers because I feel so dirty." As an attorney, however, she knew there were always two sides to every story. Deep down, maybe she wanted Christine to give her a reason to forgive her. August returned to her chair and sat. "Talk. Tell me how you could even do this."

Christine swallowed hard, then began without raising her head. "I liked the money and the prestige. Luis introduced me to powerful people. I told myself I was helping our practice, and then I told myself I was carrying the practice on my shoulders because I was bringing in the most money. He made me feel important. I don't know when...it became more intimate. You and I were arguing all the time. Luis was very gallant and attentive. He seemed to want the same things I did."

"And that was reason enough to set me up for him to blackmail?"

Christine shook her head, finally raising her eyes to meet August's. "You have to believe me. When I found out that Raphael was listing you as the attorney on those nonprofits that they were using to launder money, I went to Luis and demanded he leave you out of it."

She shrugged to try to wipe her nose on her sleeve since she couldn't raise her hands. August reluctantly tugged some tissues from a box on the table next to them and wiped her face for her.

"Thanks. Anyway, he said you were too much of a wild card. So, I told him that I'd break it off with you and dissolve our partnership so he wouldn't have to worry about you. Then he turned into someone I didn't know." Christine shuddered. "He said he already didn't worry about you because he'd been fucking your girlfriend for months and had evidence you were laundering money. So I told him I was done with him if he didn't leave you alone." She nodded to her right sleeve. "Pull my sleeve up."

August stood and addressed the deputy. "I'm just going to look at her arm, okay?"

He nodded, and she lifted the short sleeve of the jumper to expose a dark bruise clearly indicative of fingers curled around her bicep.

"He grabbed me and threw me to the floor," Christine said. "I have more bruises where he put his knee in my back. He...he said I was his any time he wanted me and he would kill you if I tried to leave him." Christine bowed her head and began to sob.

August's head and gut churned. "Was that the night you came home at three in the morning but wouldn't talk to me?

Christine nodded, still sobbing.

August swallowed. She wasn't sure she wanted to know. She closed her eyes against the image of Christine on her stomach with Luis Reyes pinning her to the floor. She barely got the words past her clenched teeth. "What did he do to you?"

Christine cried harder, tears and mucus dripping into her lap. August waited.

"He raped me," she finally said.

August stood, nearly toppling her chair, and swallowed down the bile that rose in her throat. If she ran into Reyes before Pierce Walker could put him in cuffs, she'd kill him. No. She wouldn't kill him. She'd tie him up and cut his pecker off. Then she'd phone Walker and tell him where to find him. She hated Luis Reyes. And now she wanted to hate Christine for inviting this viper into their lives, for all the things she'd done that led them to this grimy room in the county jail with both their lives in shreds.

Hate, however, was hard for August to embrace. She pitied the woman bowed before her, but she couldn't remember what it felt like to love her. This wasn't the smart, engaging Christine who'd once won her heart. This was a woman who had been seduced and broken by her addiction to money and power.

August drew more tissues from the box and cleaned Christine's face again. She even helped her blow her nose, like she would a child. Even if Christine had been fucking Reyes behind August's back, Reyes didn't have the right to force himself on her whenever he wanted. "I'll call Thurmond Evers and ask him to take your case."

Christine nodded. He was high profile, one of the best defense lawyers in Dallas. "Thank you." Her eyes and nose were red when she finally looked up. "Thank you for coming, August. If it was the other way around, I'm not sure I would have. I knew you would, though. You always were a better person than me."

Christine might have been partly right, but August couldn't let her shoulder all the blame. Somewhere along the way, she'd become so involved in her career and their practice that she'd quit paying attention to the people around her. She'd checked out of their relationship enough that she didn't even notice something was wrong until it was too late. She'd never made time to visit Julio and The White Paw wranglers who'd been so important to her as an adolescent. Now, Julio was gone.

She had to do better. Teal was right. This was her ranch, and she needed to start taking on the responsibility for running it. BJ was as old as Julio, and he was shouldering all the management work. Hell, she hadn't even asked about *his* health. He could have a bad heart like Pops and she wouldn't even know it.

She started to shut down her computer session, then stopped. She should begin by keeping an eye on Teal. The last thing they needed was a crazy ex-husband showing up, creating a police report that Reyes could find in public records to locate her. She logged out of her sign-on and in as "guest." Nope, Teal hadn't erased her browsing history. She'd send an email to Steve tomorrow, asking him to do a little more digging on Teal.

Ah. Miss Crawley had been doing a little checking herself. August flipped through the websites Teal had viewed. Hmm. That black suit always was one of her favorites. Wonder if Teal liked it? She smiled to herself. She was about to click on the next link to her name when something else caught her eye.

Oh. She had been looking at hats. August pictured Teal with a light-brown Stetson riding low on her brow, her shining black hair tucked behind her ears and flowing across her shoulders. The only hats Teal had worn were ball caps. They shaded her eyes but did nothing to protect her ears and neck from the sun.

August selected the one she liked. BJ had been clowning around one day and put August's hat on Teal, and it looked to fit her perfectly so they must wear the same size. She checked the box for priority shipping, entered the ranch's credit-card information, and submitted the order.

Then she sat back in the padded leather chair and smiled. *It's okay for a boss to order equipment for an employee, right? Of course, it is.*

CHAPTER NINE

"Hello? White Paw Ranch." Teal sandwiched the phone between her shoulder and ear while she packed the crew's lunch into the Coleman cooler.

"Is this August?"

"Sorry, no. She's out with the crew. I'm Teal Crawley. I'm… her assistant. Can I help you with something?"

"This is John Stutts. Could you ask her to call me? I guess tomorrow would be soon enough, but I need to talk with her. I know BJ will keep them out until past my office hours today."

"Actually, I was about to take lunch to them. I can give her your message then. I'm sure she'll have her cell phone in the truck. Does she have your number?"

"Yes. She has one of my cards. Thank you, Ms. Crawley. I'd appreciate it."

"Just part of my job."

She rang off and put the last of the sandwiches in the cooler. John Stutts. Why was that name familiar? She went into the office and found the business card lying next to the keyboard. That's why. She'd read his name on the card. Attorney. It didn't say what kind of lawyer, but he sounded worried. The article she'd read about August's law partner being arrested flashed through her thoughts. Hopefully August wasn't in trouble, too. She grabbed the card, in case August didn't have Stutts's number in her phone, and headed out.

❖

"He didn't say what he wanted?" August fingered the card. Gus and Julio had trusted John Stutts—as their attorney and as a friend—so she'd decided she could trust him to keep an eye on a few things for her.

Teal handed August two sandwiches and a small bag of potato chips. "The one with an H on it is deviled ham. The one marked PBB is your dessert sandwich." She handed Tommy the same combination of sandwiches. "No. He just asked that you call him, but he sounded like he needed to talk to you right away."

Tommy juggled his sandwiches, trying to get a better look at the contents of the second one. "What's PBB?"

"Peanut butter and banana. You guys need the protein and potassium working out here in the heat."

Tommy grinned. "Yummy." He yelled over at BJ, who was unwrapping his own sandwiches. "You hear that, BJ? Teal makes us eat healthy food. All you ever did was slap mustard and bologna on day-old bread."

"You better look in the drink cooler before you start strutting," BJ said.

Tommy gave him a dismissive wave and lifted the cooler's top. "Hey, who drank all the sodas?"

Teal put her hands on her hips. "You have two choices— water or lemonade. Soda is bad for you. If August will approve the expense, I'll order some sports drinks, too, to replace the electrolytes you sweat out while working in the sun, but no sodas."

Hawk, Brick, and Manny whooped. They liked those better than soda.

Tommy looked at August. "How 'bout it, Boss? You wouldn't want us to get heatstroke, would you?"

August swallowed her mouthful of sandwich. The deviled ham was homemade and really good. "Only for while you're out working. I'm not stocking the bunkhouse fridge so you guys can drink them all the time."

"Spoiling them rotten." BJ frowned at the men when they whooped again and began arguing about which flavor and brand was best. Then he took a big bite of his sandwich and shared a smile with Teal.

August watched the men as she ate. She was still finding her place with them. Tommy was at least ten years her junior, but Brick, Hawk, and Manny were experienced wranglers. It would take her years to learn what they already knew, and they seemed to be weighing her as a boss. Tommy appeared to be waiting to follow their lead as to whether she deserved his respect.

Teal, on the other hand, slid easily into their little group. She joked with the men but skillfully deflected Tommy's attempts to flirt. She'd been there two or three weeks and already knew enough about each of them to ask about their families or girlfriends, and to fix some of their favorite lunch foods. Pops's garden had flourished with Teal's help, and the beds of beautiful flowers Julio had cultivated were full and blooming around the ranch and bunkhouse again. Hell, even the chickens seemed happier and were laying more eggs. Why wouldn't they? August took in Teal's slender, athletic body. Her hands were always moving in graceful gestures as she talked. She wanted to catch and entwine Teal's long fingers with her own.

Teal's rich-chocolate eyes found hers. "A penny for your thoughts," she said, her words slipping quietly under the men's conversation to reach only August's ears.

Her thoughts didn't matter. Teal was leaving as soon as her cousin said the coast was clear. The last thing August needed was to add another complication in her life, and if—no, when—Reyes found where she was staying, Teal would be one more person she'd have to worry about keeping safe. August downed the last of her lemonade. "I was wondering if you were ready to start packing up. I'm curious about what John needs to talk about."

Teal tilted her head and raised an eyebrow, making it clear she suspected avoidance. "Sure. It looks like everybody's finished."

She unfurled a plastic bag and collected everyone's trash while August secured the coolers in the truck's bed.

BJ placed the calving box from his truck next to the coolers. "Since you're headed that way, swing by the heifer herd. We still have two or three that haven't dropped a calf yet."

"Will do. I'll see what John wants, and then I'll tackle some paperwork. I need to get the quarterly tax stuff ready for the accountant."

BJ huffed. "Seems like with all that schooling you did, you ought to be able to fill out tax forms instead of paying somebody else to do it."

"You telling me how to run my ranch, old man?" August put her hands on her hips and scowled at him in an exaggerated threat.

He squinted back at her. "I sure am. That's what you pay me for." He pointed at his chest. "Foreman. Ranch manager."

Teal laughed at their mock argument, and the sound of it warmed August. She mimicked him, pointing at her own chest. "Criminal-defense attorney. That would be like me saying you should be able to herd sheep just because you know how to wrangle cows."

BJ squinted at her. "Just 'cause you're the boss now don't mean you can get sassy with me, Grasshopper."

August chuckled, then pressed her hands together as if praying and bowed slightly. "Yes, Sensei."

"Go on. You gals get out of here." BJ waved them toward the truck.

August pointed the truck toward the herd BJ had mentioned, and they'd bumped across the pasture for several minutes before Teal spoke.

"Criminal-defense lawyer, huh?"

Shit. She'd said that without thinking. Really, though. What difference did it make if Teal knew what she did before she'd turned rancher? She'd already looked her up on the Internet. Damn, she should have finished checking which websites she'd viewed. How much did she already know? "Uh, yeah. In Dallas, where my parents live." *Might as well answer the next question before she asks it.*

Teal nodded and stared out the window of the truck. A long silence stretched between them as they bumped along across the eighty-acre pasture. Did Teal need an attorney? Or did she have a problem with defense lawyers—attorneys who defended a lot of guilty criminals? A lot of people did until they needed the services of one.

"A penny for your thoughts," she said, echoing Teal's earlier query.

Teal glanced at her, offering a small smile. "It's nothing. Just reflex from my old job."

That was a conversation opening she couldn't resist. The herd appeared in the distance, black blobs against a copse of shade trees bordering the creek, and August turned the truck that way. "What kind of work did you do?"

Teal looked thoughtful. "I took care of things for my boss. I guess you could say I made things happen."

"Made things happen?"

"Arranged meetings, travel, kept her up to speed on issues… and on rumors that would affect her work."

"Sort of a right hand."

Something August couldn't decipher flickered across Teal's face. Hurt? Disgust? "Yeah. That, too."

"So, what had you thinking about that now?" August stopped the truck near the herd but didn't move to get out.

Teal seemed to hesitate and then turned in her seat to face August. "How about a deal? If you tell me what you were really thinking when I asked earlier, I'll tell you what was on my mind."

Teal's tone was gentle and held no challenge, but her honesty caught August off-guard. What were they doing? They were edging closer and closer to the curtain that separated their personal lives. Something told her Teal Crawley was much more than a ranch cook, and August wanted to snatch the curtain back to see everything about her. But if she did, Teal would be able to see her, too. Maybe a peek?

"I was watching you with the guys. You've fit in with them well in only the few weeks you've been here."

Teal didn't seem surprised. "And?"

August shifted to stare out at the herd. The cows were watching the truck, a few ambling toward them in anticipation of feed. "And, I'm still working out my relationship with them. Hawk was starting out as a young wrangler my last summer here before college, so he knew me as a kid and now I'm his boss. BJ and Pops have known me since I was a little kid. On top of that, I think it's the first time any of them have worked for a woman." She squinted. Was that an untagged newborn next to that heifer on the left?

Teal pursed her lips and nodded. "That's exactly what I was thinking about."

August's brain stutter-stepped. "Thinking about what?"

"Your relationship to the men."

August frowned. "What about it?"

Teal took a deep breath. "Well, I'm probably overstepping my role here, but I did learn a few things working in my previous job that could be helpful to you."

Okay. This definitely had her interest. "I'm always willing to listen to advice. But, as my mother once told me, I mostly do what I want."

Teal cocked her head and flashed a quick, toothy smile that made August's stomach do a pleasant little roll. "Don't take this the wrong way, but I think you should speak to BJ about how he talks to you in front of the men."

August searched her memory to replay their conversation. "You're referring to when he reminded me that he was the ranch foreman."

Teal shook her head. "Before that. He told you to stop by and check this herd for newborns. He should have asked if you would have time to do it. And, even though he knew you as a child, he shouldn't use those childhood nicknames for you in front of the men." She gave August a pointed look. "And you shouldn't respond by calling him Sensei when he refers to you as Grasshopper."

"You're saying I shouldn't joke around with the men?"

"No. Not at all. But you should be careful that the men know who's boss. That's you. BJ and the rest of us work for you."

She was right. August stared at the herd again. Yep, that was a newborn. "You're right. I'll talk to him." But how should she approach BJ about this? She'd think about that later. "Right now, though, we need to tag that baby over there." She opened her door. "Come on. You can help me catch it."

August was impressed as Teal moved calmly among the herd to the other side of the young mama and raised her arms at the right moment to keep the heifer from moving away when August crept up from behind to grab the baby. Damn. It was a bull calf and heavy. She shifted her hold on the struggling little beast and cursed when she realized she hadn't put the weighing sling into place beforehand. But Teal was a step ahead of her, already fitting the scale's bracket into the stake slot of the truck's fender.

The calf was a lively one, nearly knocking August off her feet with his struggling, while his mother followed behind and bellowed at her baby's kidnapper. Teal quickly slid the sling around the calf and attached it to the scale's hook to relieve August of his weight.

"Whew. Thanks. He's a big one." August shook her head. "I'm glad BJ isn't here. He'd never let me live this down. I was thinking so hard about what we were talking about that I forgot to lay everything out." She had to almost shout to be heard over the racket of the calf yelling for his mother and the heifer answering. "Can you hold him for a minute?"

"Sure." Teal steadied him in the sling, scratching behind his ear and talking to him until he quieted a bit.

"You're pretty good at that."

"Grew up on a dairy farm, remember?"

"Right. I have a hard time picturing you as a milkmaid."

Teal wrinkled her nose at the term, then shifted a sizzling gaze from August's boots, slowly up her denim-covered legs, slim hips, long-sleeved T-shirt, and bandana to her Stetson. "I don't have any problem picturing you as a cowgirl," Teal said.

August half-shrugged to wipe the bead of sweat trickling along her jaw on the shoulder of her shirt and quickly laid out the ear tag and other instruments on the tailgate. Wasn't it unusually hot for June? She hesitated over the scalpel and castration forceps. She'd have to handle her first castration solo. She knew the procedure. She'd watched BJ do it at least twenty times in the past few weeks, but the thought of putting scalpel to flesh still made her queasy. She could feel Teal watching her.

"You sure you want to castrate this guy? I don't know much about beef cattle, but he seems pretty big for a newborn. He could be worth keeping for breeding stock."

August swallowed down her jumpy stomach but didn't look at Teal. "No. We're not breeding to his sire again. He throws big babies, but they don't grow at the normal rate. So, by the time they go to market, they're the same weight as the other steers. You run the risk of a small cow having a big baby, with no gain at market time."

Teal smiled but didn't say anything when August swabbed the calf's skin with a numbing agent before tagging and tattooing his ear. She recorded the calf's weight and other information while August changed into clean gloves and swabbed the calf's testicles with a disinfectant. Teal cleared her throat when August pulled a slim syringe from the calving box and injected the top of the scrotum sac with a local numbing agent. "My daddy never bothered with that. He said it was money that didn't need to be spent when they'd forget the pain in a day or two anyway."

August didn't look at her. "Most ranchers don't, but like I told BJ, it's my money to spend."

"I'm glad you do. It always bothered me to hurt them." Teal's soft words were almost lost among the restless lowing of the calf's still-hovering mother. She wrapped an arm around the calf still suspended in the sling and held onto its near hind leg so it didn't kick out at August.

August picked up the scalpel and held it next to the skin. Just cut the scrotum open, pull out the testes, apply the forceps to crush the...Just a quick slice. Right through the skin. She swallowed. One quick slice. Damn it. She closed her eyes and swallowed again. She couldn't do it. She was going to throw up.

"Since he's numb and all, would you mind if I tried it?"

August looked up, sure that her face must be all shades of green. Teal held tightly to the calf but gave no indication that she'd noticed August faltering in her task.

"I've banded goats and pigs before. I know it's not the same thing, but I've watched my dad castrate surgically—like you're about to do—a million times. You could walk me through it. I mean, if you don't mind."

They stared at each other for a long moment. "Glove up. I'll hold the calf."

Teal smiled and donned a pair of latex gloves from the tailgate. She took the scalpel, and then August took hold of the calf and they began. August verbally walked her through the procedure. She had no problem watching. She just couldn't put the blade to skin and cut. Teal was quick and her cuts so sure that August suspected this wasn't the first time she'd done the procedure. The calf barely indicated any discomfort at all and was soon released back to his mother.

Neither spoke once they were back in the truck, until August pulled up to the ranch house and cut the engine.

"Thanks."

"I should be thanking you for the practice."

"Come on, Teal. I'm not stupid. You've castrated a calf before."

Teal's mouth curled in a small smile as she ducked her head and looked up through thick lashes. "Not precisely. First time on a beef calf."

August shook her head but returned the smile. "Ah. A lawyer should know to read the fine print."

Teal's smile grew. "Exactly."

When August parked in front of the ranch house, she noticed the box left by the front door. She turned back to Teal. "You up for a ride after dinner? We can go check on your calf to make sure he's still okay."

"I'd love that."

"Okay. Let's get these coolers inside."

"Corrine put it off as long as she could, but she's not the only one in the Register of Deed's Office, you know. She had to go ahead and file the deed to close out the probate on Julio's will."

"Okay. Thanks, John."

"Maybe you're giving this guy Reyes too much credit. Why would he be looking for new property in your name? People trying to hide don't go around buying property."

"Reyes is a typical drug lord. They only have to hire brilliant people and be ruthless enough that the smart people are too afraid to double-cross them. Someone has advised him how to launder drug money through nonprofits and stash it in offshore banks, so I have to anticipate one of his security minions knows how to set up a computer search that will ping him any time my name hits the digital network, whether I've used a credit card or a health-insurance card or gotten a traffic ticket."

"Well, for your sake, I hope not. Maybe you should hire some security for the ranch."

She sighed and sat back in Julio's high-backed leather office chair. "I'm living off my trust fund from Gus right now because all my other assets were shared with Christine and they're frozen until this investigation is over. I'm a long way from being poor, but security is expensive, and I don't know how long it will take to untangle financially from her. I want to put Gus's money to work upgrading The White Paw."

"Julio was right to leave the ranch to you, August, but your plans won't be worth a nickel if you aren't alive to see them through. At least let me talk to the sheriff. I won't give him any details, but I'll ask him to watch for any tough-looking strangers asking a lot of questions. It's a small town. Someone like that'll stick out like a bowtie on a pig."

"Okay." August stared up at the ceiling. It couldn't hurt. "I'll call you in a few days to see what he said."

"Fine. Talk to BJ. I think y'all should at least let Hawk know what's up."

"If I get a hint that Reyes has found me, I'll take off. I'm not going to put the men here in danger." She and BJ had argued long and bitterly over that.

"I'm saying just in case he catches you by surprise."

It wasn't something she wanted to consider. If she really cared that much about BJ, Pops, and the rest, she'd pack up and leave now. But she didn't want to. This was her one safe place. They were her real family, her only family now that Gus and Julio were gone and Christine had betrayed her. When Julio left the ranch to her, he left BJ and Pops in her care.

"I'll think about it," she said. "By the way, how are you coming on that new will for me? God knows, the last thing I want is for Reyes to kill me and Christine to inherit this ranch along with all my other assets."

"Well, I should have all the information I need in a couple of days."

"What's the delay?"

"Your daddy's lawyer has added some stipulations to the family trust that you'll inherit upon the death of your parents."

"Ah, yes. I'm sure they wouldn't want my lesbian partner to get any of the family money."

"More like, your daddy didn't want Julio or The White Paw to get any of that money. I've asked a probate judge to give me an opinion on it, so I can be specific in the way I write your will. He might advise that you go ahead and challenge it now, but it shouldn't keep us from putting together a will for you in the meantime."

"Okay. Well, thanks for letting me know about the deed."

"August."

"Yes?"

"If you've got a gun, load it and keep it with you."

"I do, and I will."

But she didn't have to think about that today. She stood and closed the office door, then found the stiletto Julio kept in the desk drawer. Damn, she missed him. Dark and handsome, Julio was the stereotype of a Latino prince. And, the man loved fancy knives. She chuckled to herself. Who else would keep a stiletto in his desk to open mail? She looked at the box. Or a special gift?

August slit the tape carefully and flipped back the flaps to reveal the smooth, soft, latte-colored felt. She lifted the Stetson from the box. It would be the perfect complement to certain beautiful dark-brown eyes.

CHAPTER TEN

Teal ran cold water into her bathroom sink while she stripped off her shirt and bra. She felt sticky with sweat even after the past few hours cooking and eating dinner in the house's air-conditioning. She soaked a bath cloth in the water and washed the dried perspiration from her face, neck, and breasts. God, that felt good.

Even though the sun was sagging toward the distant mountain peaks, the afternoon had cooled only a little. She had to keep the boots and jeans since they were going riding, but she put on a clean bra and a sleeveless V-neck cotton pullover. She stared at her reflection, then went back to her bureau and dug through a set of bandanas that'd been there when she moved into the room. One of them matched the blue-green of her shirt perfectly.

She returned to the bathroom to tie her hair back with it, then changed her mind as she stared into the mirror. She tied the bandana around her neck in a jaunty knot instead. She'd leave her hair down. August seemed to like it that way. Not that silent and sexy would do anything about it. But, God, she wanted her to. Damn that ex-law partner. She'd left August as skittish as a newborn colt. When something wasn't working in her life, Teal always found it best to cut her losses and put it behind her. Just like she'd left that mousy farm girl behind when she drove off to college. Just like she was going to put Senator Lauren Abbott behind her. Teal winked at her reflection. Maybe August needed a little push to dump her baggage, too. They both deserved something fun in their lives.

Teal found August waiting for her on the porch. She had changed into a sleeveless shirt, too, since the sun was low enough that sunburn wasn't likely. White with Western pockets and pearl snaps instead of buttons. She looked good. Teal licked her lips. Tasty. August was watching her with a question in her eyes. Surely she hadn't been out of circulation so long she didn't know when she was being cruised.

August was wearing her usual weathered, dark-brown Stetson but held another, lighter-brown one that looked new. "Thinking of breaking in a new hat?" Maybe that had caused August's pensive expression.

August smiled and held out the one in her hands. "Nope. This one's for you. Try it on."

"Really? For me?"

"Yep. Those ears of yours are getting crispy. I can't have you suing the ranch if they wither and fall off because you've been wearing a ball cap to deliver lunch to the wranglers every day."

"I've been using sunscreen, but I think I sweat it off after about ten minutes in this heat."

"It's never this hot so early in the year. The past month has been a record for the Panhandle." August gestured at the hat. "See if it fits."

Teal finger-combed her hair behind her ears the way she'd seen August do and settled the hat on her head. It fit firmly over her brow. She grinned at August. "How do I look?"

August stared.

"August?"

"Uh, great." Her response was a little hoarse, and she cleared her throat. "You're a natural cowgirl."

"I love it. Thank you." She was mindful to tilt her head so the brims of their hats didn't collide and gave August a quick peck on the cheek. "My ears thank you, too."

August's neck and ears reddened, but she smiled. "Let's go check on that calf."

❖

The wind that rippled the pasture grass was hot, but at least the air was moving. The grazing herd had left the shade near the creek. Teal spotted her calf, napping in the grass near his mama. They dismounted and dropped the reins of the horses. Trained to ground tie, they'd stay while Teal and August walked closer to make sure the calf was only sleeping. The heifer stopped feeding and watched as they approached. She bellowed, then positioned herself between them and her calf as he roused and stood.

"She's a good mama," Teal said. Cows that were not successful breeders or failed to nurture their babies properly would go to the auction yard along with the steers or cows too old to breed.

August nodded, her eyes roaming across the open pasture.

"Now what are you thinking about?" Teal kept her voice soft, hoping a gentle probe would finally entice August to talk. She watched August scan the clouds building in the distance. She already could feel the air thickening with humidity. Thunderstorms were a near-daily occurrence this time of year.

August's eyes stayed on the horizon. "I was thinking how I'm going to change things around here."

"Change things? Oh. You mean like using a local anesthetic when you castrate babies?" She smiled when August ducked her head and blushed.

"That calf would still have his balls if you hadn't been with me."

Teal took a chance and stepped close to hook her arm around August's. "Yeah. I know." When August didn't pull away, she slid her hand down August's tanned forearm and entwined their fingers, giving August's hand a slight squeeze.

"I've done a lot of things. I shot a drugged-out guy in the leg once when he came in our law office, threatening one of my paralegals. They'd been dating, and she dumped him when she found out he was a druggie. When he pulled a knife and started for her, I didn't think twice about pulling that trigger." She shot a sideways glance at Teal. "But I just can't slice through warm skin with a razor." She didn't release Teal's hand but turned to face her. "Hell, my only grade in college below an 'A' was in biology lab. They wanted us to dissect fetal pigs, and I just couldn't do it. I flunked that part of lab and didn't flunk the entire course only because I aced the written test from studying drawings. Stupid, huh?"

"I think that's incredibly sweet." She held August's gaze, watching as her expression went from shy to serious. Teal gently disengaged her hand from August's to give her breathing room. "So, what other things are you planning to change as ranch boss?"

August's expression lightened as her gaze wandered the open pasture again. "Normally, that little guy we tagged this afternoon would stay on the ranch until after he was weaned from his mother. He'd be about a year old, give or take a month. Then he'd be sold to the finishers, who would fatten him the last few months of his short life."

Teal liked a good steak as well as the next person, but she didn't like to think about why animals were raised on a farm or a ranch. Even on a dairy farm, the youngsters unfortunate enough to be born bullocks had a ninety-nine percent chance of ending up in butcher wrap. "You're going to make a pet out of him?"

August barked a short laugh, then spread her arms toward the open field. "This ranch can support a lot more cattle than Julio's been keeping." She put her hands on her hips and faced Teal again, her eyes bright. "I'm going to tap into the growing demand for grass-fed beef." She shrugged. "I am a rancher, and people are always going to eat meat. But my cows won't go to a crowded feedlot when they're a year old, where they're stuffed with high-calorie meals without room to exercise, then slaughtered at fourteen to sixteen months old." She shook her head. "My cows will spend three years roaming my lush pastures. Then they'll only be sold to a packing house that I'm satisfied is set up so their last hours aren't spent in fear, and they'll be killed quick and humanely."

Teal smiled but shook her head. "They'll call you that crazy woman rancher who's too soft to make any money."

"Nah. They'll call me that fancy-pants rancher who sells her beef for crazy-high prices to yuppie idiots in Ca-LEE-for-NI-yay and NU-york Ci-TEE."

Teal laughed so loud at her exaggeration that the herd startled, most raising their heads, and some moving a safer few yards farther away to graze.

August's smile was blazing under the gray clouds.

"I think you'll be a huge success," Teal said. She meant it.

August tilted her hat back and scanned the clouds again. "We should head back. An open prairie isn't a good place to be during a lightning storm."

"Not up to storm-chasing on horseback?" Teal wasn't ready to go. She'd just gotten August to open up a little. But the sky was looking a little scary. "It's so humid, let's keep it slow unless it starts to rain."

They mounted up and walked the horses side by side. August kept sneaking glances at her. "What?"

"Nothing." August shrugged and smiled. "The hat looks really good on you."

Teal tugged it lower on her brow and straightened her shoulders in exaggerated cowboy style. "Why thank you, ma'am. You're pretty fetchin' yourself today."

August laughed again. Teal loved the throaty sound.

"I told you about my plans for the ranch," August said. "Your turn to tell me something about yourself."

Teal hadn't expected this. What could she say without revealing too much? "I don't really know what my future holds. I'm going to work for my cousin for a while, and then I think I'll head back to the city...a different city and take a similar job, but I'm not sure what. I like organizing and making things happen."

"I bet you'd be good at running a nonprofit."

"Mmm. I don't necessarily want to be in charge. I prefer being the wizard behind the curtain."

August frowned. "You don't seem shy to me."

"Maybe it's a holdover from my awkward-farm-girl upbringing."

"Were you home-schooled or something?"

"No, nothing that radical. But my father was…is very strict. We never went hungry and always had adequate clothes. But we weren't allowed to waste money on brand-name clothes, electronic games, or buying books when we could check them out from the library. Things like that."

"That's not such a bad thing. Too many kids today have their heads in those electronic games or their smart phones all the time."

How could she explain her father? "My mother had a scholarship to a small but prestigious art program at Earnhardt College in Virginia. She was very good. In fact, she'd just won a special fellowship to spend the summer studying in Italy after her junior year. Then her mother died. Her father, who always thought her aspirations as an artist were silly, demanded that she come home and help raise her four younger brothers. Her scholarship and fellowship went to other eligible students. She was little more than a house slave to her father and her four brothers, so when my father proposed, she jumped at the chance to marry and get away from them."

Thunder rumbled in the distance, and the air felt like humid slurry they were wading through.

"So, did she paint again after she married? Did you inherit her talent for art?"

Teal shook her head. "No. I didn't." Her mood was darkening with the clouds. "And she didn't paint. My father agreed with her father. He wouldn't let her spend the money for paints because he thought it was a frivolous expense."

Thunder sounded again, closer this time, and the horses' ears worked nervously back and forth. They picked up their pace to walk faster, but August reined her mount back, and Teal's bay automatically slowed again to match the stallion's pace.

"Mom would sketch little things for us kids on scrap paper or in our notebooks sometimes. So one Christmas, my sisters and I decided to pool our money and buy Mom some paints and a canvas as a gift. She was so surprised, she cried."

August smiled. "What'd she paint? Wait, I bet she did a portrait of you and your sisters."

Teal didn't smile back. "My father made her return the paint supplies to the store for a refund. He said the money would be better spent on something more practical, like a new dress or shoes."

"She should have told him to fuck off."

"I think her father and brothers had already taken all the fight out of her." Teal looked at August. "But I swore I would never be that woman my mother had become. I never talked to my parents about college. I just applied, lined up my scholarships, and when the day came, I packed my suitcase and walked out the door. I told my sisters and mother good-bye, but I left before my father came in for lunch."

"You've never gone back?"

"At first, I'd try to go home for holidays, to see my mother and sisters. But my father would make the time so miserable for all of us, I went less and less. I haven't seen my mother in five years. My sisters have visited me, or I've arranged to meet them somewhere for a weekend now and then."

They were quiet for a while, nothing but the soft sound of hoofbeats and the rumble of thunder intruding into the silence.

"Do you have any siblings?"

"One brother. But we aren't close." August offered a tight smile. "He's exactly what my parents want in an heir. My parents, my brother...they love the urban environment, cutthroat business, and Dallas society. They hated Gus, this ranch, and anything to do with horses and cattle. I never fit in with them. I felt more at home with Gus and Julio."

"If you aren't close to your family, why'd you go back to Dallas after you graduated law school?"

The muscle in August's jaw worked for a long minute, and Teal was about to withdraw her question when she finally spoke.

"Because Christine insisted that our best chance at starting a successful law practice would be in a city where there were plenty of criminals to defend." She paused. "And I guess I wanted to prove something to my parents and flaunt Christine in front of my brother." August's expression was guarded.

Teal realized that although the attraction between them screamed, neither had admitted her sexual orientation yet. In fact, she'd deliberately misled them to think she was straight, so August was waiting for her reaction. "Christine was more than your law partner then? She was your lover?"

"Yes."

"I'm guessing that didn't go over well with your parents?"

"No. It didn't. They weren't especially religious, though, so they tried to ignore it as a phase and allowed my brother to torment me over it."

"My sister, Gray, came out to my parents, and they forbid her or any of us to speak about it again."

August nodded. "I wish it'd been that easy in my family. My parents sent us to a private prep school where my brother was captain of the boys' lacrosse team and I was captain of the girls' soccer team. There was this one girl he found out I was crushing on, and he persuaded her to pretend she was interested until I made a move. Then she told everybody that I was a pervert who tried to kiss her. It made high school miserable for me, so I tested out of as many classes as possible and left for college early."

"That's where you met Christine?"

"I dated a lot of women as an undergraduate. Then I met Christine our first year in law school at Duke. Barrett, my brother, practically drooled when he saw her."

Teal grew uneasy as August's expression hardened, her mouth a tight, grim line. Was this a side of August she'd been blind to, like she'd apparently ignored Lauren's real personality? Had August used Christine?

"You dated her to get back at your brother."

August jerked as though Teal had hit her, and then her shoulders slumped. "No. I loved her." She looked away, and Teal could no longer see what was in her eyes.

"How long were you together?" she asked softly.

"About ten years." August shifted in her saddle but didn't look at her. "Until a couple of months ago."

The rumble of thunder grew louder, and a fat drop of rain hit Teal's forearm. She could see the ranch complex in the distance now. Another boom of thunder was accompanied by a flash of lightning tearing across the sky.

"Better make a run for it," August said, kneeing the stallion hard without waiting for Teal.

They were both drenched by the time they made it into the wide corridor of the huge main barn. The dark storm clouds seemed to have followed August inside as she hooked the stallion into crossties and wordlessly unsaddled him. Clearly, their discussion was over. Teal wished she hadn't brought up Christine. On the other hand, she was glad the ice was broken. Maybe they could get past it after August stewed a bit.

She put her saddle and bridle in the tack room to clean later and lost herself in brushing down her horse. What was his name? If she was going to ride him every time, she should know him as more than the big bay horse. She unclipped him from the ties and put him away in a clean stall, making sure the water bucket was full. The stallion and August were gone from the wash stall when she stepped back into the corridor. Given August's mood, Teal decided to clean her tack and head inside. A cool shower and a good book sounded pretty good.

Teal was mentally thumbing through the contents of her ebook library to decide her next read, when she stepped from the brightly lit corridor into the dark tack room and smacked right into August. "Oh." It was like running into a wall, a wall with soft breasts and smooth, bare arms that Teal gripped to keep her balance. "I didn't see you." They stood there for several long seconds. "Why are you in the dark?"

"I just turned the light out, then remembered I put my hat down over there." August gestured with a tilt of her head but didn't move away. "Then when I started out again, you smacked into me."

Teal didn't move either. August's eyes, gray as the sky outside, bored into hers. Was August going to kiss her? If she didn't, Teal would. But August stepped back and the moment was gone.

"I'm going to clean my tack," Teal said. "You don't have to wait for me if you're done."

"I wiped down both. Pops will give them a good cleaning tomorrow." August looked down the corridor to the barn's open end. "Looks like the rain has let up. Let's make a run for it."

They made a mad dash for the house, then shook droplets from the water-resistant Stetsons and shucked off muddy boots to leave on the porch. When Teal paused breathless just inside the door, they once again were standing close and alone in a semi-dark room. The air was thick with anticipation, apprehension, and possibilities neither was willing or brave enough to voice.

August took a step backward. "I've got some things to go over in the office."

"I think I'm going to grab a shower and climb in bed with a book. Those chickens get up early for their breakfast." Teal lifted the hat she held in her hands. "Thank you for the hat. I love it."

"You're welcome." August looked like she wanted to say more, but then she gave a curt nod. "Good night, Teal."

Two quick, unthinking steps and Teal's hand was on August's cheek, her lips brushing August's in a quick caress. "Good night."

Teal quietly closed her bedroom door and collapsed against it. Why the heck had she done that? She hadn't had the courage to look into August's eyes to judge her reaction. She'd just spun on her heel and escaped down the hallway. August might still be standing there in the dark living room. Or she might be in the office right now, telling BJ that he had to put her on the next bus to New Mexico.

She remained slumped against the door for several minutes. What was she waiting for? Did she think August was going to come knock on her door, then kiss her senseless when she opened it? This wasn't one of those romance novels she was always reading. Things didn't really happen that way. Nobody was that romantic in real life.

She pushed off the door with a sigh and tossed her new hat onto the bed. It was sweet that August had bought it. On the other hand, you could think of it as creepy that she was checking up on Teal's browsing history. Too bad August used a personal log-on so Teal couldn't check her history.

After her shower, she slid into some soft boxers and a thin racer-back tank. She'd taken her time, enjoying the soapy lather, washing her hair, shaving her legs. Those small physical pleasures always made her feel better when her mind was littered with unresolved mental and emotional detritus. Still, a small headache was beginning across her forehead, probably her sinuses swelling from the humidity of the storm. She found her decongestant tablets, but she needed a bottle of water from the kitchen. Maybe she should throw on a shirt over her thin tank top. Nah. She'd be quick. Everybody else was probably in bed by now.

Teal opened her bedroom door and slipped into the hall, only to come face-to-face with August, still in her damp jeans and sleeveless shirt white against her tanned arms. The yellow glow of a lamp filtered through the partially open door of August's bedroom behind her. Her blond hair, barely darkened by the rain, was slicked back to fall around her collar.

Clutching the pills in her hand, Teal felt nearly naked as August's gaze roamed over her bare legs and very short boxers. She wondered if her nipples were visible under the thin, white ribbed tank, because she'd swear she could feel them harden as August's eyes lingered there. She opened her mouth to say something.

August stepped forward, gently grasping Teal's nape and pressing her against the door she'd just closed. Before words could come, August's lips were on hers, hot and insistent. Yes. Teal hooked her fingers in the belt loops of August's low-riding jeans and held on. August still smelled of horses and saddle oil, sun-warmed flesh, and cleansing rain—things that were real and honest. Teal hummed as she opened to August's hungry, exploring tongue. Sweet Jesus, her knees were actually going weak. She clutched fistfuls of August's shirt to steady herself, then jerked the shirt's tail from August's jeans. She wanted to feel her, to feel the hot skin of her long, firm back.

Suddenly August's hands were on Teal's, gently breaking Teal's grasp on her shirt as she withdrew, sealing the kiss with a final soft caress of her lips against Teal's. She touched Teal's cheek. "Good night, Teal."

Teal watched, disbelieving, as August quietly went into her bedroom and closed the door. The dark of the hallway was pierced only by her heart pounding in her ears and thumping against the wall where her nearly bare shoulders were still pressed, until the flicker of a hallway night-light startled her.

"Good night, indeed," she whispered to the empty hallway.

CHAPTER ELEVEN

A ugust sat in Julio's office chair, the padded leather soft and worn with age, and stared at the framed photo of him and Gus. They were young men in the photo, dressed in chaps and long-sleeve Western shirts with their hats tilted back on their heads. Julio's was a stylish flat-brimmed favored by Hispanic cowboys, while Gus wore a practical fedora. They stood smiling side by side under a new arched gate that proclaimed White Paw Ranch. Gus held the reins of a black Quarter Horse; Julio the reins of a beautiful Appaloosa. Between them sat the ranch's namesake, a black half-wolf with one white forepaw.

"I wish you guys were here to tell me what to do," she said to the photo.

After a sleepless night, she'd deliberately been late to breakfast, showing up after she knew Teal and BJ had started eating. She'd been pleasant but quiet. Teal had watched her, so she didn't avoid her, speaking or looking at her when necessary, but didn't engage her either. She'd eaten hurriedly and then excused herself—supposedly to make phone calls before she headed out with BJ and the crew.

She was such a pathetic coward, hiding in the office. But she didn't know what to say. She didn't know what she wanted. She knew what she shouldn't want.

She closed her eyes. She shouldn't have paused when she started to close her bedroom door, but she could still feel Teal's lips touching hers in the living room. God, she couldn't remember wanting to kiss someone so badly. Was it like that when she and Christine first met? It must have been, but their long years together had probably dimmed that first flush of meeting. Then Teal was there, a few steps away, with long bare legs that August wanted to run her hands down, to feel wrapped around her. Her areolas were dark under the white, ribbed tank, her nipples hard knots stretching the thin material. Her mind had blanked white hot, and her next awareness was of Teal's lips, warm and soft, her tongue hot and tasting of mint. Her dark hair was silk against August's palm. She smelled of cocoa butter.

What was she thinking? Well, obviously, she wasn't thinking…at least not with her head.

She punched in the number for her computer security guy, Steve. It was still ungodly early, but the guy never seemed to sleep so she didn't worry about waking him.

"Yo, August Reese, my favorite attorney. You're logging in early."

"Ranchers get up before the chickens, Steve, but I'm not logged on the computer yet."

"Figure of geek speech."

"Oh. Sorry. I'm not geek cool sometimes."

"It's a small, exclusive club."

She liked Steve. He was off-the-charts smart and always in a good mood. "So, tell me what you know."

"Good news is that I've got your man—actually, it's a woman—who's the leak in the DEA office. Walker wants hard proof that will hold up in court, so we're setting a trap to catch her hand in the cookie jar."

"That's great. That could be a big nail in Reyes's coffin if she rolls over. Judges don't take influencing a federal agent lightly."

"Confirmed. However, now that we've located the leak, Walker wants those hard-drive copies pronto. He's starting to make noise about impeding a federal investigation."

"You're not impeding anything. Only two people know where those thumb drives are hidden—me and one other person, who isn't you." A cold nose nudged August's hand, and she stroked Rio's dark head that rested now on her thigh. Teal must be finished cleaning up after breakfast and the leftover bacon had been consumed.

"True. But he's pressuring me to give up where you're hiding out."

"I haven't told you where I am."

He made a rude noise. "Do you really think I haven't already pinpointed the IP of your computer before I hid it from anyone else trying to find you?"

"I'm sure you did. Listen to me." She slowed her words and spoke distinctly to emphasize their meaning. "I haven't told you where I'm staying."

There was a few seconds of silence. "Oh, okay. I'm on it. No matter how many times or ways Walker asks it, that's what I tell him. 'Sorry, no. She hasn't told me where she's staying.'"

"I knew you were super smart."

"Yeah, yeah." He yawned. "Sorry. Haven't been to bed yet. Anyway, I've got Walker to agree to our stipulations. You'll give the copies only to me, and I'll work with the federal geeks to extract the information to make sure the files don't erase themselves when they're opened like the originals did. I don't understand, though, why you don't just make copies of the copies."

"The further away from the originals you get, the weaker your credibility in the eyes of a jury."

"I see. So, do I need to clear my schedule for you to give your copies up to Walker?"

"Not until that leak is in a jail cell."

"Got'cha. Could be in about a week. If you don't already have a plan for getting them to me or to Walker, you need to be thinking about it."

"I might have one."

"You're right. The less we share, the less they can hold me responsible for."

"Exactly. I'm calling Pierce next to check in."

"Good idea. He's getting antsy."

"Later, dude."

"Later, August."

She ended the call and checked her watch to time the next one. Even though she'd made it clear each call to him wouldn't be long enough to be traced, she was sure he was still trying in case she got sloppy and talked a little too long. That's what she'd do if she were him.

"Walk—" He cleared his dry throat. "Walker."

She smiled. It was almost six thirty and he was still sleeping. "Did I wake you? I've had breakfast and drinking my third cup of coffee already."

"Reese?"

"Yeah. Just checking in. But since you haven't had your coffee yet, I'll be brief. Steve told me you found your leak. Lock that leak down tight, and I'll give the thumb drives you want to Steve. Not before."

"Lots of coming and going at Reyes's place, Reese. He might be about to bolt the country. We need something now to keep him from traveling." She heard his alarm beeping, then a slap and it went silent.

"Then you better work fast. I'll call again in three days."

"Reese, wait."

"You've got ninety seconds, Pierce."

"Christine wants a deal."

"That's no surprise."

"She got a little roughed up in jail. She—"

August's gut twisted. "Is she okay?" Damn, she shouldn't care, but she did. She'd once loved that woman. She'd shared a decade of her life with Christine. Rio whined, sensing August's concern.

"A little battered but no serious injuries. She won't talk about it, but we're pretty sure it was a message from Reyes. She wants whatever jail time she gets to be done in minimum security. One of those places where they send celebrity tax dodgers."

"Are you asking my opinion? Do it."

"I'd think you'd want your pound of flesh after what she did to you."

"Maybe I'm as guilty as she is. If I'd been giving her the attention she needed, Reyes would have never been able to seduce her into making bad choices."

"Before you go soft on me, think about this: would you have fallen into Reyes's trap if he'd targeted you instead of Christine?"

"Christine's not a career criminal, Pierce. You need to let her pay for her mistake and get on with her life." She glanced at her watch. "I'll call in three days."

She ended the call without waiting for him to reply and absently tapped the cell phone against her chin. Pierce had posed the question because he wanted to make sure she stayed angry enough to nail Reyes to the wall no matter how it affected Christine's case. Still, she knew he was right. She wouldn't have been susceptible to sexual advances from Reyes, but he was smart. He could have tried to lure her with flashy cars, money, or introductions to powerful people and sexy, willing women. Yet he'd sensed the weakness, the character flaw in Christine that August didn't have. No. If he'd approached her, she would have sent him packing. That's why he chose Christine to do his dirty work.

"The boys are loading up the fence panels you want. Are you ready to tell us what exactly you're planning to do with them?" BJ stood in the doorway.

"Tell them to haul the panels out to the south pasture and start unloading. We're going to set up chutes to vaccinate, but I want to show the guys a new arrangement that's less stressful to the animals. I've still got a few things to do here, but I won't be long." She pressed the tab to boot up the computer.

"You want us to wait? We're using the farm truck to pull one of the trailers. You can't drive that fancy car of yours across the pasture."

"I'll leave Rio with Pops and ride out on one of the four-wheelers." She typed in her password to bring up her desktop.

"All right then." He paused. "Everything okay?"

August looked up, surprised by the question. "Yeah. Everything's fine." She should update BJ, just in case. "John Stutts called to say they've filed the deed on the ranch. It might mean nothing, but if Reyes has someone looking, they might turn up my name in a computer search and track me here."

"I figured that was going to happen eventually. You need to start wearing that pistol I know you have. I'm going to do the same." He held her gaze. "What about the boys?"

"If they don't know and aren't armed, then there won't be a gunfight if Reyes's men show up. I don't want any of the guys hurt."

"Well, you see, that's not how we roll around here. It'd be better if they're armed and alert, because if those thugs do show up and try to take or hurt you, the guys would try to jump them anyway. You should at least give them a fighting chance."

August drummed her fingers on the chair's arm. He knew these men better than she did. "Okay. We'll put up the fence panels this morning, then come back in here for a late lunch in the bunkhouse. I've got a video I want to show them about some changes I want to make around the ranch. I'll talk to them about this then, too."

"Good enough." BJ gave a curt nod. "Now tell me why you were so quiet at breakfast and Sweet Thing was acting like you were a rattlesnake about to strike. You two have a tiff?"

"No." August frowned. "Sweet Thing?"

"I know you've been thrown pretty hard, but I've seen you eyeing her." His eyes softened. "Gals like that don't come along every day."

"She's got a boyfriend…well, ex-boyfriend."

"Well now, come to think of it, she didn't exactly say her ex was of the male variety. Pops and I just took that for granted, and she didn't correct us."

They stared at each other as she silently chewed over that possibility.

"She kissed me." August waited for BJ's reaction to her quiet admission.

He raised a questioning eyebrow and drawled out his prompt to continue. "And—"

She turned back to the computer and opened the inventory program. "I kissed her."

"Is that all one kiss or two separate kisses?"

She stopped typing and dropped her chin to her chest. "Does it matter?"

"Julio would say it does."

"Julio?"

"Yes, ma'am. He was one of those Romeo types for sure." He pointed a finger at her. "I know what you're thinking. Wasn't nobody else in his sights when Gus was here, but the months that Gus was in Dallas with your grandmother was another matter. Fair was fair, and Gus understood that."

August was surprised. It was the first time BJ had openly admitted there was more than close friendship between Gus and Julio. "So—"

"So, Julio would say if it was one kiss, then you're making her take all the chances. But if it was two kisses, then there might be hope for you yet." He crossed his arms over his chest and gave her a pointed look. "Either way, those looks she's been shooting you this morning probably mean she's wondering if you're regretting those kisses and thinking she should pack up and leave."

August blew out a breath. "She's going to leave anyway, BJ. Her cousin is expecting her." She closed the inventory program, her thoughts so sidetracked that she'd forgotten what she'd intended to do. "Anyway, it might not be safe for her to stay."

"Don't sound like to me that she's any safer at her cousin's place. So, quit making excuses and give her a reason to stay if that's what you want." He grabbed his hat from the coat tree just outside the office door. "Don't take all morning with that paperwork. We'll have those fence panels unloaded in about an hour." He disappeared from the doorway before she could answer.

Was BJ right? Was Teal worried that August was going to run her off because of the kisses they'd shared? Hell, if anything,

Teal could sue The White Paw for August pushing her against the wall last night and nearly ravishing her. She closed her eyes, reliving for the tenth time the heat of Teal's body against hers, the taste of Teal's mouth, and her low throaty moan. She'd been a willing participant. God, what Teal must think of her right now—kissing her like that, then treating her today like nothing happened between them.

But Teal was a hundred unanswered questions.

She was straight, wasn't she? Was she just curious about being with a woman? Was she a spy for either Reyes or Walker, trying to get close enough to find out where the evidence was hidden? Or was she was just the smart, beautiful woman she seemed? Did August want her to stay? Was their chemistry just two damaged egos needing reassurance? Could they enjoy each other for a short time and walk away friends?

Scratch that. Teal was a thousand unanswered questions.

First, she'd start with a question she could actually answer. What new websites had Teal been looking at recently? She logged out of her desktop and back in as "guest."

What was this? Teal had logged into the computer last night after their hallway encounter? She'd Googled August again, then browsed through images of her. Despite mixed feelings, she smiled at the thought of Teal checking her out all dressed up for those Dallas society events. Did she like what she saw? The smile faded as she scanned further down the browsing history to a *Dallas Morning News* article about the investigation into her law practice.

August didn't know much about Teal, but they had talked enough for her to know that Teal was no naive farm girl. She was savvy enough about business to give out advice—good advice—on how August could improve her image as boss. What was she thinking after reading that article?

Hmm. Several more websites. She must have been up for quite a while. August glanced at the open doorway to make sure she was still alone, then clicked on the first of several lesbian fiction websites. Well, well. This was some pretty hot erotica, free for the reading. Before she knew it, she'd lost herself in one of the stories and was shifting uncomfortably in her chair. Damn. She glanced at the time in the bottom corner of the screen. She'd better get moving. She copied that part of the browsing history and emailed it to herself for late-night reading on her iPad.

As soon as she tapped "send," she paused. Teal had an iPad, too. She could have looked up the *Morning News* article on that. Did she want August to know she'd seen it? Yes, she did. Why else would she look up lesbian erotica on a shared computer? Nobody else used the office computer but her and BJ. August quickly deleted the browsing history. Lord, BJ's old heart might not be able to take it if he stumbled onto it.

August grinned as realization struck. Teal had figured out the hat gift was the result of August's computer snooping. This browsing history was a deliberate message. The idea warmed her neck and ears. Her crotch throbbed with a genuine need she hadn't felt in years.

That was the second question answered, if she was totally honest. She didn't want Teal to leave. She stood. Damn it. She had a message of her own to deliver.

She grabbed her Stetson from the coat tree and headed for the kitchen with Rio on her heels. Her determined strides faltered when Teal, washing a frying pan in the sink, didn't turn around at the sound of her footsteps. August felt suddenly tentative and cleared her throat. Teal glanced over her shoulder but began to rinse the pan.

"I wanted to tell you that we'll have lunch in the bunkhouse, rather than out on the range like we've been doing. We'll probably be about an hour later, too...around one o'clock," August said. "I want to show the men some videos about grass-fed cattle operations and talk to them about, you know, the Dallas situation."

Teal set the frying pan in the drain rack and dried her hands on a dish towel as she slowly shifted to face her. The uncertainty in her eyes stabbed August. She didn't like knowing she was the cause of it.

"Yeah. I'm talking about what you read in the article. The guys haven't said anything, and I don't know if any of them keep up with Dallas news or just read the local paper, but I want to explain to everyone what I can. That includes you."

"Okay." Teal looked away, nervously biting her lip and twisting the dish towel in her hands, then back at August. "Anything else you want me to know?"

August hesitated, then fell into those dark eyes, so brave and, for her, unguarded. "Yeah. Just this." Two quick strides and Teal's face was cupped in August's hands. Teal's mouth was soft and welcoming to August's tongue. She wanted to forget BJ and fences and cows. She needed to forget Reyes and the trial. She ached to shut out the world and drown herself in this intelligent, beautiful woman.

August gently withdrew from the kiss, searching Teal's eyes. They were bright with desire and filled with certainty now. Her message had been received.

"See you at lunch," August said softly. She wheeled and scooped up her hat before she bucked off her responsibilities, grabbed Teal, and galloped for the bedroom. "Come on, Rio. Let's go see Pops."

❖

The wranglers had already departed for the south pasture, so Pops was in his rocking chair on the porch of the bunkhouse, enjoying his morning smoke and another cup of coffee. He eyed August. "You okay?"

She raised an eyebrow. "Yeah. Why?"

"You look a little flushed, and it ain't all that hot out here yet."

"I'm fine," she said. "It was sort of warm in the kitchen, you know, cooking breakfast with the stove and oven."

He sat forward in the chair. "Pretty, ain't she? That girl would get my motor running, too, if it could still run."

Heat rose up her neck to flood her face anew, and he chuckled. "Yup. I thought so."

"Mind your own business, old man, or I'll take you down to the old folks home and drop you off like a stray dog." August smiled and ducked her head, stealing all credibility from her threat.

Pops's chuckle became a belly laugh, then a coughing fit. Rio laid her head in his lap and whined as she licked his hand.

August narrowed her eyes at him and scowled, her hands on her hips. "BJ said the doctor ordered you to stop smoking."

"I'm too old to stop. Been smoking all my life." He scratched Rio's head and spoke to the dog. "I'm okay, girl."

August picked up the pack of cigarillos resting on the arm of his chair. "You could at least smoke something with a filter and try to cut down some." She smiled as a sudden idea came to her. "How about we let Rio help?"

Pops eyed her. "Rio?"

August held out the pack to the dog. "Go hide." Rio grabbed the pack of cigarillos and took off running for the barn.

Pops stared after the dog, then at August. "Durn your hide. Where's she taking my smokes?"

"She'll hide them and only go fetch when I tell her. I'll let you have one twice a day. You've already smoked your first. You can have another after supper."

Pops waved a dismissive hand. "I've got more."

Rio returned, her tongue lolling in a big doggie grin.

"Got a stash, huh?" August held the door to the bunkhouse open. "More, Rio. Go find."

The collie disappeared into the bunkhouse, and Pops stared after her suspiciously.

"I'm headed out to the pasture," August said. "But I'm going to leave Rio to keep an eye on you."

Rio reappeared with a box of cigarillo packs in her mouth.

Pops frowned at her. "Maybe I don't want that meddling dog around."

"She'll be good company. Besides, we'll all be back in for lunch. We're going to have a ranch meeting after we eat."

"A meeting?"

"Yep. I've got a few changes I want to make, and I'm going to lay it all out at one time for everybody so I can answer any questions."

He squinted one eye at her, then nodded. "Good enough. I was going to dig potatoes this morning anyway. Since that dog is so smart, maybe I'll teach her to dig 'em up for me."

"All you have to do is show her. You'll be surprised at what she understands."

Teal sagged against the sink and cast about the kitchen. What had she been doing? Lord, she couldn't remember. August's kiss had stolen her ability to think, shaken her equilibrium, and quite possibly—she dabbed at her throat with the dishcloth—broken the air-conditioning unit. Last night's kiss in the dark hallway was one thing, but being kissed like that in broad daylight was another matter. She closed her eyes, reliving the fire in August's eyes as she strode forward, feeling August's hands on her face, August's hips pressing into hers.

She threw the dishcloth onto the counter and cut a quick path through the living room to her private bathroom, slamming the door closed and propping her back against it. She opened her jeans in one swift movement and shoved her hand inside, moaning as her fingers found the ache and began a swift massage. Eyes closed again, she could taste August's tongue in her mouth. In Teal's mind, August didn't pull away, didn't end the kiss. It was her fingers snaking down Teal's belly, sliding against Teal's slick, swollen flesh. Then she was pushing Teal's jeans down and lifting her up onto the kitchen's counter. She was jerking Teal to the edge of the counter, her grip firm on Teal's thighs to spread them wide, and then her mouth hot and—

Teal realized the loud thump had been her head slamming back against the door as her vision and her fingers catapulted her to quick orgasm. Chest heaving, she opened her eyes, almost startled by the wanton woman who stared back from the bathroom's mirror. This was pathetic. She had to stop. Last night after her reading session and again today. August was driving her crazy. She'd never wanted a woman so much. Maybe it was all this fresh air and exercise. She'd never hungered for Lauren like this, not even during their first weeks. Lauren had been heels and business suits, wine and five-course dinners, a master in the power game of lies and strategy and getting what she wanted. August was different. She was golden sun and rich earth, sweat and horses, blood-pumpingly sexy and achingly tentative. God almighty. She should run the other way. Run fast. No. She had to sleep with her. Yes. Sleep with her, by God, to get August out of her system.

Teal made a plan while she washed up. August had a private sign-on, so she couldn't check to see what she browsed on the Internet, but maybe she could find a few clues about what she liked in her bedroom. She slipped across the hall.

August's room was neat but not obsessively so. The queen bed was made, but the closet door had been closed to hide the jumble of boots, athletic shoes, and overflowing laundry hamper. Teal stuffed the dirty clothes into the hamper and set it by the door to take to the washroom.

A towel hung a bit haphazardly in the bathroom, but none were on the floor. Teal smiled. The cap was neatly replaced on the toothpaste, which was appropriately squeezed from the bottom. No problem there. She pursed her lips. Also, no hints. Her cosmetics amounted to a preference for standard Ivory soap. No perfumes or bath oils. No tub for that matter. Only a walk-in shower.

The iPad on the bedside table requested a password when she turned it on, so she switched it off again. Darn. She picked up the television remote and hit the power button. Hmm. August had been watching the food network. That was interesting. She'd never shown any interest in cooking. Then she spotted the printer on the small secretary's desk under the window. A single sheet of printed paper lay next to it. Bingo.

August apparently had printed the recipe for a butter rum cake. In the page's margin, a note was written in August's bold cursive:

Angela, a client's mother in Dallas used to make these cakes for me because it's my favorite. What would you charge to bake one? Or do you know someone in town who bakes them?—August

The printer was also a copier, so Teal made a quick duplicate. She heard voices in the kitchen and checked her watch. That would be Brick's wife, Angela, and her cleaning crew. Just the person Teal needed to see.

CHAPTER TWELVE

S o, we ain't gonna ship these steers out after we wean them? We're gonna feed them for three years?" Doubt was written all over Manny's rugged features. At least it wasn't the same wariness they'd all shown as they watched her set up the video about raising grass-fed beef.

"Yes." August watched the men exchange incredulous looks. Except Hawk. He sat quietly against the wall, watching her. "We'll still sell breeding stock every year, so there'll be some income. I have my own financial resources, so I intend to invest the money Julio left back into the ranch. My plan is to develop a White Paw brand and sell directly to top-level outlets. An old college chum is a big-deal chef in Chicago and has already put me in touch with some contacts there, in New York and Atlanta. There's plenty of interest."

Manny, Tommy, Brick, and Pops stared at her, not really comprehending. Hawk, as usual, was hard to read.

"What she's saying is that we're going to start raising specialty beef and sell it to some high-priced restaurants that cater to people who'll pay extra because somebody tells them it's fancy meat." BJ wasn't anxious to change the way they'd been doing things for years, but she'd discussed her ideas with him at length, and he had her back when it came down to doing it. "Nobody here is going to lose their job. There'll be plenty to do even though we won't be shipping calves to market every year. We'll just be doing some different things, or the same things a different way. Could be, we find out we need to hire another man—"

"Or woman," Teal said.

BJ nodded. "Or woman to handle all the work."

"I heard people won't buy grass-fed beef because it costs too much and doesn't taste as good without enough fat marbling in it," Brick said.

"It's true that grass-fed beef sells at a higher price unless you buy in bulk. We'll start out just shipping to restaurants or a few premium distributors. But we'll offer bulk sales to individuals through a website, and maybe a few places locally. Eventually, I want to have our own meat-packing plant or contract someone to partner with who'll do things our way."

Teal looked up. She'd been busily scribbling in a small notebook. "You could introduce your brand at some community events in Amarillo, Lubbock, and Dallas to start out. Offer to cater an event or give away cooked samples at a community festival. Set up a White Paw booth at the Texas State Fair and sell jerky, or steak on a stick, or kabobs." She waved her pen, her eyes bright with excitement. "Get your celebrity chef friend to come down and do a cooking demonstration with your beef. The Dallas media would eat that up." She stood and began waving her arms around. "You could make a video about how the cows are raised and handled in a more humane way, like you using local anesthesia to castrate while other ranchers don't."

August grinned at Teal's excitement, then made a face at her last suggestion. "I don't think people want to watch a calf get castrated while they're chewing on White Paw beef."

The men laughed, and so did Teal.

"I didn't mean you should show the video at the food booth. Well, you could, but a sanitized version. The long version could go on the website. You could put cooking tips on the website, too."

"Those are great ideas." As impressed as she was by Teal's brainstorming, August couldn't help but shrink a little from the enormity of it. She wouldn't exactly be retreating to the quiet life of a small ranch operation. She'd be building what could evolve into a corporation. Did she want to do that? Did she want to shoulder that alone?

Tommy still shook his head. "I don't know. We spent all morning putting up fence panels for a vaccination chute that has no corners. The old square paddock and chute have been fine all these years. How come you want to change things around?"

Hawk finally spoke, his eyes never leaving August's. "Because it is the right thing," he said. "It's more kind and gentle to the animals who give their lives to nourish us. The rounded paddocks are less stressful and remove the risk of them bunching up in a corner and causing an injury. When you avoid crowding them into muddy feed lots and stuffing them full of additives, hormones, and grain to fatten them quicker, and make changes in how they're handled on the ranch and at slaughter, the end product is a healthier, leaner meat."

"Julio would'a done it."

They all turned to Pops. August thought he'd fallen asleep in his recliner during the video she'd shown them on the big-screen television. Apparently not.

He sat forward, resting his forearms on his knees, and looked around the room at each of them. "Julio had talked about it fifteen years ago, but there weren't enough buyers out there." He jerked his thumb toward August. "And he didn't have the connections this one does."

August hadn't expected an endorsement from Pops. If they hadn't had an audience, she would have hugged him. She looked at her wranglers. "Julio depended on you guys, and I'm hoping you'll stick with The White Paw. If you get behind me on this, each of you will receive a bonus of one percent of The White Paw's profits the first year we sell grass-fed beef. In addition, you'll each receive two head of mature beef. You can sell them, put them in your freezer, or keep them for breeding stock to start your own herds. If you keep them, I'm willing to negotiate some grazing terms so they can stay on The White Paw until you have your own pasture for them."

Manny and Tommy sat straighter and exchanged surprised smiles. Hawk gave her an approving nod. "We're in," Brick said, answering for all.

August held up her hand, palm out, when they started to rise from their seats. "One more thing I need to discuss with you. But before I do, I need each of you to give your word that what is said here stays on this ranch. You cannot discuss it with anyone."

They settled back in their seats, checking each other's reaction.

Brick was the first to speak up. "This secret. It's not anything illegal that would get us in trouble with the law by knowing and not telling, is it?"

Tommy snorted. "Yeah, Brick. She's gonna grow a side crop of marijuana in the chicken-manure pile."

August shook her head and smiled. "No. I would never ask you to do anything illegal."

"You have my word," Hawk said.

The rest chimed in one by one, and BJ nodded for her to begin.

"I think most of you are aware that until I got the news that Julio had passed away and left the ranch to me, I was practicing law in Dallas." August's gaze rested on Teal. She was ashamed to admit how stupid she'd been. But something in Teal's eyes told her it would be okay. She was admitting that she'd let Christine dupe her. But telling them was letting them have a stake in her as well as the ranch, or giving them the option to leave for their own safety. She cleared her throat. "What you don't know is that just before I got the news about the ranch, my law partner was arrested and our offices closed. There's an ongoing federal investigation into some cases handled by my partner and a junior associate, who is the son of the biggest client our practice handled. Or, I should say, my partner handled. There'll be a big trial sometime in the next year, and I'll be called to testify."

They were quiet for a moment as they digested the information.

"They didn't charge you with anything? Or did you make a deal so they wouldn't arrest you, too?" She was glad Brick asked, rather than gossip and conjecture behind her back.

"My paralegal brought the malfeasance to my attention, along with information that my partner and the client were doctoring paperwork to implicate me if I ever found out."

"So, how did the cops find out?" Tommy asked.

"I gathered evidence from our office files and beat them to the punch. I turned them in."

"Why do I think this is more than you being worried that we'll hear about it and think you were involved?" Hawk was always the perceptive one.

She avoided looking at Teal. This part wasn't in the newspaper article. "The client, the man the feds are still gathering evidence to arrest, is very dangerous."

"Who is this bad guy, and what's he into?" Brick had a wife and kids. If any of them left, she would expect it to be him. He had to think of his family's safety.

"I know he's laundering money through fake nonprofit organizations with off-shore bank accounts. The feds can't prove it yet, but they believe it comes from importing and distributing cocaine from South America." She paused. "His name is Luis Reyes."

"Sweet Jesus, Mary, and Joseph." The others watched Manny as he looked skyward, crossed himself, and kissed the Catholic medallion hanging around his neck.

"Witnesses have mysteriously disappeared or suddenly refused to testify in past cases that involved his employees." She gave them a grim smile. "But when I got the call about Julio, I left Dallas in the middle of the night. Nobody knows I'm here. Not even the feds. They wanted to put me in witness protection until the trial."

"You've been here for weeks. Why are you telling us now?" Hawk asked.

"Because John Stutts called me yesterday to say he can't delay filing the deed to the ranch any longer. If I was Reyes, I'd have Internet-search alerts set up in case I surfaced. The deed will trigger that and give him a new place to look for me. His men could show up here." She held up her hands. "If they do, I don't want anyone to be hurt. I would ask you to stand down and not put yourself in harm's way for me, but to alert authorities as soon as possible. BJ and the sheriff have the number of the DEA agent who should be contacted."

The men shifted in their chairs, sharing looks but staying silent. Finally, Brick stood. "Most of us had already been making plans for other employment when old Julio's health began to fail. We figured this land would be sold off to developers like most of the other ranches."

August held up her hand. "I understand that you have a family to protect, Brick. There'll be no hard feelings if you feel you have to leave. Anybody who does leave will get three months of salary to tide you over until you settle in somewhere else. I wish I could do more, but I have to keep the ranch going."

He glared at her. "I was going to say that we were relieved when you showed up here wanting to ranch rather than sell the place. I think I speak for all of us. We're not going anywhere. And if you think we intend to stand by and let those drug dealers drag you off, you don't know nothing about The White Paw. We stick together."

The men all nodded, an occasional "that's right" or "you bet" thrown in for good measure.

August shook her head and was about to object when BJ stood.

"Here's the deal. Until this pig swill is behind bars, I want everybody armed and carrying a two-way."

She couldn't let them do this. "BJ—"

It was Pops, though, that settled the issue. He stood, his gnarled hand grasping her forearm to forestall her argument, and met her glare with unfaltering steel. "Would you stand by and let them haul off one of us?"

"Of course not, but—"

"No buts. You're part of The White Paw family, and we take care of our own. Just say thank you."

She still wanted to object, but the determination on their faces told her it wouldn't do any good. She looked at Teal, who offered a small smile and slight nod. Then she took a moment to look into the eyes of each man. "Thank you," she said.

❖

Teal licked a bit of the butter-rum glaze from her finger. Yum. This recipe had turned out even better than it sounded. Angela had suggested a few minor changes and was glad to drive Teal into town for a quick shopping trip to gather the necessary ingredients. She'd baked the cake before lunch and managed to sidetrack August, who'd smelled it cooling when she'd popped in to wash up before heading to the bunkhouse to set things up for the post-lunch meeting.

August's decision to include the men in her plans for the ranch's future and to share her personal dilemma seemed to tear down any reservations they had about her as a boss. They were full of questions about the changes she wanted to make, and she showed them another video about Temple Grandin, an autistic woman who had been changing the way meat-packing houses operate so animals were less stressed and slaughtered in a humane way. That was when Teal managed to slip away and finish her dinner preparations and glaze the cake.

"I'm heading out," BJ said, stopping to peer over Teal's shoulder. "That sure smells good. Maybe I should take some with me."

"Maybe you can have some when you come home tonight," Teal said, slapping at his hand when he tried to drag his finger through the glaze puddled at the base of the Bundt cake.

He looked over the kitchen bar where the three of them always ate. Cloth napkins, wineglasses, and taper candles weren't their norm for dinner. He winked at her. "I could be late." It was his usual poker night at a tavern in town. "There's a certain lady I keep company with occasionally. I'll bet a big piece of that cake would get me breakfast at her house if I don't linger at the cards too long."

"You old dog," Teal chuckled but cut a quarter of the Bundt and transferred it into a plastic container.

"What? Didn't think this old dog could still hunt?"

She laughed at his implication. "On the contrary. I'm sure none of the widows in town are safe." She handed over his cake. "Good luck, although I'm sure you don't need it."

He laughed, too, and headed for the door with his cake in hand. "Good luck to you tonight, too." He paused as he settled his hat over his brow. "The skittish ones, you just have to keep after them smooth and steady."

She watched him leave, staring at the door even after he'd gone. Problem was, she didn't feel so steady. She had no idea what she was doing. She'd never actually pursued another woman. Not even Lauren.

"Those must be some serious thoughts." August stood across the kitchen, slouched against the large stainless-steel refrigerator. Her hair was still damp from a shower, slicked back and draped across nearly bare shoulders. The racer-back black ribbed tank clung to her small breasts, her nipples hard peaks in the air-conditioning. She wasn't wearing a bra. In fact, Teal had noticed that August rarely wore a bra. Faded jeans sagged along her slim hips, and bare feet peeked from under the hem that dragged the floor. God, could she get any sexier?

"Uh. Oh. I'm sorry. What?"

"I was just wondering what you were thinking about so hard."

Teal let her eyes wander slowly down August's length and back up to her face. "I'm sure it must have been important, but I can't seem to remember right now." August's appearance had stolen more than her thoughts, and her words sounded a bit breathless.

August sniffed the air. "Something smells really good." She pushed off from where she was propped and sauntered forward, her eyes never leaving Teal's. "What's for dinner?"

"Beef stroganoff." Teal lifted the lid on a large skillet and turned off the flame under it.

"One of my favorites." August edged closer. "But I smell something different. Something sweet."

Teal ran her finger along the inside of the bowl on the counter and held it up without breaking their gaze. "I made dessert. Butter rum cake. Want a sample?"

August's mouth was warm as she sucked the buttery sweet glaze from Teal's finger.

Teal nearly moaned as a jolt of pleasure rolled through her groin. She swallowed hard. "How does it taste?"

August's eyes darkened. "You tell me." She closed the final distance between them, and her lips were soft against Teal's. Her tongue, sweet and buttery, played against Teal's. Her hips pressed against Teal's in a slow, languid roll.

Holy mother. Teal wasn't a religious person, but kisses from August might change her opinion about the possibility of heaven and perhaps a goddess, after all.

August eased back from their kiss and trailed her mouth down Teal's neck.

Teal closed her eyes to concentrate on the tingle racing down her arms and swelling her breasts. "I could serve dessert first if you want."

August stopped and briefly rested her forehead on Teal's shoulder. Teal rubbed her hands along August's long, lean back.

"What is it?"

"I'm sorry," August said, stepping back. "I'm out of line. You're an employee—"

But Teal wasn't going to let her back away. She cupped August's face in her hands and drew their mouths back together. August stiffened, then relaxed and opened to her. Teal swung them around and backed August against the counter. She pressed her hips against August's and smoothed her hands down August's soft, strong shoulders. She palmed August's small breasts and tweaked her hardening nipples through the thin cotton tank. They were both panting when she retreated, her mouth still a breath away from August's. "I want you so bad I'm about to combust."

She'd never been so desperate, so wanton, but she had a sudden inspiration. Teal stepped back and stripped off her shirt. August watched silently, her chest and neck flushing as Teal reached behind to release the hooks on her bra and let it drop to the floor.

"Teal."

"I want you, August." She reached for the bowl of leftover icing and smeared the buttery glaze on her nipples. "I'm the chef, and I say dessert first."

August grabbed the back of her tank and yanked it over her head to bare her chest, too. Then her mouth was on Teal's breasts, her tongue hungrily bathing the glaze from her nipples. Teal dropped her head back and held onto August's shoulders. "Bed," she gasped. "I want to feel you naked against me."

August didn't cease from her pleasurable task but slipped her arms around Teal and under her hips, lifting her. Teal reflexively wrapped her legs around August's hips as she walked them out of the kitchen, their meal still on the stove.

❖

August carefully lowered Teal onto the bed, kissing down her smooth belly as she removed Teal's jeans and panties. August dropped the clothes to the floor and straightened where she stood beside the bed. The setting sun seeped in past the open blinds and glowed soft across Teal's naked body. She was so beautiful.

Teal stared back, her dark eyes half hidden by thick lashes, and August slowly opened the fly of her jeans, button by button. She hooked her fingers in her briefs and slid them from her hips, then kicked them aside. She stood for a moment, letting Teal take her in. Teal licked her lips, and August's belly clenched at the signal. Teal wanted to taste her. Yes. She wanted to taste Teal, too.

She began with her tongue along the arch of Teal's foot, then mouthed on the sensitive inside of her ankle. She gently flexed Teal's legs up and apart as she crawled onto the bed between them, pausing to kiss and suck the pulse at the back of her knee. Teal trembled when she trailed kisses upward along the inside of her thigh, then spread her wide to nibble at her swollen clit. She dipped lower and plunged her tongue inside, coating her tongue in the salt and musk that was all woman, all Teal. She held firm as Teal's hips surged upward.

"August, please. I've wanted you for so long." Teal's fingers tightened in her hair. "Don't tease. Not this time."

She clamped the tender flesh gently in her teeth to stay the flow of blood as Teal's clit plumped to near bursting, then slid her fingers inside and stroked. She relaxed her jaw and licked at the surging flesh as Teal's heels hit the bed and her hips lifted again. As August sucked, her spirit soared when Teal's breath faltered and then held and her body bowed taut. She smiled and stroked as Teal's orgasm and voice let loose. She was a screamer. The knowledge that she caused that exclamation of appreciation swelled her ego and her sex. It drove her hunger. She wanted to hear it again and again.

She continued to stroke as she kissed a path up Teal's belly, nibbled on Teal's tasty breasts, and kissed along her neck. She withdrew and entered again with three fingers, stretching her wide and thrusting deep. She pressed hard against the rough spot that many women found pleasurable. Teal gasped.

"August, August." Teal moved with each thrust, wrapping her legs around August, opening further to her.

August laid her thumb against the side of Teal's sensitive clit and reared up, bracing on one arm and curling inward to rub her own throbbing clit against her knuckles as she pumped her hips into Teal.

"August, I'm going to, I'm going to—" Teal drew in a deep breath.

"Come for me, Teal." August clamped her teeth together as sensation gathered in her groin and swelled. She pumped and stroked, pumped and stroked. "Come with me. Come hard."

She couldn't hold it any longer.

"August, oh God." Teal arched again as she climaxed.

Orgasm bucked August, and she rode it out with a yell until her insides unclenched and she collapsed on top of Teal.

The quiet seemed unnaturally loud with both their hearts beating wildly. August shivered when the air conditioner blew a frosty stream across her sweating body. She stirred. She must be crushing Teal, but she didn't want to move. She wanted to stay inside her forever. She wiggled her fingers.

Teal moaned. "Can't. I need some recovery time." But Teal's arms came around her, stroking her back.

August lifted her head from Teal's shoulder and smiled as she wiggled her fingers again. "Are you sure? Sometimes all you need is a different position."

Teal lifted her head and kissed her.

August took it as an invitation and kissed her back, battling her tongue against Teal's and humming her approval. Teal's arms tightened around her, and then they were rolling and Teal was on top.

"A different position is a good idea," Teal said, her voice syrupy rich, her words thick with intent. She closed her eyes and moaned as she clenched August's fingers inside one last time, then withdrew from them. She pinned August's arms at her side and moved down her body with her mouth, tasting nipples, tonguing her navel and nipping the inside of her thigh to make room for where she wanted to be.

August closed her eyes when Teal's mouth found her. Sweet Jesus, it'd been a long while since she'd felt pleasure like this. "Teal, sometimes it takes me a while like this. Especially the second time."

Teal hummed. "You taste so wonderful."

"Oh, right there. God, that feels good."

Teal abandoned the spot and sucked her. "Just relax. I'm in no hurry." She slipped a finger inside, then two, and stroked.

"Yeah, I like that." Christine had never had the patience to really please her.

Teal flicked her tongue against the exact spot she'd found before, and August twitched.

Ten years and Christine never seemed to remember that her most sensitive place was on the left side of her clit. Teal had marked it the first time. She grabbed Teal's free hand and squeezed. "Don't stop. A little harder inside and I'm going to come."

Teal lifted her head. "Are you ready? Because I could do this all night."

August groaned. "Please. I want to."

Teal sucked her and stroked a few times before stopping again. "You want to come or you want to do this all night?" The teasing in her voice nearly sent August over without her tongue and fingers.

"I need to come now, and maybe all night, too."

Teal hummed as if considering the request, but her strokes were firm and deep. And when she lowered her head, her tongue was strong and unerring. Gut-clenching sensation boiled up in August's groin and burst forth to flow through her body in wave after wave.

As her orgasm abated, August floated in a pool of utter satisfaction. She'd forgotten what it was like to be totally sated, to have another woman desire her so completely and make love to her with such hunger.

Teal's soft voice penetrated August's fog of contentment. "Hey. You still with me?"

"No. I think you killed me. I'm sure I heard angels singing."

Teal laughed and August smiled. She loved that sound. She drew Teal close. "I don't want to get up. I'd like to stay in bed, naked, with you all night. But I was too nervous earlier to eat lunch, so I'm starving. And BJ will be coming home soon from his poker night."

Teal smiled and wiggled her eyebrows. "It cost a quarter of the rum cake I baked for you, but BJ won't be back until morning. He's spending the night with a lady friend."

August was surprised. BJ had never mentioned having a lady friend. "Really?"

"Yep." Teal propped up on one elbow and trailed her finger down August's chest, between her breasts. "So, how do you feel about eating in bed?"

August couldn't stop her slow smile. "Isn't that what we've been doing?"

Teal slapped her lightly on the chest. "That's not what I was talking about. Give me five minutes to reheat some stroganoff, and I'll bring dinner in here." She slid out of bed and pulled on her jeans.

"I love picnics, but let me help. You get the stroganoff, and I'll get the wine and dessert." August cast about for her jeans, too.

"I thought we just had dessert."

August stopped, her jeans halfway up her legs, and looked at Teal in exaggerated horror. "There's a limit?" She was pleased that her antics again triggered Teal's throaty laughter.

"I certainly hope not," Teal said.

Chapter Thirteen

Teal snuggled deeper into the warm body spooned against her back and entwined her fingers with the ones resting between her breasts. August's deep, even breathing caressed her neck and shoulder. Teal never thought she'd feel such absolute contentment.

They'd been tentative with each other the first night BJ had returned, standing in the hallway at bedtime, shuffling their feet. Finally, August had held out her hand.

"Sleep with me?"

Teal slipped her hand into August's, and they wordlessly picked up where they'd left off the evening before. August didn't hesitate the next day. As they said good night to BJ, August took Teal's hand and led her again into her bedroom. They'd slept together every night since. BJ never commented, and a week later when his poker and date night came around again, it seemed like it had always been that way.

But would that change…tomorrow, or next week, or next month?

August had unfinished business with Christine. And what would August say when she discovered that Teal had lied about who she was? Not exactly lied, but she hadn't been fully truthful. August stirred, and Teal realized she was squeezing the hand she clutched next to her heart too tight. The icy ball of fear in her chest roiled her stomach. Oh God. She was falling in love with August.

Really falling in love. She thought she'd loved Lauren, but now she realized she'd only been riding a high of hormonal attraction and infatuation with the power Lauren wielded in Congress. She didn't want to be on August's arm; she wanted to be in her skin, in her head, in her heart.

What was she going to do if August wasn't feeling the same, didn't feel the same when Teal finally told her the truth? She felt sick at the thought. She took a deep breath. Plan B. She always had to have a Plan B.

The Washington political jungle seemed so morally bankrupt and disgustingly disloyal now that she'd spent these past weeks with real, honest people. She couldn't go back, couldn't remember why she'd ever wanted to be part of it before.

She'd been brilliant at marketing a candidate, but could she market an idea? She'd been researching August's idea for a grass-fed-beef operation. Maybe she could study other organic operations—dairy without hormones. She could cash in her nest egg and maybe talk her sister, Gray, into joining her in the business venture, but turning farmer would be a constant reminder of August.

She closed her eyes and, since her brain didn't seem to want to shut down, tried to think through some details of her fallback plan. Her thoughts, however, only returned to the woman warming her back—August, tall and sexy in chaps and her Stetson pulled low over her gray eyes; August, head flung back and mouth open in a soundless gasp as orgasm grabbed her, then groaning and bucking as it flowed through her; August, face soft in the moonlight as she worked her magic fingers and watched for the pleasure on Teal's face.

Teal grew wet and aroused as the scenes flickered through her brain. Her hips and belly reflexively clenched, and warm lips moved across the ridge of her shoulder to her neck. She trembled. August never forgot Teal's neck was one of her erogenous triggers.

"I thought you were asleep." August's voice was low and husky.

"Sorry. I didn't mean to wake you."

"No, I'm sorry. If I'd been paying attention, I'd never have dropped off with you still wanting."

"I…I don't know what's wrong with me. I can't seem to get enough of you. I'm sorry."

"Never apologize for wanting me, for wanting more." August disentangled their hands and trailed her fingertips lightly down Teal's stomach. "Let me take care of you, baby."

August slid her fingers into Teal's damp curls, unerringly finding her swollen flesh. Teal closed her eyes and brushed her hair back to expose more of her neck to August's feasting mouth. August tugged at her earlobe with her teeth, and a jolt of sensation shot down to her clit. God, she could come like that. It wouldn't take much. Bells were already ringing in her head. Wait. The ringing was real. "The phone."

"Let it go to voice mail." August's fingers swirled over the spot that made her gasp.

But the house phone rarely rang. Teal summoned every ounce of her waning willpower and cupped August's hand to still it. "BJ isn't here, and it could be an emergency. It could be Pops."

August instantly rolled onto her back and grabbed the phone from the table on her side of the bed. "Hello?" Teal felt August's tense body relax. "Angela, hey. No, I wasn't asleep yet. BJ isn't here. What's up?"

Teal could hear Angela's muffled voice, fast and urgent as August listened.

"Okay. Listen. BJ's in town. Call his cell. Do you have that number?…Tell him to meet me there. It's halfway between us… No problem. I'll be there in ten minutes."

Teal scrambled out of bed as August rose, pulled on jeans, and rummaged in her dresser for a shirt. "What's wrong?" She began to dress, too. Had Reyes or his henchmen found August? No way was she letting August go off alone, even if BJ was going to meet her. "Is it Reyes?"

August flashed a wry grin. "Nope. Just a cowboy who needs his posse around him. There's a roadside bar halfway into town that's a local hangout. Apparently, Tommy's had too much to drink, and a biker whose group was passing through has been hitting on Tommy's date. Tommy's trying to take on the whole group. The bartender called Brick. He's on his way, too, but asked Angela to call BJ to give him a hand. The biker isn't alone, and the bartender is afraid they'll make hash out of Tommy if we don't get him out of there."

They climbed into the farm truck, and Teal barely had time to click her seat belt into place when August gunned it down the dusty drive, squealing the tires as she turned onto the blacktopped highway.

❖

The lights of the Lock & Load roadhouse were a beacon in the black, moonless night, and August fishtailed into the gravel parking lot, sliding neatly to a stop next to Brick's truck. Damn, she still had it. Her blood sang like she was a teen again, cocky and sure, as she trotted to the door with Teal hurrying to keep up. Before she went inside, she stopped, took off her hat, and handed it to Teal. She quickly braided her hair back while she talked. "Stay behind me unless things start flying. Then I want you to find a safe spot near the door or behind the bar." She tucked the braid into her collar and took her hat from Teal, settling it low on her head. "Don't worry about me. I've done this before."

She didn't see BJ's truck yet, but she wasn't going to wait. After all her haste, she sucked in a deep breath and sauntered casually inside. She was just in time, too. The biker wasn't the stereotypical middle-aged bald guy. His sleeveless jean jacket was open to reveal a chest as muscled as his tattoo-covered arms, but he had a young, handsome face. Tommy's date was smiling uncertainly at him while Tommy tugged at her arm. Brick was trying to persuade both that it was time to leave, but the girl didn't look convinced. The other bikers had taken notice and were gathering to watch the show.

August tucked Teal away at the end of the bar and strolled into the fray. "Everything okay here, Brick?"

"Hey, August." Brick moved behind Tommy, keeping a steadying hand on the young wrangler's shoulder, so August could take up a position beside him. "I think Tommy's had one beer too many, so I was thinking I'd give him and Penney a ride. I'll drop Manny off here on my way home so he can drive Tommy's truck back to The White Paw."

August nodded. "Well, since Teal and I are here, how about you take Penney to her house, then go on home to Angela. I'll drive Tommy back to the ranch to sleep off the beer, and Teal can follow in his truck."

"Even better."

"Not so fast." The buff biker grinned at Penney. "I don't think sweet thing is ready to go home, are you, darlin'?"

He might be good-looking, but obviously Neanderthals had raised him.

Penney didn't seem to notice. She smiled up at him. "I'm still a little thirsty," she said with a flicker of her mascara-laden eyelashes.

Did she actually bat her eyes at him?

"I'll buy you a cola on your way to your daddy's house," Brick said, wrapping an arm around her shoulders to guide her toward the door.

The biker had other ideas. He wrapped a meaty hand around Penney's arm. "I say she stays."

The tavern's door swung open and BJ strode in. "Got a problem here?"

"Just making sure we don't," August said, checking quickly that Teal was still in a safe spot as the other bikers edged closer. She focused on the buff biker again.

Penney seemed to have decided she'd bitten off more than she could chew and was trying to squirm out of the biker's grasp. "You're hurting me," she whined.

Geez. August would never understand why straight women loved to light fires when they had no intention of cooking. Tommy shook off Brick's hand and surged forward, but August blocked his path, stepping between the biker and Tommy.

"Look. We don't want any trouble. I'll just take them out of here and you can get on with your night." She put her hand on the biker's wrist but tried a different tactic when he didn't release his hold on Penney's arm. "The girl is underage. Ask the bartender. I'll bet he's been serving her nonalcoholic beer all night because he knows her ID is fake."

"I am not!" Penney thrust out her over-sized bust as evidence of her womanhood. "I turned twenty-one last month."

August almost rolled her eyes. Apparently, the boobs were real. The silicon was in her head, replacing brain cells.

The biker grinned. "Then she'll be staying."

August spoke low but clear as BJ moved to her side. "Brick, get these two outside. BJ and I will take care of things in here."

"I'm on it."

At that instant, she gouged her thumb into the biker's wrist, and Brick yanked the girl free, dragging her and Tommy toward the door.

"What the fuck?" The biker jerked back and shook his hand, then leaned into August's personal space, his eyes narrowing. "You shouldn't have done that."

The other bikers laughed. Their eyes gleamed as they formed a threatening semicircle around August and BJ but taunted their fellow biker. "What's the matter, Buck? You gonna let that woman boss you like she does those cowboys?"

The buff biker snarled at their insults, pushing his face closer to August's. "I'm going to teach you a lesson for that, bitch."

"We don't want trouble, mister. Why don't you stand down, and we'll clear out." BJ inexplicably moved a few steps away, putting space between him and August.

"You'd do best to get out of the way, old man. I'm thinking that since this bitch ran off the best-looking woman in this dump, I'll just have to settle for a little fun with her."

August grinned. "Put your hands on me, short dick, and I'll show you how much fun I can be."

The bartender groaned and squatted behind the bar to begin punching numbers on his cell phone.

"It's about time you called the police," Teal said, whispering as she kneeled beside him. She couldn't believe he'd waited this long.

The bartender gave her a disgusted look, then spoke into the phone. "Hey. You know where that catalog is that I use to order new tables and chairs? I'm going to need it. August Reese is back in town. She and BJ are here, fixing to mix it up with a gang of bikers. Yeah. Well, I need some new furniture anyway. This way, The White Paw can pay for it."

Teal stared at him in amazement. "That wasn't the police."

"Hell, no." He gave her an irritated look. "That was my wife. I'm not calling the cops. They'll write a report that'll show up when my alcohol license comes up for review. I don't need that. Those bikers won't go whining to the cops either. If they need medical attention, they'll just say they fell off their bike after drinking too much."

Teal was incredulous. "Are you crazy? That's a woman and an old man against eight bikers. The smallest one has to weigh two-fifty." She began to search for some type of weapon. Didn't bartenders keep a shotgun or something stashed under the bar?

They both peeked over the top of the bar at the sound of a loud crash. August was standing with her back to the crowd, and the biker was on the floor at her feet, shaking his head. BJ had her back, eyeing the others as they hooted and laughed.

"She's a wild one, Buck. Maybe you should let one of us show you how to handle that kind."

Buck stood and dusted himself off. He grinned. "I'm just getting started." He dove for her, but when she ducked to flip him over her back again, he grabbed hold to take her down with him. She threw a quick elbow between his legs and he howled, releasing her in time for her to complete the flip and land him once again on his back, where he writhed and gripped his crotch.

Another biker made a grab for her. She blocked his arm and punched him in the nose. An awful crunching sound was followed by a torrent of blood as he staggered backward.

The rest of the bikers closed in, and BJ joined the action. His wiry frame seemed no match for the muscled bulls, but he struck with speed and accuracy that stunned Teal. The bikers appeared like clumsy giants as he spun and weaved among them, punching and kicking knees, throats, faces, and other vulnerable parts.

Suddenly, Teal realized she was watching a strangely choreographed dance. BJ and August were back to back, moving in sync to dispatch the bikers surrounding them. At one point, BJ snatched up two short legs of a broken chair, then tossed August the long leg of a smashed table, and they used the wood as weapons. Using the table leg like a staff, August swept a biker's knee, then downed him with a blow to the head. BJ wielded the chair legs in a blur that battered ribs, elbows, and heads.

It was over all too quick. No bikers and only one table remained standing.

August turned to BJ and bowed. "Sensei, it was my honor to be at your side again."

BJ returned the bow. "Grasshopper. I am pleased to see you haven't deserted your training." They grinned at each other. "You always were my best student."

"Wow," Teal said, rising from her hiding place. "That was amazing."

August grinned, using her shirttail to wipe the sweat from her face. "That's why BJ calls me 'Grasshopper.'"

BJ stepped over a groaning biker. A few of them were beginning to sit up. "You want us to stay until they clear out?" he asked the bartender.

Tank burst through the door. "Oh, man. I missed it, didn't I?"

August laughed. "Yeah, you did, buddy. Who called you?"

"Penney. That girl's trouble, but she's my cousin." He laughed. "She couldn't believe Brick left you two here alone with these roughnecks."

"Y'all go on," the bartender said. "Tank can hang around until these fellers can drag themselves out to their bikes, and I've got Betsy here in case they try to cause any more trouble." He reached into the stockroom doorway at the end of the bar and retrieved a double-barrel shotgun. Right. That was the next place Teal would have looked.

❖

August's body still hummed with adrenaline as she drove Tommy, whom she found snoring in her truck where Brick had left him, back to the ranch. Her eyes were constantly drawn to the headlights in her rearview mirror—Teal following in Tommy's truck. She wanted her, wanted her in the worst way. Would Teal understand? August had experienced a split second of uncertainty when she realized Teal had watched her commit violence on those men, then relaxed at the wonder in Teal's eyes. Not that August condoned violence, but the martial-arts lessons had been necessary when she'd come out in high school and discovered that some men saw lesbians as a challenge to be physically converted or conquered.

She parked by the ranch house and watched Teal pull up next to the bunkhouse, where she was met by Hawk. He took the keys to Tommy's truck and walked Teal over to where August was shaking Tommy awake.

"I've got him, Boss," Hawk said. His white teeth flashed in the dim light. "Sorry I missed the show." He hauled Tommy from the truck and held on while he found his balance.

August was surprised. "News travels fast. I thought Brick had already left to take Penney home."

"Yep. He did. But Chuck Wheeler was tucked in that corner booth, recording the whole thing on his iPhone. He sent the video to me." He eyed her, then bowed slightly. "No rust on your skills. Anytime you feel like a little practice, I'd be honored to spar a few rounds."

"Thanks. I'd like that."

He nodded. "Then I'll take this upstart off your hands and let you get on with your evening. Good night."

August watched Hawk guide Tommy's stumbling path back to the bunkhouse. She could feel Teal's gaze on her. Maybe since she'd had time alone in Tommy's truck to think, Teal had decided their little display wasn't all that cool. She wasn't ready to see what Teal's eyes held for her. Instead, she blindly held out her hand, and when she felt Teal's fingers lace with hers, she led her inside and down the hall to her bedroom. Teal apparently didn't feel the same uncertainty.

The moment they stepped inside, Teal slammed the door closed and spun them so August's back was against it. Her mouth was hot and demanding, her tongue pushing past August's lips and thrusting past her teeth. August's body damn near ignited with the onslaught.

"Off, get these clothes off." Teal ripped August's shirt open, her fingers grappling to divest August of her bra. She growled. "I love that Western shirts have snaps instead of buttons."

"Teal." August almost winced at the pleading in her voice, but she was a pressure cooker about to explode. "God, I need you."

Teal was already tossing off her own shirt, and then her mouth was on August's breast sucking hard, nipping lightly. Her fingers found the buttons on August's jeans and worked them open with quick precision. Then she paused to slide the jeans down August's hips slowly. "I really love it when you go commando."

"Teal. Oh, God."

Teal worked August's turgid flesh with her mouth, stroking and sucking.

"I'm going to—"

But Teal stopped, thrusting her fingers inside. August groaned as she was filled below and Teal's tongue again filled her mouth. Teal's bare breasts were soft as they pressed against hers, but her jeans were rough, rubbing August's bare legs as she thrust her fingers and her tongue into August's body, capturing her, claiming her. The orgasm came so fast, so hard August was drawing a breath one second and exploding the next. But the climax only fed her need.

Before she'd fully come down, she jerked Teal's fingers from her body, picked her up, and tossed her onto the bed. She toed off her boots to step out of her jeans, then tugged Teal's boots off, throwing them across the room, and jerked Teal's unfastened jeans down her legs. Both completely naked, August fell on Teal, her sweat-slicked body meeting Teal's soft, cool skin. She feasted on Teal like a starving animal, tasting, touching nearly every part of her. She didn't think she'd ever satisfy her hunger for this woman. August plunged her fingers into Teal's tight sex and pumped.

"Your mouth. I want your mouth."

She would not, could never deny Teal. Brushing her face across Teal's fragrant curls, she probed with her tongue as she thrust with her fingers. When she found the hard knot growing at the top of her clit, she sucked it in, and Teal's body bowed as she screamed out her orgasm.

"Not enough," August said urgently.

Teal wrenched free and rolled onto her belly. "Your thumb inside, your fingers on my clit."

August loved a woman who knew what she wanted. She also loved a great ass, and Teal had a superior derriere. She planted kisses along Teal's back and nipped her buttocks as she thrust sure and steady. She pressed hard against the rough spot under her thumb pad and felt Teal's clit swell again.

"Oh, yeah, babe. Right there. Just like that." Teal raised her hips slightly to give August a prime view and better leverage. "Don't stop. God, that feels good."

Stop? Nothing could make her stop. She needed more.

August straddled one of Teal's legs and pumped against her firm buttock. Oh, yeah. She could come again. Being commanded to take Teal like this was primal and beyond erotic.

"Yes, yes. Don't stop, don't stop. Harder."

Teal's body tensed and she screamed into the pillow. Another thrust, another, and August was howling along with her. She collapsed only when Teal went limp. Their hearts pounded against each other as though trying to break out of their physical prisons and meld.

"I think I'm done," Teal said, her voice weak.

August carefully withdrew and rolled off Teal. She stared up at the ceiling, willing her breath and heart to slow.

"God, I don't know where that came from." Teal's voice held a bit of uncertainty. "Was it okay?"

"More than okay. It was…amazing."

Obviously reassured, Teal cuddled against her side and soon was fast asleep. As she well should be. It was late, no, early the next day. August had been up most of the night fucking and fighting and fucking. So why wasn't she sleepy, too?

Because her mind couldn't shut down. Teal had incredibly tapped into a part of August that Christine had never sensed, never understood. August wasn't sure she understood herself until now. But that's what scared her. She'd connected with Christine in a haze of hormones, too. Was that how it always happened? Was she always going to be led around by her ovaries? Talk about the lesbian U-Haul cliché. She wasn't even technically finished with Christine, and she was falling for Teal. Wait. This was just sex. She wasn't falling for anyone. She can't get involved. Reyes would use Christine against her if he could. *He doesn't need more leverage.* And, what did she really know about Teal? BJ hadn't asked for references from her last job. Teal had a ten-year blank in her past that she always managed to talk around.

August looked down at the woman slumbering on her shoulder. Teal's long-fingered hand splayed across August's belly, fingers that moments before had been inside her, commanding her, pleasuring her. Her sex clenched at the thought. Teal was incredible all right, too incredible. And August was in so much trouble.

CHAPTER FOURTEEN

The men were gathered around the big-screen television when August strolled into the bunkhouse Saturday morning. She knew Tommy had Saturday calf watch and wanted to make sure he was up fulfilling his duties rather than nursing his hangover.

"What's so interesting?"

The men stepped back so she could see past them. It was a video of her and BJ roughing up the bikers. Grainy, and a poor angle, but it was them. Oh, yeah. Chuck and his iPhone. The thought hit her like a hammer.

"Holy crap! That isn't going viral, is it?"

"It should." Brick grinned. "But Chuck has only about six followers on his YouTube station, and four of them are standing here."

"Make him take it down. That could lead Reyes straight to me."

Hawk's eyes widened. "Damn it. She's right. I can do that. I set up his account for him because he's too stupid. I know his password." He began typing on the laptop that was feeding the video.

Tommy came through the front door and groaned. "Haven't you guys watched that enough?" He dropped his gaze to the floor when August turned to face him.

"You check all the herds already?" She kept a firm tone. She wouldn't cut him any slack for being young and foolish.

"Yes, ma'am. All but the west pasture. I'm headed there next, but—" He clutched his stomach as it let out a loud growl. "I needed the bathroom." He glanced about desperately and ran for the toilet when August waved a hand to shoo him in that direction.

"Boy has the runs something powerful," Pops said. "Mixing beer and liquor will do it."

Manny reached for his hat. "Guess I'll check the west pasture for him."

But August held up her hand. "No, he did the drinking. He'll pay the price. That's what Gus made me do. I never forgot it." She turned to Pops. "But get some toast or some kind of bread and some Pepto-Bismol in him before he heads out again. The cows aren't running off anywhere in the next hour or so."

Pops nodded but eyed her. "Need anything else?"

"Yeah. I'm going into town with Teal. I want to talk to John Stutts about some stuff, and Tank said he has the check for her car now. I didn't figure you'd mind if I left Rio with you."

Pops's face lit up, and he slapped his thigh for Rio to sit next to him. "I never mind her company. She can help me dig some potatoes out of the garden later. She's getting pretty good at it."

August shook her head. "She's supposed to be a herding dog, not a gardening dog."

Pops stroked Rio's head. "Well, nobody needs a one-trick pony, now do they?" He looked up at August. "You git on. We'll be fine."

"Don't stay out in the sun too long," she said, pointing at Hawk, then Pops, to indicate Hawk should enforce her order. She turned her palm out to Rio. "You stay with Pops, girl." It was an unnecessary command. Rio had been at August's side for the past six years, since she was a puppy. But she seemed to sense Pops needed to be looked after and had gravitated to the old man over the past few weeks, with August's approval. They were both important to her.

August stepped back into the glare of the noon sun and settled her hat onto her head as she surveyed her surroundings. The heat wave smothering the Panhandle remained relentless, the recent storms evaporating as quickly as they rolled through. But she loved this land. When she closed her eyes, she imagined she could hear the hooves of a thousand bison on the long, flat prairies and the songs of the tribes echoing off the red mountains of the Caprock. Everything and everybody important to her was here at this ranch. Maybe it was time to admit that Teal might be part of that, too.

❖

The streets of the small town were inexplicably crowded with people and cars. Teal stared down Main Street. It was blocked to traffic and filled with tents and pedestrians.

August cursed. "I forgot about the annual arts festival. I can't believe so many people turned out in this heat wave."

"An arts festival? Do we have time to browse through the booths? I'd love to see what the local artists have to offer." She hadn't had to touch her savings since hiring on at The White Paw. In fact, she'd added a few paychecks to her stash and was about to pick up another check for the sale of her car. She could relax a bit because her short-term investments would mature in a few weeks and she could easily buy another car. Or truck. Maybe she should consider one instead. She'd ask Tank about it.

August shrugged. "I need to see John Stutts to tie up some loose ends on the ranch property. You go ahead, and I'll catch up to browse with you if he isn't in his office."

Teal shook her head. "It's Saturday. He won't be working."

August gave her a smug look as she navigated side streets to reach Tank's junkyard. "He's an attorney. Of course, he will."

"Bet you a buck."

"Whoa there, Miss Big Bucks. Throwing that car money around already, huh?" August parked in front of Tank's garage, and they both hopped out of the ranch truck.

Teal shoved August playfully and skirted around her to enter Tank's shop first. "Hey there, Tank."

"Hey, look here, fellas. Two beautiful ladies." He pointed to his chest. "Come to visit me. Yep. Here to visit old Tank." He turned to a group of three retired men sitting in the gossip corner. "But you better watch out for the blonde's right hook."

"Very funny, Tank." August smiled at the men. "How are y'all today?"

"Good."

"Not too bad."

"Day's getting better." The last answer came with a wink.

Teal smiled at the old guy. "Have you guys been down to the festival?"

"Nope. Been there, done that." The oldest of the three frowned. "Can't even get lunch at the diner because of all the idiots coming in from out of town just to buy a few trinkets."

"Are you going?" the winker asked.

"I'd like to browse through the booths," Teal said.

"Then look for my granddaughter. She's selling pottery, and her friend in the same booth is selling blankets her Apache grandmother taught her to make."

"That sounds interesting. I'll do that." She turned to Tank. "But first, you have some money for me?"

"I do. I got the fella to give me cash since you don't have a local account and the nearest branch of the bank he draws from is thirty minutes away."

"Thanks, Tank. You're awesome."

He hitched his jeans up. "Yep. That's what the women tell me."

August hooted. "You wish. Did you forget about that time I caught you and Joey skinny-dipping?"

Tank's ears pinked and he glanced over at the gossip corner, then came around the counter to place an envelope in Teal's hand and hustle them toward the door. "Thanks for coming by. Y'all have fun at the festival." He pushed them out the door but lowered his voice for his parting shot. "I told you the water was extra cold that day."

Teal covered her mouth to stifle the laughter bubbling up as she realized what must have happened.

August grinned at him. "Just kidding, buddy. I've never heard any complaints from Bunny."

Tank straightened and puffed out his chest at the mention of his wife. "Damn right."

They both laughed at Tank's bravado and waved as they got back into the truck. August steered toward downtown and found an empty parking space near Stutts's office. She gestured toward the colorful avenue of tents. "Go ahead. I'll catch up with you."

Teal tucked her folded envelope of cash into her front pocket. She loved Southwestern crafts. She strolled through the booths, smelling homemade soaps and buying some gourmet dog treats for Rio, then suddenly became aware that she was being followed. She thought she saw the young man lift his phone and snap her photo, so she faced him and glared. His face reddened and he shrugged with an apologetic smile. She relaxed. She'd been followed by admiring boys a few times when she was a college student, and he looked young enough.

She spotted a booth displaying pottery and Native American blankets and headed that way, but August intercepted her.

"That didn't take long," Teal said, holding out her hand.

August stared at Teal's upturned palm. "What?"

"I expect that John Stutts wasn't in his office, and you owe me a dollar."

August squinted one eye at her. "Technically, I never answered your challenge for a wager, therefore no verbal contract was made."

Teal wiggled her fingers. "Fork it over, Counselor."

August shook her head but dug a dollar from her pocket and slapped it in Teal's palm. "Just because I like you."

The festival crowd flowed around them as Teal tilted her head, her mouth suddenly dry. "Do you?" They both knew she was asking more than a simple question.

August's eyes softened and searched hers. "Yeah. I do."

Teal held her gaze. "I like you, too," she said softly.

August leaned closer. Good God. She was going to kiss her in the middle of this small Texas town. And, as those gray eyes darkened and drew near, Teal knew she was going to let her. She barely registered the clicking sound among the crowd noise.

"TJ. TJ Giovanni."

Caught off-guard in a vulnerable moment, Teal reflexively turned toward the loud male voice. A camera shutter whirred as it recorded photo after photo.

"I told you it was her." The boy who had taken her photo earlier stood next to man with a real camera around his neck. He had media written all over him.

She was momentarily frozen, then smiled at the man and approached. "I'm sorry. Were you yelling at me?"

"That's right," he said, holding up his camera. "And this photo is worth a sweet twenty grand at least. The tabloids are still looking for you."

"I hate to burst your bubble, but you must have mistaken me for someone else."

"No, I haven't. If there's any question, I have face-recognition software that will confirm it."

August was instantly at her back. "I don't know who you are, mister, but you can't take photos of private citizens and publish them without their permission."

"And who are you?"

"I'm Miss Crawley's attorney, and I think you'll want to hand over that camera so I can delete any photos you've taken of her right now."

He peered at Teal. "Crawley, huh? I can't believe nobody looked for you under your old name."

Teal didn't answer, but August held her hand out for the camera.

The guy pulled back. "No can do. Your friend here is considered a public figure, so I can take her photo any time she's in a public place and sell it to whoever pays my asking price. If you're really an attorney, you know that already." He turned back to Teal. "How about an exclusive interview, TJ? Don't you want to tell your side of the story?"

"There's nothing to tell." Teal turned and headed for the truck, but he followed.

"Come on. You're just going to let the good senator smear you all over Washington and come out smelling like a daisy? There've been rumors for years about her and her husband's affairs, but nobody has been able to catch one of them until now."

August caught up to them and shoved the guy back. "Leave us alone."

"Roughing up the media, Counselor?"

Teal tugged at August's sleeve. "Let's just get out of here."

They began walking again, but the guy kept dogging them.

"Don't be a victim, TJ," he called as they climbed into the truck. He snapped several more photos of them as August slammed the truck into reverse and backed away with tires squealing out of the parking lot.

This was bad, so bad. August said nothing the entire twenty-minute ride to the ranch. When they arrived, she banged out of the truck and strode into the house without waiting for Teal.

Teal climbed out of the truck slowly, her heart seizing. How could they be happy and carefree an hour ago, staring into each other's eyes and nearly confessing their feelings, and now their bond had seemed to vanish. She had to go to August and explain. But explain what exactly? That she'd purposefully concealed her identity? That her notoriety would probably put August and everyone at the ranch in danger? Maybe she should just leave. One of the guys would drive her to the bus station. But she couldn't go without talking to August.

August wasn't in her bedroom, the kitchen, or the den. Teal finally found her in the office. She'd Googled TJ Giovanni and was reading the news accounts.

"August." Teal propped against the door frame and stuffed her hands in her pockets to hide their trembling.

August kept her eyes on the computer screen, refusing to look at her. "Well, looks like I just can't get out of my own way, can I? Sucked in again by a pretty face."

"No. I'm not Christine. This isn't the same."

August whirled the chair around, her gray eyes dark as a thunderhead. "Isn't it? You lied to me."

"I didn't. I am Teal Crawley." She couldn't stop the tears welling in her eyes. "Giovanni is my mother's maiden name. When I was a college student applying for jobs, I thought it sounded more professional. TJ Giovanni was who I thought I wanted to be, but since I've been here—"

"God almighty. I can't believe I missed all of this on the national news. I was just so wrapped up in what was happening to my law firm." August stood, her voice rising with her. "You had to know the danger you were putting me and the guys—BJ, Pops and all the others—in if you were discovered."

"I didn't know at first. I read the articles and knew you were a witness in a trial, but I didn't realize you were in real danger. Not until you explained the situation to all of us. By then, I'd found a home here." Her hand shook as she lifted it to touch August's cheek. She needed desperately to connect with her, to make her understand. "I'd come to care for you and couldn't bring myself to leave."

August jerked away and then slid past Teal to escape the office. "I need to be alone to figure out what to do next."

Teal waited until she heard the front door slam, then ran to see where August was going. She watched her stride into the barn, then emerge a short time later on horseback. She sighed. At least she didn't go tearing off in the truck to get drunk somewhere or drive carelessly and end up in an accident.

She wandered into her bedroom, the room where she hadn't slept in more than a week. It was the first place she'd felt safe since that awful day Lauren had left her stunned and naked. The gash in her heart widened as she faced the reality that she had to leave this haven. The tears came slowly at first, leaking from her eyes and trailing down her cheeks. Then she fell onto the bed, buried her face in the pillows, and sobbed.

❖

The sun was setting, and August felt like her life was sinking with it as she guided the stallion into the barn. She'd played out a dozen different scenarios, but only one option was actually viable. *She* had to leave. She was the one bringing danger to the ranch, to the men she cared about. To the woman she couldn't bring herself to hate.

She loosened her mount's girth and leaned against him, inhaling the familiar and comforting scent of horse sweat and damp leather. He lowered his head to nuzzle her leg.

It'd been surprisingly easy to walk away from Christine, even as destroyed and pathetic as she'd appeared in that jail visiting room. She'd lied to August, concealed things that destroyed their practice and could have landed August in jail with her. But, worst, she'd morphed into a person August didn't know—one who traded sexual favors, willingly at first, with Reyes in exchange for power and money. Their intimacy had meant so little to her that she had shared it with someone else.

What was Teal's crime? August hadn't shared everything with her at first either. She'd let her work here without explaining the danger. If she'd told Teal before their attraction had taken hold, would Teal have stayed? She might have opted to leave, knowing what it would mean if the media tracked her here.

Damn. No matter how much she wanted to walk away from Teal with the same sense of justice she'd felt when she left Christine bruised and pitiful in a prison jumpsuit, she couldn't. And the toughest part was still to come. She had to convince Teal to stay, to look after BJ, Pops, and the ranch while she gave herself up to Pierce Walker and witness protection for God knows how long.

She turned to grab the stallion's halter from its hook but froze at the dark silhouette standing silently in the arch of the barn's entrance. Teal.

August hated the distance between them. She wanted to pull Teal into her arms, to turn back the clock and erase the past afternoon. But she was acutely aware of the sweat that trickled down her bare arms, leaving wet tracks in the fine sheen of red dust on her skin. She was a dirty mess, literally and figuratively. Distance was exactly what she needed. Part of her was afraid that if she touched Teal, she wouldn't be able to leave. She'd have to stay and take their chances if Reyes's men found her.

Teal's voice shook when she spoke. "I'm packed, but the guys refused to drive me into town before I told you I was going."

August returned the halter to its hook and slid her hands into her pockets so she wouldn't reach for Teal. "I—" She wasn't sure how to begin. "I'm the one who has to leave."

"August, no." Teal's quick response was choked. "This is your home. I'm so sorry." She turned to the side, and because she was no longer backlit in the doorway, the dying light revealed her tears.

The tenuous control that kept August from running to her faltered, and August reached deep for her lawyer persona. Teal was practical. She'd make that argument. "I've thought this out carefully, Teal. Reyes's men are looking for me, for the evidence I have. No matter what leads them here, I'm still the one bringing the danger to everyone." She shifted her feet, hesitating over the next part. "So, I need to ask a favor. I need you to stay. BJ isn't young, and Pops shouldn't be left alone all day every day while the men are out working. His heart is weak, and he forgets things. He could end up burning the bunkhouse down."

Teal wiped her hands over her face and took a few tentative steps toward August. "No. Stay, August. We'll face it together like we all planned before."

August wouldn't be swayed this time. This was best. She'd been weak before to let them talk her into staying. "No. I'm not going to endanger anyone else."

"But where will you go?"

She sighed and stared down at her boots. "I'm going to call Pierce Walker, the DEA agent, and let them put me under witness protection until they can lock Reyes away."

"How long?"

She shrugged. "It could be months, or several years. Depends on how good Reyes's lawyers are at delaying trial."

"August, no."

Teal's warm hand on her forearm undid her. She looked up into brown eyes, soft and pleading, and drew Teal into her arms. She closed her eyes and tried to memorize the perfect fit of their bodies together, the soft scent of Teal's shampoo, the silky texture of her hair against her cheek. "I've already decided, but I need to know you'll keep things safe here until I can come back."

Teal's arms tightened around her. "I can't stand the thought of you leaving, but I'll do anything you need of me." Teal lifted her head from August's shoulder, tears again wetting her cheeks. "I…I'm so scared for you. Promise you'll be careful and come back. You have to come back."

At that moment, August knew she would. They needed to sort out so much more. Teal's past. August's future. Secrets they each kept from the other. But more than the ranch, more than her chosen family here, she was staring at her reason to find her way back to The White Paw, no matter how long it'd take. "I will," she said, lowering her head and sealing the promise with a brush of her lips. It wasn't enough. Teal opened willingly, desperately as their kiss deepened and conveyed feelings, swore vows they couldn't yet put into words.

Suddenly Rio jumped against August's legs and nearly knocked them to the ground. "Rio, what the hell?" August struggled to catch Teal and steady them both. Rio barked sharply and ran to the other end of the barn, where Pops was leading Teal's big bay in from the paddock.

"You gotta hurry," he said. "Tank called. Reyes's vermin are headed this way."

August was confused. "What are you doing?"

"The best way to hide from those city rats is to head for the country. We done figured this out." He ducked into the tack room and returned with the bay's saddle, dropping it at August's feet. "Both of you need to skedaddle."

"I'm not leaving you guys here to face Reyes's men alone."

"They ain't going to bother us much when they find out you ain't here."

"And where do you expect me to go?" August began saddling the bay despite her protest, while Teal retrieved the gelding's bridle and swapped out his halter.

"Caprock Canyon. It's been a while, but you used to know those trails like the back of your hand. BJ's calling that DEA guy, but you two gotta stay clear of those goons until the cavalry can get here."

"Wait, wait." August held up her hands. "I thought we were saddling a fresh horse for me. Why should Teal have to go?"

Pops gave her an incredulous look. "Girl, those pictures of y'all in town were on the television a minute ago, and it ain't hard to see what's between you two. You think they wouldn't use her to pull you back in?" He limped into the barn's small office.

Teal raised her hand to her mouth. "Oh, no. August, I'm so sorry."

August reached for her. "No. I'm sorry to mix you up in my crap."

"What's done is done," Pops said. He tossed a bedroll at August and began tying a second one behind the bay's saddle. He nodded toward a backpack he'd dropped on the ground with two large water bottles attached to the sides. "Slide that on. You'll have to be your own pack horse. That's got your climbing equipment and enough freeze-dried meals and protein bars for a few days."

BJ strode into the barn and handed August's holstered pistol to her, and she clipped it to her belt. "Extra bullets are in the backpack." Then he handed over her hiking boots and tossed Teal's boots to her. "These will serve you better in the canyons."

August stared at him. "You guys had this planned all along."

He shrugged. "Somebody told me you always need a Plan B, and maybe a Plan C." He winked at Teal, then turned back to August. "You need to hold on to that one. She's a pretty smart catch." He glanced back toward the door. "It's getting pretty dark, but stick to the fence line and go quiet until you're far enough away. Leave Rio. Pops will send her to find you when the coast is clear."

They turned the horses toward the back of the huge barn and mounted up. Pops murmured a quiet "stay" command to Rio, and August looked down at BJ. "You be careful, old man. Don't do anything crazy and get yourself hurt on my account."

BJ smiled and waved a dismissive hand in front of his face. Then he stepped back and peered up at her. "Listen to the wind and the earth. Be open to your spirit guide. The White Paw is with you."

"Always."

❖

They barely glimpsed the cloud of dust and the outline of a large SUV as it turned from the highway onto the ranch's long gravel drive. August led them behind the equipment barn and bunkhouse, then along the outside of the large paddock's board fence. The sky grew darker with each measured, quiet step their horses took, and the horses inside the paddock, expecting food, followed along to further conceal them from the ranch complex. When they reached the end of the fence, the night had fully enveloped them.

August gestured for Teal to come alongside. "I know it's dark, but we're not safe until we get off this flat prairie and into the canyon. The bay should be able to keep up, so stick as close as you can."

Teal's nod was confident. "Don't worry about me. I'm right behind you."

They both started at the distant pop of gunfire, and August swore. She immediately wheeled the stallion to return to the ranch, but just as quickly, the big bay gelding blocked her path. The stallion jerked to a stop, dancing in place.

"I've got to go back." Her heart pounded and her mind raced with what could possibly be happening. BJ and Pops were closer than family to her. She was responsible, too, for Hawk, Manny, and Tommy. They were hers to protect. Thank the stars Brick was at home with his family. She tried to guide the stallion around the bay, but Teal grabbed one of the stallion's reins and held on tight. "Let go!"

"No, August. I won't." Teal's eyes were fierce. "I won't let go. God forgive me, but I won't let them have you."

August settled the stallion, and they stared at each other.

"You need to trust that BJ knows what he's doing," Teal said quietly. "Trust all of us, sweetheart."

She'd trusted Christine. That's what had landed her in this mess. She closed her eyes and dropped her chin to her chest. She was so torn she wanted to cry. She wanted to be a little girl again and run into the arms of the most honorable person she'd ever known, the one who'd never broken a promise, who'd dried all her tears, who'd always stood with her against her parents' efforts to change her into someone she wasn't. What would Gus do? An unexpected breeze brought the scent of bison and sun-warmed rock. She could almost hear the wind whistle between Caprock's peaks like a native flute, and the large, dark shape of a half-wolf with one white paw formed in her mind. The wolf turned and loped toward the red mountains. The wranglers had each other for backup. Teal only had her. Gus would expect her to keep Teal safe.

With the burst of gunfire still echoing in her ears, she made her decision grudgingly. She opened her eyes. Teal was watching her. "Okay." She turned the stallion away from the ranch but hesitated one more time. "Teal, just in case—"

"Don't. We'll get out of this. There'll be time later when the media and drug dealers aren't chasing us, when it's just the two of us."

August nodded and kneed her stallion into a cautious lope, keeping a protective ear to the echoing hoofbeats at her back.

CHAPTER FIFTEEN

The black SUV idled in front of the ranch house, the outlines of the men behind the dark-tinted windows not moving.

BJ lifted the radio to his mouth and spoke quietly. "Hold your positions. If things go sour, step out and show yourselves. We're just trying to run them off. I don't want any of you in court explaining why you shot some guy in an ambush."

Hawk, Manny, and Tommy were hidden in strategic positions with rifles trained on the SUV. The sheriff was on his way, and the fancy-pants DEA guy was coming from Dallas. Walker had asked about landing a helicopter at the ranch, so BJ figured all they needed to do was stall thirty or forty-five minutes for the sheriff.

He'd grown up watching the old Western movies and television shows that romanticized showdowns. He allowed himself a grim smile. He was the Rifleman. He was John Wayne. He was Marshal Dillon. Okay, maybe he looked more like Robert Duvall in *Lonesome Dove*, but he was better than all those guys. His time in Vietnam as a young man had inspired him to combine Asian martial arts with the Native American mysticism that was his boyhood fascination. He was at peace with whatever was to come. Besides, he'd trained himself to be ambidextrous and could shoot accurately with both the rifle tucked under his left arm and the pistol holstered where his right hand rested at his hip. He stepped down from the porch.

The glide of a window lowering broke the stillness. In spite of all his caution, all his training, he didn't expect the gun that popped out without prelude and fired, knocking him to the ground. His shoulder burned and he struggled to breathe. His first gulp of air was filled with dust as tires crunched on gravel. His right hand wouldn't work. The rifle. He groped in the dirt around him, but a heavy boot slammed into his ribs. Shouts in Spanish and English and gunfire were all around him. Someone grabbed his collar and dragged him to his feet. The security lights of the compound wavered. His vision darkened as pain shot down his arm, then crushed his chest when an arm roughly circled him to hold him upright. The cold metal of a gun barrel was pressed to his temple. The gunfire stopped.

"How many?"

"One on the roof over there. One in the barn loft. One from the side of that long building."

BJ struggled to focus. Who was talking? The men were shadowed figures in the dim light as they gathered around him and the man he was pinned against. Their Spanish was Central American, not Mexican dialect. Manny had taught BJ the difference. Not good news. The Central American cartels made the Mexicans look like mere schoolyard bullies.

"You, on the rooftops. I will not hesitate to finish him, and then my men will burn each of these buildings unless you throw down your weapons and come out." The slender man, who stood with a bullet-proof boldness in front of the group, spoke in clipped, formal English. "I have come only for one person and something she stole from my employer. I have no interest in the rest of you. However, I also have little time and no patience. If you continue to delay me, I will kill every living thing in this compound and burn it to the ground." His voice was as smooth as a sweet brandy, his reasonable tone a contrast to his cruel message. He raised his hand and flicked his fingers.

The brute holding BJ shifted. The press of the gun barrel left his temple, and BJ gasped as blazing pain in his left calf instantly followed the gun's loud report. He'd underestimated the man sent to hurt August, and he'd failed her. His head swam with pain as he called on the coyote, his spirit animal, to rouse The White Paw.

Rio whined as Pops bent over the workbench in his garden shed, scribbling a quick note that he dropped into a small leather tobacco pouch. He wrapped the computer thumb drives in a soft cloth, then plastic, and sealed them in an empty snuff tin. He knelt and tied the tobacco pouch around Rio's neck, then held the snuff tin out to her. "You know what to do, girl. Hide. Then go find August."

The dog licked his hand and whined again.

"I'll be fine. You just do what I said." He shook the tin for emphasis. "Hide." Then he touched the pouch tied around her neck. "Go find August." He struggled to his feet. "Damn knees." He took only a second to gain his balance, and then he opened the shed's door a few inches. The long bunkhouse stood between the shed and the open compound where the others were. The shadows were still. He pushed the door outward and whispered his urgent command. "Go, girl. Go."

The black border collie shot out of the shed like a bullet and disappeared into the dark night.

Pops studied the buildings a moment longer and then moved silently toward the back door of the bunkhouse.

❖

Tank shook his head and slammed his fist against the side of his pickup. "Bunch of pussy-assed—"

"Careful there, honey pot. I know you're demeaning your own incompetent gender, but don't use the sweet words of my sex as insults." A muscular, tattooed woman swung down from the passenger side of the monster truck and came around to stand in the yellow gleam of the headlights.

His shoulders slumped as he faced his wife, Bunny. "I'm sorry, Bun. You know my bad upbringing comes out when I'm under pressure."

"I would'a thought August had pounded all of that out of you when y'all were teens."

"My daddy had twice as long to beat it into me before I met August." He gave her a beseeching look. "You know I'm not like that. I'm just so worried."

She tossed her ponytail behind her shoulder and rubbed her hand over his massive back. "I know, sugar. I'm worried, too. I'm not about to go back to my sister and tell her that drug dealers have harmed her boy Tommy. Take a minute and let's think this through."

Sweat plastered his T-shirt to his back, and she pulled it free to fan it a little. Only Bunny would touch his sweaty shirt to let some cool air next to his skin, and he loved her for doing it. He had known she was the woman for him the first time he'd taken off his shirt and she didn't recoil, but purred over his overly furry physique. Her touches helped him focus, and Tank studied the situation before them.

It'd taken an eternity to convince the sheriff that he needed to pull resources from the town's biggest event of the year. Most of their county's meager law-enforcement personnel were committed to the long festival weekend, so the sheriff had been able to free only the four deputies who had been through SWAT training. They'd piled into the sheriff's car and the SUV that carried the team's gear and headed to The White Paw ranch with Tank and Bunny following. Halfway there, someone had put out law-enforcement stop-sticks that punctured the tires of the sheriff's car and sent it into a spin. The deputy driving the SUV hadn't been able to stop quickly enough and had plowed into the police cruiser from behind. The SUV had little damage, but the cruiser's trunk had tangled into the SUV's bumper, locking the two vehicles together.

"I should have gone by the Lock & Load and rounded up a bunch of boys with shotguns," Tank muttered.

"Just put them deputies in our truck," Bunny said.

"Hey," Tank yelled at the deputies. "Get in back."

The sheriff put his hands on his hips. "I can't leave all this equipment out here unguarded."

"Then you stay. We'll take the boys with us," Bunny said. She pointed to the deputies. "Grab your gear quick and get in, or we'll leave you behind."

Tank almost laughed as the deputies ignored the sheriff and scrambled for their gear.

The sheriff wasn't laughing. "Wait. I don't know about this." But the last man was already climbing up the rear bumper into the bed of the monster truck. "Well, okay. I'll radio for assistance. Johnston, you're in charge."

One deputy saluted. "Right, Sheriff."

"Don't embarrass me," the sheriff yelled at his men as Tank backed the monster truck and the big wheels churned up the desert sand when they went off-road to skirt around the two disabled vehicles.

❖

"What in blue blazes?" Pops hunched his shoulders and shuffled into the common area of the bunkhouse, grumbling as he stared at BJ, unconscious and bleeding all over his clean floor. "I told August not to let you idiots carry guns. Which one of you fools shot BJ?" He glared at each of the wranglers in turn, then squinted and moved closer when his eyes rested on the Hispanic man holding an AK-47 across his chest. "Who the hell are you?"

"We are here to see August Reese. But I'm afraid your colleague was not very welcoming."

Pops turned from the gunman to squint at the slender man with dark, hard eyes—a study in black from his slicked-back hair to his expensive boots. The visual screamed danger, but his voice was smoothly hypnotic. Pops ignored him and shuffled into the kitchen. The gunman and another man standing near the door pointed their guns at him when he began jerking open drawers. "I just cleaned that floor, damn it, and he's bleeding all over it." He pretended not to notice the guns leveled at him as he gathered a stack of dish towels and the kitchen shears before shuffling back to BJ. He tossed the items down next to BJ and pointed to Hawk. "I can't get down on the floor, so you cut those jeans and tie a bandage around that leg."

Hawk held out his hands and knelt cautiously when their guests didn't object, then began to staunch the bleeding. BJ moaned as Hawk tightened the bandage, but the bleeding had slowed.

"Get that shoulder, too," Pops said, keeping an eye on the ringleader. Why were they letting him stall? Surely they knew reinforcements were on the way.

The slender man stepped forward. "No need." He gestured to the gunman, and the nose of the AK-47 was immediately pressed to BJ's forehead. "You will tell us where August Reese is hiding or you will die one by one, beginning with this man." He tugged his sleeve up and checked his watch. "You have thirty seconds."

Pops made a show of turning to look at the gun pressed to BJ's head, then back to the ringleader. "Why didn't you ask before? August has gone camping."

"Camping?"

Tommy looked horrified. "Pops!"

Pops stepped closer to the hard-eyed man, peering into his eyes as if he could see his dark soul. "Don't believe I caught your name."

The man's lips slid into an oily smile. "Cobra, but some know me as The Snake." His breath hissed through a gap between his front teeth when he said "snake."

Pops sucked on his own front teeth, then pointed to them. "I know a dentist who could fix that for you, Mr. Worm." He pointed to the floor. "Be sure you get up all that blood, Hawk. I ain't mopping this floor again already." He turned back to Cobra.

"A snake is just an oversized worm in my book." He limped back toward the kitchen. "I like worms, though. They break up the ground, and worm poop makes good fertilizer." He leaned over the bar that separated the main room from the kitchen. "They make good bait, too, when you're going after a big fish. And from where I'm standing, you're just a worm working for the big fish everybody is trying to catch."

Cobra snatched the handgun from another of his henchmen standing nearby and pointed it at Pops. "The only worm, old man, is that she-man you putas follow, and the big fish has sent me to gobble her up. Now, tell me where she is or I'll start with you, then your friend on the floor, then the rest until the boy—" he swung his Glock toward Tommy—"pisses his pants and tells me anyway."

"Won't work."

"No? I guess you won't be around to find out." He rotated to again aim at Pops.

"I'm the only one who knows where she went."

Cobra stood as still as a statue.

Pops continued as though Cobra hadn't nearly squeezed the trigger that would've ended his life. "Well, me and BJ, who you've incapacitated and can't talk."

"That's not true." Hawk spoke quietly. "I know, too. I overheard you talking to August."

"Me, too." Manny, who had been completely still and silent, spoke up.

Tommy looked at the two of them. "Me, too."

Pops shook his head. "You're all lyin' and you know it." He shuffled around the bar and looked down at BJ, then up at the man who still had the muzzle of his weapon pressed against BJ's forehead. "I don't think he's going to jump up and run." He put his hands on his hips as he faced Cobra. "Caprock. They're headed for the canyons."

"Pops, no." Tommy looked like he was going to cry, but Hawk and Manny only tensed. If they didn't give Cobra the information, they were as good as dead. Giving him the facts, though, might also cost them their lives. Pops had anticipated they would know that as well as he did. Pops held Cobra's gaze as he studied him. He'd lived a long life and didn't fear what might come. But he had to try to save the others.

Then Cobra smiled that oily smile again. "You think I grew up in the city and won't follow them." He handed the Glock back to his henchman. "I grew up in the jungle, not the city streets." He pointed to Manny. "Tito, take the Mexican and ready three of their horses for the trail."

"They probably have faster transportation in the equipment barn." Tito also wore a large silver buckle on his belt in addition to Western boots.

"It's also louder and will be useless in the mountains."

"Three horses?" Tito shoved Manny. "Are we taking him with us? You know I hate the smell of Mexicans."

Cobra turned a cold stare on the man. "Are you questioning me, Tito?"

The man froze, then seemed to shrink away. He pushed Manny toward the door. "No. I, uh, I…if the third is to be a pack horse, I won't need a third saddle."

"We'll take the Mexican with us. We don't have a map of the canyons. I'm betting he knows his way around them."

"You ain't going to find tracks in the dark," Pops said. "If I was you, I'd start out at first light from inside the state park."

"I'm no fool, old man. It would take much longer to find her if we go in at a different entry point. We will track her from here."

"I know the canyons," Hawk said. "Better than Manny."

Cobra eyed him. "Yes, I expect you are better at many things. But I can't take a hawk into his natural habitat and expect him to remain on my arm. Your Mexican friend will need less watching."

The guy with the AK-47 gestured at Hawk, Tommy, and Pops and then spoke in Spanish. "What about these putas? I can take them out back."

Cobra closed his eyes, his chest rising and falling in an exaggerated sigh. "I must talk to Luis about hiring his inbred relatives." He spoke in English, which the man didn't understand, judging from the blank expression on his face. Then Cobra spoke in Spanish. "Give me your gun and go wait outside."

When the man hesitated, Cobra pinned him with the same cold stare that had cowed Tito. The man held out his AK-47 and slunk out the door, the two other henchmen following. Cobra turned to Pops, Hawk, and Tommy.

"My men will drive you to a remote location and dump you so that you will have a long walk back to civilization. You may take a backpack of water."

Hawk frowned. "Why?"

Cobra cocked his head as if he, too, was considering this. "Because the senseless slaughter of locals will anger the local police and give them too much of a reason to pursue me. I only wish to delay you long enough to finish the job I was sent to do. August Reese is not local. They will be incensed, but none will crusade to avenge her as they would you."

Tommy's face reddened. "August is worth a thousand of you. We're not going to stand by and let you take her."

"There is nothing you can do about it."

"We know who you are. You hurt her, and I'll never stop until I find you."

Pops shook his head. Idiot. Another misplaced crush on August. He should have seen it coming. When Tommy had passed out mid-sentence after his night of drinking at the Lock & Load, he'd been jabbering on about August kicking those bikers' butts.

Cobra slung the gun's strap over his shoulder and drew his phone from his pocket, tapped the screen a few times, and held it up. There was a photograph of Brick and his ten-year-old son at the ballpark. He swiped the screen to bring up a photo of Brick's daughters, six and eight years old. "Beautiful children, no? If they were my children, I would have them guarded every minute of the day. The sex-trade people, disgusting perverts that they are, love beautiful children like these."

"You lay a hand on those children, and *I* will hunt you to the ends of the earth," Hawk said, clenching his fists at his side. "In this life and beyond."

Cobra lowered the phone. "Money can buy many things. Who can say how children disappear, never to be found again?" He shrugged. "But it happens." He swept his hands out, palms up. "Silence can buy many things, too." He stared into the eyes of each man. "Will you keep them safe with your silence? Or will you tell the police who visited you and then worry every day that your friend will wake up to find his children gone?" They remained mute, and he gave a curt nod. "This is how we do business and ensure loyalty in my country."

He put the phone away and pointed the AK-47 at Pops. "Get a backpack and fill it with bottles of water. No quick moves. I'll be watching." He gestured to Hawk and Tommy. "Pick up your wounded friend and put him in the SUV."

The vehicle was large, and Hawk sat in the back cargo area where they'd laid BJ to keep him as comfortable as possible. Pops and Tommy sat in the backseat with one of their kidnappers.

"Are we going to leave them like the Snake said?" The man in the passenger seat spoke in Spanish to the driver. Pops stared out the window, careful to give no indication he understood.

"The Snake is not our boss," the driver said without taking his eyes from the road. "Luis Reyes is our boss, and I don't think he would like loose ends. I think these four are loose ends."

The first man nodded and turned his attention to the road. "Then we are in agreement."

❖

"Honey pot. I don't think you should be standing right out there in the open. What if those guys are on the roof or something and take a shot at you? Just 'cause we have some of your tiny swimmers in cold storage don't mean I want to lose my P-I-D."

Tank stood in the middle of The White Paw compound, staring into the shadowy edges of the security lights' illumination. He swept his gaze from building to building. "There's nobody here. I can feel it. Nobody's here. Dang it. I knew we took too long."

"Tank?" One of the deputies sidled close so Bunny, who was surveying the scene from her seat in the cab of the monster truck, wouldn't hear.

"What?"

"What's a P-I-D?"

Tank grinned. "Personal insertion device."

"Huh?"

"My dick, you moron. She's rather fond of it and is reminding me that she wants me to live long enough to have children the natural way, not in a doctor's office."

"Oh."

"Stop thinking about my dick."

"I wasn't. God."

"Then stop thinking about my wife."

"I, uh…"

Tank shoved him. "Just kidding, man. Find anyone at the barn?"

"No, but I see a lot of empty saddle racks. That doesn't mean much since we don't know if they're usually full."

A second deputy came around the back of the house, while a third came out the front door. "All clear," the third deputy, Johnston, said. He stepped off the porch, then stumbled. "Hey, look here." Johnston pulled a small flashlight from his utility belt and shone it on dark, irregular spots in the dirt walkway leading up to the steps.

Tank walked over and squatted to touch the darkest spot. His finger came away red with blood. "This isn't good."

A fourth deputy burst from the bunkhouse and called to them. "In here. Lots of blood."

Ten minutes later, a thorough search of the chicken coop, Pops's garden shed, and the equipment barn determined that no humans were in the vicinity. Tank and Johnston conferred.

"We should report back to the sheriff," Johnston said.

"Are you kidding? There's blood, but not enough for six people, so obviously they took some live hostages. We don't have time to go back to get the frickin' sheriff."

"We have no idea where they went. How are we going to chase after them?"

Tank shook his head. "Don't take a genius to know they didn't head back to town because we came that way and didn't see 'em." He pointed down the driveway. "So, we go back to the highway and turn right."

"There's an all-points bulletin out on their SUV. The Texas Rangers will pick them up."

The big engine revved behind them, and gravel crunched as Tank's truck jerked to a stop next to them. Bunny poked her head and shoulders out of the driver's window and yelled down at them. "Y'all can stand there jawin' all night or you can get in this truck. I'm going after the bad guys." She revved the engine again.

Tank ran to the passenger side, yelling over his shoulder at Johnston. "You better hop in the back because she won't tell you twice."

The other deputies were already scrambling up the rear bumper and pulled Johnston over the tailgate just as Bunny hit the gas and spun gravel in a semicircle to whip the big vehicle around and speed back to the highway.

Chapter Sixteen

August slowed the stallion to a walk again. They'd kept up the pace for several hours, alternating twenty minutes at an easy lope with ten minutes at a walk. But these were cow ponies, conditioned for short bursts of speed, not endurance rides. A white, salty foam of sweat coated their leather tack and lathered their flanks. She twisted in her saddle to check on Teal. Her head bobbed sleepily with the big bay's movements.

"Hey," August said quietly.

Teal looked up and yawned, then belatedly covered her mouth. "Sorry. I think I can understand how cowboys say they slept in the saddle. Time to pick up the pace again?"

"No." August reined her horse in a circle to come alongside the bay. "Almost time to rest." She pointed ahead and to the left. "There's a small pond over there and a trail on the other side of it that leads into the first canyon. I know a place just inside where we can stop and catch a few winks before we start climbing."

"Climbing?"

"Yeah. We're taking the high-canyon trail. It's pretty steep and rough. We'll turn the horses loose to find their way back to the ranch."

The clouds had moved off, and the moon now lit their path and glinted off the dark water of the small, spring-fed pool at the foot of a steep cliff. The horses drank deeply as August freed them of their saddles. She propped the saddles under a small overhang and covered them with the ground cloth in her bedroll.

Teal's eyes followed her every movement. "Shouldn't we hide them better? That will be pretty easy to see in daylight."

August refilled their water bottles in the pool and dropped purifier tablets into them. "That's just to protect them if we get a cloudburst. If they see the saddles, they've already tracked us from the ranch, so it's not giving anything away. I've got a few tricks to lose them on the high-canyon trail."

August led both the horses back and forth along the base of the cliffs to lay down a confusing pattern of hoof prints before she removed their bridles and stowed them in her pack.

She shouldered their backpack and helped Teal tie their bedrolls together at the ends so she could fit them over her head like shoulder pads. It would be a comfortable fit but uncomfortably hot to carry them that way. The backpack was much heavier, so August figured they would suffer differently but equally.

Teal looked at the cliffs rising before them, her expression a determined mask. "Okay. Let's do this."

August led them left of the obvious entry point on the other side of the pool, using a handful of trail mix to get the horses to follow. When they reached a sliver of an opening in the cliff, she fed the mix to the horses and shooed them away, effectively covering her and Teal's footprints with their hoof prints. The horses went a short distance and lingered uncertainly before the stallion shook his head and started off at a trot for the ranch. The bay followed.

They hiked for another twenty minutes with nothing but the sound of their boots on the sandy path breaking the stillness of the night before Teal spoke again.

"Do you think they'll try to come for us tonight?" she asked.

"I have no idea, but I've learned not to underestimate Reyes." August hoped they would because she was tired of looking over her shoulder. No matter how it ended, she was relieved that Reyes was finally playing his cards so they could end this game. Still, she worried about the other players possibly involved. "If he's mixed up with a Central-American cartel, though, I'm mostly worried about who those guys would send to protect their interests."

"I'm trying to wrap my brain around some drug dealers chasing us on horseback."

August was only half listening. She was searching the steep incline on her right. *Ah. There.*

"I know I'm babbling. I'm just so tired." Teal stumbled into August's back and grasped onto her backpack to keep from falling.

"No, it's okay." She pointed to the small ledge she'd spotted. "I'm climbing up there to set our alarm so we can catch an hour or two of sleep." She shrugged off her pack and emptied it. "Find as many rocks as you can fit into the pack."

She and Teal gathered small and medium-sized rocks to fill the pack, and August added a coil of dark twine from its previous contents, then slipped into a climbing harness. Teal helped her heft the pack onto her back, and she began to free-climb.

"That pack is too heavy. Be careful," Teal said.

The rock wall appeared solid, but amazingly, after twenty years, the shallow indentions for hand and toe holes that she and her friends had chiseled into the rock remained.

"Not to worry. I'm an old hand at this." When she came alongside the short, narrow ledge, she tested the eyelet still anchored into the rock wall and smiled. Still solid. Who knew that kids playing at war games in those canyons could someday save her life? She hooked her harness into the eyelet to free her hands, then swung the pack around to begin her task. She neatly stacked the rocks vertically on the slim ledge, tying one end of the twine around the largest at the base. "Don't touch that twine," she called down to Teal as she dropped the rest of the coil downward.

Teal was waiting anxiously when she reached the bottom and shucked off the harness. "Are you going to tell me what you're doing?"

"When Tank and I were teens, a group of us used to come to the canyons and split up into teams with our paintball guns and play war games. This was a trap we set for our opponents—only we used hollow Christmas-tree ornaments filled with paint instead of rocks."

While Teal put their supplies back into the pack, August carefully threaded the twine through another eyelet long ago imbedded in the rock, then tied it off at a third one on the opposite side of the trail. She stood and pointed to the twine that now stretched across their path. "When the other team came through and snagged the trip wire, it would yank loose the wedge holding the ornaments on that small ledge, they'd roll off, and...splat. Anybody standing down here would get hit and coated with paint, effectively 'killing' several at once. Those rocks aren't big enough to really hurt anyone but will create enough noise to let us know someone's on the trail."

"What about other hikers?"

"This isn't a park trail." August pointed toward a dark ridge some distance to their right. "That's the upper canyon trail." She helped Teal step over the twine and led her another five minutes down the trail that was little more than a sandy path at the bottom of a wide gorge. Narrow gorges had periodically forked off to the right or left, but August ignored them until they reached the fourth opening on the left. That path angled upward for a bit before it leveled out. "This is where we'll rest. If we hear our alarm go off, we have several possible escape routes."

August watched Teal spread out her bedroll, then wordlessly laid hers at the top for a pillow. Despite the heat, they snuggled close. Teal was tense against August's side, and August tightened her arms. The night was so sticky hot, she wasn't sure where her sweat ended and Teal's began. Exhaustion winning out over adrenaline, she'd started to drift toward sleep when soft words drew her back to wakefulness.

"I'm scared, August."

She touched her lips to Teal's damp brow. If she wasn't so tired, she'd kiss away every bead of sweat, lick away every worry that had Teal's beautiful body strung tight as a bow. "Don't worry, baby. We'll be okay."

Teal clutched the front of August's T-shirt. "I can't lose you. If you have to go into witness protection, I want to go with you." She loosened her hold. "I mean if you want me to be with you."

August rolled up on her side and captured Teal's mouth in a deep kiss. This was no time to stoke their libidos, but she needed Teal to feel how much she wanted her. Teal whimpered when August pulled back to caress her cheek. "The smart thing would be for you to stay at The White Paw, but I'm not sure I could stand being without you."

Teal's eyes were dark pools in the moonlight. "I know I said there'd be time to say it later, but you have to know I've fallen hopelessly in love with you."

August closed her eyes. She could deny it. If she didn't admit it, maybe it wouldn't hurt if this didn't last.

"August?"

The fear in her whispered name jolted her to a quick decision, not that she'd actually had a choice. She opened her eyes and started to say what was on her heart, but Teal wasn't looking at her. She was looking past August's shoulder to the entrance of their small side trail.

"Where's your gun?" Teal whispered so softly, August could barely hear her.

Stupid, stupid, stupid. The gun was beside their bedroll, and when she'd rolled up to kiss Teal, she'd put her back to it. She mentally calculated the seconds it would take for her to roll over, grab the gun, and begin firing. Not enough time to stop them from shooting Teal as soon as she moved. "How many?" She, too, kept her voice barely audible.

"One. It's an animal. All I can see is a dark shape and the moonlight reflecting in the eyes. It could be a wolf or coyote or mountain lion. I can't tell."

August relaxed a little. Better than a human wolf with a gun. A low whine pierced the night, and August cocked her head. "Rio?"

They both relaxed at the answering woof.

August rolled onto her back. "Come here, girl."

The collie was on August in a heartbeat, licking her face and yipping her happiness at finding her. She spared a few licks for Teal, too.

"She's sure a sight for sore eyes," August said, then wrinkled her nose. "But I don't know what you've gotten into. You reek."

"Phew. She smells like she's been in the garden with Pops." Teal ruffled Rio's fur. "I was imagining a mountain lion about to jump on us. Does this mean we can go back already?"

August sat up and retrieved the note Pops had tied around Rio's neck, then unclipped the pen light from where it hung on the outside of the pack. She read quickly. "Son of a bitch."

"What does it say?"

Everything in August wanted to go back. But the horses were probably halfway to the ranch by now, and Pops's note warned that BJ had been injured and Reyes's hit man would likely be headed her way soon.

"It's just a warning that the bad guys are coming for us. Pops said he'd try to delay them a bit. We already have a head start and will be traveling faster since we know where we're going. Still, we shouldn't rest too long." She stared into the darkness for a moment, then pulled out her cell phone.

Teal looked at her like she'd lost her mind. "Surely you can't get a signal out here."

"No, just setting an alarm." She was never so glad she'd downloaded those nature sounds on a whim. She set the alarm for an hour before dawn and turned the wake-up sound to "hawk's cry." She made room on the bedroll by her feet and pointed. "You're sleeping down there. Even that's a little too close, considering the way you smell." Rio curled up in the spot indicated, and August lay back, holding her arms open in invitation to Teal. "We've got one hour to sleep."

"I doubt that I can. Or that you can either."

"We have to try because we're going to need the energy tomorrow. We can relax now because Rio's hearing is a lot better than ours. She'll wake us if anything sounds unusual." She wrapped one arm around Teal and rested the other within inches of her gun. She wouldn't make that mistake twice.

❖

Bunny stomped on the brakes and whipped onto the road's shoulder at the sound of hands slapping against the back window of the truck's cab. She shot her husband an irritated look. "These guys are gettin' on my last nerve."

Tank gave her an apologetic shrug and lowered his window to twist around and poke his head out. "What?"

"Back there, on the left." Johnston pointed behind them. "I thought I saw some tire tracks, and it looked like some of the sagebrush had been knocked down."

Tank dug a dusty set of night-vision binoculars from the glove box and scanned the landscape. A flat prairie led to some not-so-distant hills, both covered with scrubby trees and spotty undergrowth. A small cloud of dust kicked up near the hills. "There's somebody out there, all right."

"Hold on." The men hardly had time to heed Bunny's warning when the big truck made a U-turn and rolled slowly back down the two-lane blacktop. She turned the air-conditioning off and rolled her window down, too, since Tank was hanging out of his, scanning the road shoulder with a mag light.

"There." Tank pulled back and pointed. The tire tracks were faint on the hard-baked ground, but it was clear from the crushed underbrush that something big had made a winding path around the largest of the scrubby trees.

"Lord, I don't know how I missed that." Those deputies weren't so bad after all.

Tank wedged himself through the window to shout instructions to them. "There's no way they'll miss this big rig coming after them, but you guys stay down where they can't see you. We'll stop when we get closer and let you crawl out the back and spread out in the trees." He grunted as he squeezed his belly and wide shoulders back through the window to settle in his seat, then gave her a thumbs-up. Good thing she had Tank around. He was the yang to her yin, and she loved every pound of his big, hairy body.

Bunny backed the truck up and swung wide to follow the SUV's path. "Yee-haw." She grinned at Tank as she wrestled the steering wheel and shifted into four-wheel drive. "I love goin' off-road." They bounced around the cab, and cursing accompanied the loud thumps in the back as the truck navigated the ditch.

The SUV's path through the brush was clear, and although their monster truck was much wider, the scrubby trees barely topped the big tires that rolled over them like they were twigs. Still scanning the horizon with the night-vision binoculars, Tank suddenly edged forward in his seat.

"Holy shit, baby doll. They're headed toward us, not away."

Her breath caught. "That's not good, sweet cheeks. That means they've already dumped our boys out there." A lump grew in her throat at the thought, and her voice cracked. "I don't know what I'll do if something bad happened to Tommy." She slowed to a stop. "My sister is so much older, he's more like a little brother to me than a nephew."

"I'll skin every one of them alive if they harmed one hair on that boy's head," Tank said, wrapping her in a one-armed hug.

"Thanks, sugar." She soaked up his love for a few seconds, then gave him a squeeze before pushing him away. "Now you and the boys git. I'm gonna block their path so you can pick them off."

"You be careful and keep your head down, sweet cakes." Tank turned his puppy-dog eyes on her. "I don't want nothing happening to you."

She gave him a quick peck on the lips, then handed him a rifle from the gun rack behind them. "You stay safe, too, big guy. I need my teddy bear."

With a wide smile, he slid out of the cab to the ground and joined the deputies. She watched them disappear into the brush on either side of her and then turned her attention to the task at hand. The top of the black SUV was still moving toward her through the ground cover. She smiled. While she could easily see them from her tall vantage point, they wouldn't see her until she was nearly on top of them. She began to sing softly. "A hunting she will go, a hunting she will go. Hi-ho, you're road kill-o, when Tonka rolls right over you." She waited until the SUV drew close so that she didn't get too far from her guys, then revved the 5.7-liter Hemi pushrod V-8 engine and barreled ahead.

The SUV slammed to a stop, and she rumbled within inches of its hood. She didn't want to give them room to go around her. The SUV sat for a moment, then began to back away. She drove forward, keeping less than a foot between them. It stopped and so did she.

She needed to buy some time for Tank and the boys to get into place. She reached for the mike attached to the dashboard and flipped the switch from "CB" to "loudspeaker."

"Listen up, you crackheads. A little birdie told me you took some friends of mine for a little joyride. Only it might not be so much fun for them and it's past their bedtime, so just let them out of your car and I'll take them on home."

The night was dead quiet, not even a cicada sounding in the stillness, so it was easy to hear the hum of the window being lowered. Without hesitating, Bunny stomped on the gas and braced herself for the impact. She ducked as a bullet shattered the windshield and another pinged off the bull guard that protected the front of the truck. Then the truck tilted as the big wheels began to crawl up onto the SUV's hood. The SUV's back tires spun in the dirt as the driver tried to back out from under the monster truck, but the truck was too heavy. Bullets ricocheted off the plates welded underneath to protect the truck's underside when off-roading.

When her tires reached the windshield, the SUV doors flung open and three men jumped out, all firing at the truck. Bunny ducked as low as possible when a bullet whizzed past her ear and embedded itself in the cab's ceiling with a thunk. That was too close. Then the loud crack of rifle fire ended any further shooting. Her Tonka rolled over the SUV, crushing the hood, top, and back into the body of the vehicle. She hoped to hell she was right that none of The White Paw guys were in there. By the time she got the truck turned around, Tank and the deputies had the three men on the ground, belly down with their hands cuffed behind them.

She jumped from the truck and walked over to them. "Tell me nobody else was in that truck."

Tank turned to look at the SUV. Its roof was flat against the body, and all four tires were blown. "I sure hope not, sweet thing. If they are, we're going to need a pry bar to get them out."

"Everybody okay?" she asked.

Tank laughed. "Who knew these guys could shoot the wings off a fly at fifty yards?"

The deputies all grinned.

"We been hunting rabbits together since we were kids," Johnston said. "These guys don't move half that fast."

She smiled back at them, then walked to the nearest prisoner. "Where's my nephew, Tommy?"

The man turned his head away from her.

Bunny narrowed her eyes. "I can see that my honey bear here didn't warn you that I'm taking hormones because we're trying to have a baby. If you think too much testosterone makes a man mean, you should try injecting an overdose of estrogen in a woman." The man's forearm was bleeding where he'd been winged by one of the deputies. She placed her heavy biker boot on the wound and shifted her weight onto that arm. The man screamed.

Johnston frowned. "Miss Bunny, you can't be torturing the prisoners after we have them in custody." He took a step toward her but stopped when she glared at him.

"Uh, Johnston. You don't want to mess with her. She's not lying about those hormones." Tank backed away a step. "I suggest you just turn your back. Then you won't have anything to report."

Johnston hesitated, then backed away, too. "I think I need to water the flowers." He turned and disappeared into the scrub.

The second deputy stared after him, then followed. "Me, too," one said. "Bouncing around in that truck makes you have to pee."

The third deputy hesitated. "I hear a tree calling my name, too." He hurried to join them.

Tank chuckled. "Nothing like female hormones to send men running." He put his hands up when Bunny turned her glare on him. "I'm staying. Somebody needs to tape their mouths so they don't get the coyotes howling."

"Don't bother. I want his buddies to hear him scream so they'll know what's in store for them." She stepped down on the man's arm again. He clenched his teeth to muffle his scream this time. "I'll ask one more time. What did you do with my nephew?"

"We didn't kill him," the man gasped.

"Shut up," one of the other men said. "Another word and it'll be your last."

Bunny left the man she'd been questioning and strolled over to the one issuing threats. "Really? Maybe you want to tell me, tough guy."

The man twisted to stare up at her, his eyes full of hate. He spit on her boot. "I'm not afraid of you, bitch."

She closed her eyes and sucked in a deep breath. "Okay. I'm tired of this game." She held out her hand. "Give me your knife, sugar."

"Now, honey pot. We can explain the gunshot wounds, but the sheriff might not understand if you cut them up, too."

"Oh, I'm not going to cut him. I just need access to a few dangly bits."

Tank gulped. "I was afraid that was next." He withdrew a long switchblade from his pocket and handed it over. "You want the calf bar?"

"It's in the back next to my calving box."

Tank returned from the truck with a three-foot-long, two-by-two board that had leather cuffs attached to each end. He buckled the man's ankles into the cuffs and straightened. "I think I'm going to find a tree to water, too."

"Coward." Bunny chuckled as he hurried away. "He never can watch when I have to castrate a calf." She flicked the knife open, planted her knee on his lower back, and slid the knife under the waist of the man's pants.

"Fucking bitch. Get off me." He struggled under her weight, but Bunny was a big woman. Bigger than this man if he'd been standing.

The sharp blade cut neatly through his jeans and underwear. She kept cutting until he was exposed from waist to mid-thigh. He struggled harder when she reached between his legs and squeezed his scrotum.

"Bitch. I will kill you." His scream and red face only made her laugh and squeeze again...hard. He struggled to find a way to pull his legs together and protect his tender organs, but the calf bar held him fast.

"Where's my nephew?"

The man panted, then rattled off a string of curses in Spanish.

"You know, those three years of Spanish in high school sure are paying off because I know exactly what you just called me." Keeping her knee on his back, she placed her other foot between his legs, his testicles under her heel, and applied a little pressure. He screamed, drool dripping into the dirt under his cheek, and she raised her heel. "I'll give you one more chance before I crush your balls under my boot. Where is my nephew?" When his reply was another Spanish curse, she stepped down a little harder.

"Stop, stop. About a mile back the way we came." Tears rolled down the man's cheeks.

She stood, closing the switchblade and shoving it into her back pocket. "Now, was that so hard? You're only a little bruised. If my nephew isn't alive and well, I'm coming back with my calving box, and all three of you will be singing soprano in the prison choir."

Tank and the deputies emerged from their hiding places. "Come on, Bun. Let's go get Tommy."

She nodded, suddenly tired and ready to let him take his turn at being in charge. It was one of the things that made them work as a couple—each was able to step back or step up, depending on what the other needed. She thanked the stars again for sending her the perfect mate.

Two of the deputies stayed behind, and Johnston settled on the hood of the truck, clinging to the bull guard with one hand and holding the mag light in the other. Bunny held back the tears until Tank had helped her into the passenger seat of the truck and climbed into the driver's side. He leaned across the console, his beard stubble tickling as he held her face in his big hands and kissed away her tears. "Damn hormones," she said.

But her tears sprang from the fear gripping her heart, not hormones, now that they were moments from finding her older sister's son, the kid she'd loved like her own since she didn't yet have a child. These drug dealers were really bad men, and she was terrified of what they might find.

Chapter Seventeen

Exhaustion won out, and it seemed they had just fallen asleep when the hawk's scream sounded so close that Teal nearly jumped out of her skin. August's arm tightened around her.

"It's okay. That's my phone alarm."

Teal sat up and pressed her hand to her chest in a half-conscious effort to calm the frantic thumping of her heart. "Warn me next time." She twisted to look down at August. It was true that the night was darkest before dawn, but August's cell phone, also awakened by the alarm, still glowed next to her head. Her eyes were closed, her beautiful features etched with weariness. Teal had already learned in the few nights they'd spent together that August liked her first few moments of wakefulness to be slow and quiet. She bent over her, brushing her lips against August's, but August reached for her and deepened their kiss. Teal's belly tightened and her sex throbbed to life. She gently disengaged after a moment and smiled when August blinked sleepily and smiled.

"That kiss almost made me forget the rock that's been poking me between the shoulder blades for the past hour," August said as she sat up.

"Mmm. It must be the match to the one that was digging into my ribs."

They stood and stretched, then chuckled quietly as Rio did the same. August disappeared into the dark while Teal rolled their bedding into one long bedroll and tied it to sling over her shoulder. It would be heavier than two bedrolls, but she could switch shoulders periodically if necessary and would be cooler than having both shoulders covered. She wiped at the sweat already beading along her upper lip. This was supposed to be the coolest hour of the day, but the air was so heavy it was hard to breathe. She could only imagine what it would feel like at noon.

When August reappeared, she handed Teal a small spade, the penlight, and a tissue. "The tissue is biodegradable. Follow along the right edge of the cliff and look for the shallow hole I dug. We don't want to leave any obvious evidence, so after you use the spot, throw your tissue in with mine and fill the hole."

Teal hurried to comply and wordlessly accepted the bottle of water and protein bar August handed her when she returned. She gobbled down both and tucked her trash into the pack August had already shouldered. She started to pick up the bedroll when August stopped her.

"Give that to me."

"You can't carry everything, August."

"I can when I'm taking the shorter trail and you'll need to move at a faster pace." She led Teal back to the main trail. "The main trail meanders a bit and curves back to the left where this side trail, which is actually a shortcut, meets up with it again. I'm not the runner you are, so I'll play pack mule and take the short route while you lay down tracks on the main trail. Take Rio with you." She handed the pen light to Teal.

"How far?" It scared Teal a bit to split up.

"About an hour from here."

It was a good idea, and the sky was beginning to lighten, which lifted her fear a bit. "Okay. See you soon."

"Wait. Jog with short steps until you see another trail on your right, then run down that trail a short distance, retrace your steps, and take off full speed down the main trail. That will buy us a little more time while he investigates the side trail." August pulled her close and kissed her again. "Most of all. Be safe." She knelt to pet Rio. "Go with Teal, girl. Guard."

Then August stood, shouldered the bedroll, and started down the side trail.

Teal sucked in a breath and began a double-time, short-stepping jog she sometimes did for conditioning. She smiled at the abundance of footprints it left behind. "Figure that out, Mr. Badass," she said to nobody. Rio seemed to think the odd jog was a game, running ahead and circling around behind her, tail held high like a happy plume. She yipped a couple of times but quieted when Teal held her finger to her mouth. Teal smiled. The extra dog prints would further confuse their trail. Before long, they came to the side trail August had mentioned and she walked normally until she rounded a few curves, then took off her shoes and backtracked in her socks at the base of the cliff that bordered one side of the trail. When Rio caught on to the idea, she had the dog walk in front so her socked feet would smudge out the dog prints, too.

Back on the main trail, Teal was tying her shoes on when she heard a distant rumble and the echo of curses. Someone had found their tripwire. She made a mental note of how well sound traveled in the maze of canyons and hurriedly finished with her laces. She stood and motioned for Rio to follow. This time, she stretched her long legs in an effortless run, driven by the fear of who might be following and the need to have August by her side again.

❖

Water was filling Pops's ears as he tilted his head back to keep the pond's rising level from filling his mouth and nose. He'd lived a long life, and this wasn't how he expected it to end.

Reyes's men had ignored Cobra's orders. They apparently amused themselves by coming up with creative ways to kill people so had bound their hands and tied large rocks to their feet. While one guy stripped to his underwear and dragged each of them into the deepest part of a large creek they'd come upon, the other two built a dam of brush and rocks downstream. They reasoned that

Hawk was the most likely to find a way out of their deathtrap, so they tied the still-unconscious BJ to him to further confine him. The water had initially come only to their chests, but the level was rising fast.

Tommy burst to the surface again, gasping for breath. He'd been trying to hold his breath long enough to pretzel his body and untie his feet with his hands behind his back. He looked over at Pops. "God damn it." He panted a few times. "I'm trying, Pops. Just hang on."

Pops was the shortest and knew he couldn't hold out much longer. He gritted his teeth against the pain as arthritis cramped his neck and back. "It's not your fault, son. I've lived a long life. I'm okay with this."

"No. I can do it. I know I can."

Pops stared up at the star-filled night sky. Julio and Gus were waiting for him up there. "They say drowning is the most peaceful way to die. It's almost like just going to sleep after that first big gulp to fill your lungs."

"Pops, no." Tommy sucked in a big breath and disappeared under the water again.

"Hawk."

"Yeah?"

"Be sure he knows it wasn't his fault."

"I will. Go in peace and look for us, my friend. We might be crossing right behind you."

Pops took one last look at the stars, closed his eyes, and dropped below the water. He pushed all the air out and sucked the cool, clear water into his lungs.

❖

The trail twisted around to an east-west direction, and Teal could see the sun rising at the end of the narrow canyon. She sighed in relief at the sight of August sitting where the side trail reconnected with the main trail. Her shortcut must have been a lot shorter than she'd implied. Teal lengthened her strides, her smile growing as August stood and waved. Her eyes on her goal, she didn't pay much attention to the odd buzzing noise. Suddenly, Rio slammed against her legs, and Teal tumbled to the right of the trail.

"Rio, what the—"

Rio had a large snake in her teeth, growling fiercely and shaking it for all she was worth.

"Rio, drop it." August's command held a note of fear. "Come."

Blood spattered the trail, but the snake slithered off to the left, into a wide crevice. She hoped the blood belonged only to the snake, but Rio's limp and bloody front leg confirmed her worst fear. "No."

August knelt next to Rio. "Damn, girl. This is bad. Really bad."

"August, no." Not Rio. God, no. Not Rio. "I didn't see it. I was looking at you. Oh, God."

"Most snake bites don't kill," August said, but her face was pale and her hands trembled as she opened the bedroll and began cutting it into wide strips. "It's good that it's on her leg and not on her throat. Swelling is the biggest danger, but she needs to get to a vet as soon as possible."

"How are we going to do that?"

"You're going back. I'm making a sling because you'll have to carry Rio. The more she exerts herself, the faster the venom will circulate in her bloodstream. She's actually pretty light for her size." August worked fast, cutting and tying the sling around Rio's slender body so that she could be carried like a backpack.

"This is crazy."

August fitted the contraption around Rio and stood. She grabbed Teal by the shoulders. "I raised her from a puppy. This dog has stuck by me when my family and my partner didn't. Please, Teal. I need you to do this."

"If I go back, I'll run right into Reyes's men."

"I'm pretty confident they're on the main trail. I didn't hear anyone following me on the shortcut. You'll go back that way."

"Then what? We let the horses go."

"If they entered the same way, they either had horses or a Jeep. I'm sure they didn't leave themselves stranded. I hope that growing up on a farm, you know how to hot-wire an ignition if they drove a vehicle."

"Sure I do, but don't tell my probation officer."

August stared at her.

"Just a joke to break the tension."

August shook her head and laughed despite their situation. "I—" She stopped and glanced away. "I owe you for this."

"What are you going to do?"

"Lead them down this trail, climb up to the Caprock Canyon hiking trail, head for the nearest populated area, and get a ride to the ranger station to have the cops pick me up." She lifted Rio so Teal could slip the makeshift straps over her shoulders.

"Please be careful." She kissed August.

"You be careful." She took Teal's hand and placed her cell phone in it. "Keep checking for a signal and call for help. If you can't raise BJ or any of the guys at the ranch, stay away from there. Head for the highway and call Brick to come pick you up. He's at home today with his family, thank God, and not involved in all this." She tugged the gun clipped to her belt free and attached it to Teal's belt. "There's a shot already chambered, but the safety is on. Remember what we practiced and don't hesitate to use it. If I'm wrong and you do run into Reyes's men, they won't hesitate."

"But that leaves you with nothing."

"I know a million hiding places in these cliffs. That's my weapon." This time, August kissed her. "Go."

Johnston pointed to the left, and Tank turned the big truck, finding the SUV tracks in his headlights. The vegetation was thinning, and the trees were a bit taller. He caught a flash of movement as the truck's beams bounced when his left tires rolled over a large rock.

"Look there. I see somebody." Bunny released her seat belt and scooted to the edge of her seat.

Tank gunned the engine, and Johnston's butt bounced into the air as they zoomed over the remaining rough terrain. He'd barely stopped when Bunny was out of the truck and Johnston was jumping to the ground.

Tommy, his hands still bound, was struggling to drag a huge rock from the creek. He was crying but didn't stop his efforts as they ran to him. "Help me. God, you've got to help me."

Then Tank saw what was dragging behind the rock Tommy was pulling onto the shore. He ran to lift Pops's limp figure from the water as Bunny cut the bindings that tied him to the rock and cradled him like a baby while she cut the rope from his hands.

"You've got to help him. Do CPR or something." Tommy knelt beside Pops and pushed weakly on his chest with his hands, even though they were still bound together. "I don't know what I'm doing."

Johnston pushed him out of the way. "I can do it." He turned Pops's head to the side and began pumping hard on the old man's chest. "Miss Bunny, get down here and do this while I try to put some air into his lungs." He showed her how to count and alternate with his efforts to push air into Pops's water-filled lungs.

Tommy protested. "He's got a bad heart. You're going to bust it if you bang on him that hard."

Tank put his hands under the younger man's arms and lifted him to his feet. "It ain't beating at all right now, Tommy. She has to thump on it that hard if she's going to get it going again."

"A little help would be appreciated." Hawk's voice pierced the dark. Tank shone Johnston's spotlight out over the creek to where Hawk was using his chin to hold BJ's above the water.

"Give me a knife," Tommy said. "I'm already wet."

Tank took the knife from Bunny's pocket and offered it and the mag light to Tommy.

"You keep the light." Tommy pointed downstream. "Go find where they plugged the stream and unblock it."

Tank hesitated when Pops suddenly coughed and vomited water onto the ground.

"He's slipping. Tommy. I can't hold him much longer." The uncharacteristic urgency in Hawk's voice and the splashing as Tommy plowed back into the creek spurred Tank to move. He found the small dam, put the light down, and began throwing rocks and brush in all directions until water again poured unimpeded to the rest of the creek.

When Tank returned to the group, Bunny had already laid the backseat of the truck's crew cab flat, and Hawk and Tommy were gently lifting BJ up to lay him next to Pops. Tank shook his head. "I know I told you that feature was useless because we were both too tall to use it for a camp bed, but now I'm glad you insisted."

Bunny put her hands on her hips. "I told you it's for our young'uns so they can play back there or nap when we drive all the way to Tucson to visit my mother."

"You think of everything." He hugged her, relieved that her Tommy, who was hovering over Pops and BJ to make sure they didn't get tossed around too much on the way back to the highway, was okay. He climbed into the driver's seat. "Think you can raise some help on that CB? I doubt we have a cell signal out here."

She gave him a pointed look. "We would if you hadn't signed us up with that jack-leg service where your aunt works."

He sighed. "I know, but I didn't have a good excuse not to. Now I do. I'll get us switched over as soon as everything settles down."

They both glanced back to make sure Johnston and Hawk were securely in the bed of the truck, and then she picked up the CB mike as he carefully backed up and turned to retrace their route.

"Breaker, breaker. This is Cottontail. Anybody out there with a signal got their ears on?"

"Go ahead, Cottontail. This is Glory Rider. You're wall-to-wall and treetop tall."

"I've got a ten-thirty-three on highway two-five-six, a few miles west of two-seven. I need a flying meat wagon for two pronto and a couple of grown-up bears. We're off-road in a green monster but will be heading west if we don't see anybody when we hit two-five-six."

"Copy that. Relaying your ten-thirty-three."

❖

Jogging bumped Rio against her back and caused the dog to struggle to get free of the sling, so Teal settled for putting her head down and walking as fast as possible. She hadn't gone far when she rounded a curve in the trail and stumbled over a Hispanic man sitting on a boulder with one leg stretched across the trail and the boot off his other so he could massage his foot. He whipped his handgun from his shoulder holster before she could regain her balance.

"Well, well. What have I found?" He stood, keeping the gun aimed at her chest as he slipped his foot back into the boot.

Teal cursed herself for not being more careful. Somehow, she needed to talk her way out of this. She'd spun bigger tales in Washington when her Congresswoman had been caught in a bad place, so she should be able to handle one dumb drug dealer. She schooled her expression and turned on the charm. "Hi. Are you lost? Because this isn't a regular park trail, and you don't look like you were out for a hike." She pointed to his Western boots.

"Cut the crap, lady. I know who you are. Cobra will be pleased. You might not be the target, but you're the next best thing, according to our information. Hands in the air."

She raised her hands upward, her eyes on the gun pointed at her. But when he reached to take August's gun that was on her belt, Rio snapped, nearly sinking her teeth in his hand. She barked an angry warning and struggled to get free of the sling so she could go after him.

"Son of a puta. I'll shoot that mutt."

Teal held out her hands. "No, please. She has a hurt foot. She probably thought you were going to grab it. Here, I'll give you the gun…slowly, grip first."

He pointed his gun at her head but nodded his consent. She slowly pulled the weapon from its holster and handed it to him. He tucked it into his belt and gestured for her to turn around. "Now we'll go find your girlfriend, too."

❖

August stopped at the sound of Rio's barking. Damn. Teal must have run into trouble.

She shrugged off the backpack and took her climbing gear from it, pulling on the harness that had a variety of climbing gear attached to it. She hung three slender ropes from it and stowed the backpack in a deep crevice, then trotted back to where they'd parted ways. Teal wasn't in sight yet, so she free-climbed fast, stretching from nook to ledge without pause. The first ledge was about forty yards above the ground, and she moved silently along it until she spotted them. Only one man. Teal and Rio appeared unharmed, so he must be planning to use them to get her to give up. Careful not to loosen any rocks that could alert them she was above, she moved back to the main trail and looked in both directions. Nobody else was on the trail as far as she could see.

She would follow along from her higher vantage and drop down behind to ambush him at some point. She crouched low as she watched them, surprised when they turned back to the right. Why'd they do that? Had Teal convinced him that she'd doubled back?

She waited for them to pass, then climbed down to cross the side trail and up the other side to shadow them from above the main trail. Teal stumbled, falling to one knee, and Rio yelped when her swollen paw banged against Teal's hip. August couldn't hear the angry exchange between Teal and the man, but he paced impatiently while she got up slowly, then braced against a rock to sip from the small canteen she carried. Her knee was bloody.

August crouched low and hurried along the narrow ledge that sometimes wound behind boulders and other times was barely a foot wide with a sheer drop on one side and rock face on the other. When she was a kid, they'd used the path to ambush their paintball opponents. She prayed those narrow portions were still strong and didn't crumble under her weight. The ledge widened again, so she broke into a jog as she skirted a large boulder. She skidded to a stop in the nick of time, staring down at the wide crevice.

Damn. There was no way she could jump this. She studied the other side. There appeared to be another ledge much lower that jutted into the gap, shading the sand below. Then she saw it—the big snake Rio had tangled with before. It was stretched out and unmoving. Maybe it had died from its wounds. The sandy bottom seemed to be moving like boiling water, and she realized the crevice with its shading ledge was a rattler nursery. She counted at least four large snakes but couldn't guess at the number of small- to medium-sized rattlers crawling about. She'd read that several females would sometimes share a den and stay with their young for weeks.

She mentally measured the distance and uncoiled two of the ropes, tying them together. She looped one end into a lasso and gave it a few test swings over her head. It'd been years since she'd roped calves, and even though she'd been pretty good at it, the limp climbing rope was a far cry from a good, stiff lariat. She also readied a rappelling rope if she was unsuccessful. Hopefully if she could distract the gunman by trying to lasso him, Teal would take the cue and knock him down so she could rappel down and jump into the fray.

She squatted by the boulder as they approached, a baseball-sized rock in her right hand. Teal slowed and said something to the man. She backed away from the crevice. The gunman pushed her roughly, but she refused to walk past it first. Apparently she recognized it as the site of her previous snake encounter. The gunman cursed and snatched the straps of Rio's sling from Teal's shoulders so fast she was unable to catch Rio before she hit the ground with a yelp.

"No more time to waste," he yelled at her. "The dog this time. Next time it will be you." He pointed the gun at Rio, but Teal threw herself in his line of fire. August heaved the rock at the cliff on the opposite side of the trail, and the gunman spun toward the loud thump, pointing his gun skyward toward the shards of red rock splinters showering the trail.

One swing, two, and she let the rope fly. It sang through the air behind the man and dropped neatly over his upraised gun hand. She jerked the noose tight and yanked him backward off his feet. He dropped the gun in his struggle to loosen the noose with his other hand and pull free. But August shifted to the other side of the boulder and yanked again. He flew backward into the crevice and screamed when he realized he'd landed in a bed of snakes.

August threw the rope down on top of him, then quickly went to her other one and rappelled down. Teal still knelt in the path, hugging Rio to her with one arm, while she covered her eyes with the other. August grabbed the Glock the gunman had dropped and turned toward the snake den.

The man stumbled out, yelling and clawing at the rope draped in a tangle around his shoulders and arms. Then August realized it wasn't just rope. A large snake dangled from his neck where its fangs were imbedded deep into his flesh. A second hung from his forearm, flopping back and forth as he tried to pry the first snake from his neck. The one on his arm went flying, and he tore the other from his neck, then fell to his knees, his eyes wide as he stared at August. "Help me."

August pointed the Glock at his head. "That's my gun clipped to your belt. Hand it over."

"You've got to help me. My neck is on fire." His voice was a tight, hoarse whisper—possibly from swelling or maybe just fear.

"The gun."

He fumbled the holstered gun from his belt without taking his eyes from August.

Teal finally spoke. "There's a second man, August. They apparently split up. This guy got the shortcut, but the other's coming this way."

August glanced down the trail. No sign yet. She was sure he didn't run like Teal, and hopefully had been delayed by her false trail. Still, they were running out of time. "Hold this gun on him and shoot if he moves a muscle."

She tied the man's feet, then looped the rope around his torso to pin his arms by his side. She probably should have made it tighter, but she didn't have the heart to constrict his chest too much or tie his hands behind his back. He would find breathing difficult enough as his neck continued to swell. The snake's venom wouldn't kill him, but the swelling of his trachea would. When her conscience hesitated over that thought, she reminded herself that he was about to shoot Rio when she distracted him by throwing the rock.

"We'll leave you for your friend to find. Maybe he'll help you," she said. She dragged him away from the snakes and propped him against a boulder. Maybe his airway wouldn't close completely if she left him sitting up.

Realizing they were going to leave him to his fate, the man turned angry. "The Cobra is Senor Reyes's exterminator. He will not stop until you are dead."

August ignored him and lifted Rio's sling onto Teal's shoulders and clipped her holstered gun onto the waistband of Teal's jeans again. "This is not an ornament. Use it next time." She softened her admonishment with a quick kiss and tucked the man's Glock into her own belt. Now they were both armed.

When they reached the shortcut, August kissed Rio's head. Her paw was twice its normal size, and Rio whined when August started to touch it. She stopped. "Hang in there, girl."

"August, come with me. I don't want to split up again."

"No. I need to lead this other guy away to give you time."

"But—" Teal's eyes filled with tears.

August grasped Teal's shoulders. "You know the note that Pops tied around Rio's neck?"

Teal nodded, her breath hitching.

"He gave the evidence to Rio to hide. She's the only one who knows where the thumb drives are. If you won't go for Rio, then go for me. Because if you don't, everything I've given up—" Her throat tightened around the next words. "The note said they shot BJ, but Pops didn't say how bad he was wounded. We don't even know what else those goons might have done to the guys at the ranch. BJ, Rio, my career—it will all be for nothing if Rio doesn't survive."

Teal nodded, tears streaming down her face.

August cupped Teal's face in her hands, took a deep breath to center her thoughts on something more positive, and held her gaze. "And for the record, I'm crazy about you, too." She kissed Teal. "Now go. Get my dog to a vet."

They simultaneously turned and hurried down different paths, August soaring on the wings of Teal's blazing smile her confession had ignited.

CHAPTER EIGHTEEN

Cobra jogged easily along the belly of the winding gorge, his bare feet a whisper on the path of rock and sand. It wasn't the lush forests of his South American home, but he relished shedding the urban jungle for the chance to hunt where it was just him, nature, and his prey. He had stripped down to his black tank-style undershirt and loose chinos, carrying only a high-powered rifle strapped to his back, his Glock snugged in his shoulder holster, and a hunting knife and bota of water lashed to his belt. He didn't need food. He hungered only for the kill.

He slowed and drew his Glock at the sight of the figure propped against a boulder just ahead. Tito, his face pale, wheezed as he struggled to suck in air past the grotesque swelling in his neck and cheek. His eyes were wide and wild when Cobra stopped in front of him and lowered the Glock to his side.

"Help...can't...breathe." Tito's strangled words were hardly recognizable. He lifted one hand in an imploring gesture, and Cobra saw that the other was as grossly swollen as his neck. "Snakes—"

Cobra cursed this turn of bad luck. Tito was one of the few men he truly trusted. They had begun together as guards in the coca fields before Cobra earned his reputation as a ruthless enforcer and had taken Tito up through the cartel ranks with him. He stepped closer. "Don't worry. I have a serum to fix your problem, but give me some quick information while I prepare it."

He took a wallet-sized case from his pocket and knelt next to Tito. "Did you see the women?"

Tito pointed in the direction Cobra was headed.

Cobra opened the case to reveal a compact injector and three small vials of dark liquid. "August Reese. She has the dog with her?"

Tito shook his head as much as the swelling would allow and tried to suck in a deeper breath. "Snake…bit…dog. Other…take…back." Sweat ran down Tito's face. He tried to speak again but shook his head, his breath coming in short, desperate pants.

Cobra snapped one of the vials into the injector and patted Tito's leg. "They split up then?"

Tito lifted his thumb in an affirmative confirmation.

"August is still in the canyon?" He held up the injector.

Tito lifted his thumb again, then clutched at Cobra's sleeve, his throat convulsing in a desperate effort to suck in air. His mouth worked and his face reddened with the effort.

"That's good. The hunt is still on." Cobra gently pulled free of Tito's grasp and stood.

Tito grabbed Cobra's pant leg and mouthed a renewed plea for help.

"I will, my friend." He jabbed the injector into his own vein, his nostrils flaring as the military-grade stimulant flowed into his bloodstream. "That should keep me going for a few more hours. Now, time for your anti-venom." He lifted the Glock, his hand steady and aim true as the bullet drilled a neat hole between Tito's eyebrows. "Breathe easy now, my friend."

Teal was concentrating intently on the trail when the gunshot, faint but distinct in the quiet of the canyons, stopped her. She closed her eyes. Should she go back? What if August was hurt and needed help? What if the bad guy was shooting at snakes and she returned only to be captured again? What if the gunshot was August shooting the Cobra guy and going back would cost valuable time Rio might not have? She had no choice but to continue.

Her back ached from the weight of Rio's sling, but she concentrated on planting one foot in front of the other without stumbling over another rock. Blood had dried on her left knee from where she'd fallen, but it throbbed with each step. Rio had been quiet for some time now, her head hanging low next to her very swollen paw. Teal wished again there was some way she could carry her and keep the paw elevated at the same time. Teal needed Rio to be okay. She couldn't let August down. *And for the record, I'm crazy about you, too.* The words, the affection in August's eyes were all the incentive she needed. She'd crawl out of these canyons with Rio on her back if that's what it took.

The side trail's north-south direction thankfully shaded the narrow gorge from the sun, so the sudden blaze of light startled Teal. She stopped, blinking at the wall of red rock blocking her path. For a few seconds, her exhausted brain registered only the rivulets of perspiration trickling along her jaw and down her neck and the pounding of her heart that beat counterpoint to the wheeze of her open-mouth panting. Then she realized she was looking at the other side of the main gorge. She turned right and continued, so tired that urgency was the only fuel keeping her upright and moving.

She nearly cried when she stepped out onto the prairie and the noon sun glinted off the pool where they'd last filled their canteens. Had that been less than twenty-four hours ago? It felt like a lifetime. Teal shrugged out of the sling to gently lower Rio to her feet. The dog hobbled on three legs to the water's edge and drank greedily. Although spring-fed, the surface of the pool was lukewarm, thanks to the relentless sun. Teal peeled down to her underwear and waded in up to her shoulders. She didn't have time to luxuriate but took a few moments to let her body cool and soak up the moisture. Then she drank the rest of the water in her canteen and refilled it. She hadn't thought to get any of the purification tablets from the backpack, but she'd just have to chance it.

Teal dressed quickly and stood, then shook her head in disgust as she surveyed the area. She would never make a good soldier. Again, her single focus had been on the pool with complete disregard for what could be waiting for her. Movement in her peripheral vision caught her eye. A horse's rump and swishing tail were barely visible from behind an outcrop of rocks to her left. "Stay here, girl," she said to Rio.

She wouldn't be caught again. She drew the gun from her jeans and flicked off the safety as she cautiously approached. She felt a lot scared as she crept to the edge of the rocky outcrop and a little silly when she jumped around it with the gun extended in both hands like a television cop. The horses startled and backed away.

"Whoa, whoa." The muffled cry came from the man, bound and gagged, whose feet were tied to the reins of the horses dragging him as they backed away.

Teal flicked the safety and tucked the gun back in her pants in one swift movement, then added her voice to his. "Whoa, there." She kept her voice calm. "Whoa." She walked slowly to the horses when they stopped. "It's okay. Nobody's going to hurt you." She looked down at the man. "Manny? Oh, God."

Manny tried to speak when she knelt and pulled the gag from his mouth, but his voice was only a hoarse croak.

"Let me untie you and get some water." It took a long minute to work loose the rope tightly knotted around his wrists, and then she went to work on the rope binding his feet. Manny groaned when he at last was able to move his arms from behind his back, but his hands weren't working well enough yet to help her with the second rope. She finally untied the last knot.

He held out his hands for her to help him up, then leaned heavily on her, gesturing at the horses. She grabbed their reins, and he took them from her in one hand before flinging his free arm over her shoulder. "Water." His whisper was faint, but clear. "They need water. Help me."

She wrapped an arm around his waist and helped him hobble to the pool, the horses in tow behind them. When they got near, he dropped the reins, and the horses went ahead to plunge their noses into the water. Teal lowered him to sit beside the pool and offered him the canteen.

"It's straight out of the pool. I don't have any purification tablets."

Manny snorted and turned the canteen up. Water ran down his cheeks, and his throat worked with every gulp. After he'd drunk his fill, he poured the rest over his head. He handed the canteen to her and cleared his throat. "I've drunk out of muddy puddles before. There's nothing in that mountain spring I'm afraid of."

She refilled the canteen, but he shook his head when she offered it to him again. Rio limped over to lie next to him, panting.

"Where's August?" He looked at Rio's swollen paw. "Shit. What happened to Rio?"

"She was protecting me from a snake and it bit her." Teal closed her eyes to block out the gunshot that still echoed in the edges of her thoughts. "August is still in the canyons but wanted me to get Rio to a vet." She opened them and looked at the horses, realizing there were three. "So it was two guys and you?"

Manny nodded. "When I heard you in the water, I was praying it wasn't those two devils returning. Even though they tied all three horses to me, I thought it was more likely they'd tie a rock to my feet and throw me in that pool. I don't know why they didn't before, when that Cobra guy figured out he could track you in the canyons well enough without me."

Teal shuddered, then sucked in a breath. "Well, lucky for all of us that it was me and Rio, but we need to get going. Do you think you can ride?"

"Yes." He stood carefully. "I just needed the circulation to return to my arms and legs."

"Good. Which is yours?"

Manny pointed to the red roan mare. "She's mine. You should take the sorrel if Rio is riding with you. I'll unsaddle the other. He'll follow us."

"I'm going to get Rio back in her sling." She handed the gun over to Manny. "You ride shotgun."

He freed the unneeded horse, then helped lift Rio's sling onto Teal's shoulders, backward this time so Rio was cuddled against her chest. Manny took off his belt and used it to secure the sling's straps together so they wouldn't slip off Teal's slender shoulders. Then he helped her mount and climbed onto his horse. "I'll let you set the pace," he said.

❖

Tommy paced between the bunkhouse and where Hawk was pointing to BJ's blood staining the ground and recounting their night once again to two "grown-up bears," aka Texas Rangers. The sun had been rising when a medical helicopter evacuated BJ and Pops to an Amarillo hospital but was high overhead now, and he wanted to scream. The rangers had been ready to drive their Jeeps in an immediate off-road rescue, but they'd requested a helicopter when they learned August and Teal were likely already in Caprock Canyon. That was hours ago. Apparently some argument between state and federal agencies was stalling the operation.

"Damn it." Tommy threw his hat in the dirt where Hawk and a husky ranger stood and yelled at them. "We're wasting time." *For Christ's sake.*

Even Hawk, who was normally the calm in every storm, shook his head in disgust. "Go saddle two horses," he said to Tommy. "I'll get some supplies together."

"We can't have you boys meddling in an investigation," the ranger said. "I'll arrest you if needed to keep you from interfering."

Hawk narrowed his eyes. "I don't know what you're talking about, Ranger. Tommy and I are just saddling up to go check the herd. You can't arrest us for that."

The ranger wasn't backing down. "Then you won't mind if I send one of my men with you. We wouldn't want you to stumble into trouble or violate the law by accidentally carrying weapons onto state-park property."

"You son of a bitch." Tommy had stepped up and poked the ranger in the chest, ready to give him a piece of his mind, when the whup-whup made them all turn to the field just behind the house. The black helicopter had barely touched down when a man with blond hair cropped military short on the sides and wearing a dark suit jumped out and ran toward them in a crouch to avoid the chopper's churning blades.

"Where's August Reese?" Shouting to be heard above the noise of the helicopter because its pilot wasn't shutting down the engine, Pierce Walker held up the leather wallet that displayed his DEA identification.

The Texas Ranger started to speak, but Tommy refused to miss this chance.

"That's what I've been trying to tell this idiot. They took off on horseback toward the canyons, but some guy who calls himself The Snake shot up things here, then took off after her. We need to go help her, but he's too concerned about stepping on some park ranger's toes."

"Cobra was here?" Walker frowned. "Are you talking about Caprock?"

"Cobra, yes. He shot BJ, and his men tried to kill the rest of us, but it's a long story," Hawk said. "He went after August with only one of his men and Manny as a hostage." He pointed past the barn. "They all left on horseback across the prairie. August and Teal had at least an hour head start."

"One of you come with me to show us where she would have entered the canyons."

Tommy wanted to go in the worst way. He was embarrassed that August and BJ had had to save his drunken hide at the Lock & Load, and he needed to prove he could be a better man. It wasn't that he had romantic delusions about August. She was beautiful, but he clearly didn't have what it took to attract her that way. He just wanted her respect. Still, this wasn't about him.

"Take Hawk. He knows the canyons." Well, that and the fact that Pops swore Hawk had an ability most people believed was only legend.

❖

August hadn't actually managed to say the magic "L" word, but as soon as she'd given voice to a small part of her feelings, she knew it was true. As hard as she'd tried to guard her heart, Teal had easily captured it. August hadn't realized how much energy she'd been expending to hold back, but Teal's answering smile lifted a huge weight from her soul and ignited a burst of adrenaline that kept her going for the next three hours as she alternately jogged and walked. She kicked over stones and left a tiny bit of a power-bar wrapper as a clear clue for her pursuer. About thirty minutes after she and Teal had parted, her heart had nearly seized at the sound of a single gunshot. She told herself it was too loud to have come from the side trail. This Cobra guy was close. At least she prayed he was following her, not Teal.

The narrow gorge at last widened, and she knelt in the rough, wiry grass of the canyon that stretched out before her. Relief, along with exhaustion, washed through her. The cliff she would scale to the state park's upper trail and possible safety was a hundred yards to her right. But the few hours of sleep, lack of real food, and dehydration had drained her. She lurched forward onto her hands and knees, and sweat dripped from her nose and chin as she sucked in deep breaths of the hot, heavy air. After a moment, she shed her backpack and extracted her last protein bar. Her sweat-soaked T-shirt clung to her body, and her hands shook slightly as she tore open the wrapper and chewed the bar thoroughly. She drank all of the water remaining in her canteen. This canyon led to another gorge and other canyons, but this was the only one she knew that came so close to the park trail. If she couldn't scale this cliff, then her only hope would be to ambush a professional killer, and she wasn't stupid enough to think her barroom fighting experience could match his skills and whatever weapons he might be carrying.

A lone hawk's cry echoed through the canyon, and August watched it circle overhead before disappearing over the cliff she intended to scale. She squinted up at the cloudless sky. It was only mid-morning, but her skin already felt scorched by the fiery sun glaring down at her. She wanted nothing more than to lie down in the grass and sleep. The hawk circled again, his cry ringing out as he neared the cliff. His message was clear. She needed to get moving.

❖

Teal shaded her eyes and scanned the sky for what sounded like a low-flying plane. She was surprised to see the black helicopter approaching at a fast speed, but when it neared, the engine slowed to the distinctive whup-whup sound. The horses, although accustomed to darting, mooing cattle, skittered away from this huge bird when it descended and kicked up a cloud of stinging sand as it settled on the ground. Manny quickly dismounted and held the reins of both his horse and hers to steady them. Rio whined a bit but didn't stir in her sling. She thought she would weep when the chopper's blades slowed enough for the sand to settle and reveal the yellow DEA letters painted on its side.

Hawk jumped out, followed by a tall man bent low to avoid the churning blades, and ran toward them. "Teal, Manny, are you okay? Where's August?"

"The Cobra…he's still tracking her in the canyons," Manny said as he reached up to help Teal dismount while burdened with Rio's extra weight.

"Rio was bitten by a snake," Teal said. "The man with Cobra was bitten twice. We left him on the main path of the gorge that opens by the pool." She pointed toward the red cliffs that rose in the distance. "August sent Rio back with me." Rio was quiet, her body limp against Teal's. Manny released his belt holding the sling's straps on her shoulders, and Hawk helped her lower Rio to the ground.

Rio panted, unmindful of her tongue lolling in the sand, and her eyes were barely open. She grunted softly as Hawk felt carefully along her chest and throat.

"She's swelling all the way into her body. She needs steroids to stop it from getting worse," Hawk said.

"You were with August?" The tall man had a buzz cut and steely blue eyes that bore into Teal's when she looked up at him.

"Yes."

"Then you can come with us." He gestured to Manny. "He can take the dog and the horses back to the ranch."

The ranch. *The note said they shot BJ, but Pops didn't say how bad he was wounded.*

"Oh my God." Teal grabbed Hawk's arm. "BJ. Is he okay?"

He covered her hand with his and met her gaze. "They flew him and Pops to a hospital in Amarillo."

"They shot Pops?" Instant tears choked her words.

"No." He started to say more, then shook his head. "It's a long story, but they're doing all they can for both of them."

The tall man glared at them. "You two can talk in the chopper."

Teal glared back. "Who are you?" She was tired and hungry and worried to her very core.

"Pierce Walker, DEA, and you've got thirty seconds to get your butts in that chopper."

"Hawk, how far is the nearest veterinary clinic?" Teal asked.

He blew out a breath. "As tired as these horses are, it's another three hours to ride back to the ranch, then about an hour to the vet hospital in Plainview."

"How long if we flew in a helicopter?"

Hawk eyed the modified Blackhawk. He'd done a tour in Iraq as a national guardsman and ridden in more than a few of the military version. "Fifteen minutes."

Pierce was shaking his head. "You're crazy if you think you're putting that dog in that government helicopter, and even crazier if you think we're going to make a side trip to the vet right now. Luis Reyes's hit man isn't chasing August so he can shake her hand. I've spent most of my career pursuing this guy, and she has the evidence I need to finally put him away."

"Even if this dog is the only one who knows where that evidence is hidden?"

"Lady, I don't have time for games."

"August gave the thumb drives to Pops to hide, so she wouldn't be able to tell Reyes where they were even if he tortured her. Then Pops told Rio to hide them. It's a game August taught her." Teal could feel Rio's shallow breathing and rapid heartbeat against her chest, but she didn't know if her heart would survive if something happened to August. "We'll go get August, then fly Rio to a vet."

"Oh, for God's sake. Put the dog in the chopper. We're wasting time."

She looked to Hawk for confirmation that Rio would be okay for a while longer. He shrugged, his eyes apologetic, but nodded his agreement.

Teal was so tired that she allowed Hawk to buckle her into the safety harness and fit the headphones over her ears before settling in his own seat and taking Rio carefully into his lap. Pierce strapped into a seat adjacent to hers and stared at Rio.

The helicopter was roomy enough to carry eleven, so there was plenty of room for them as well as the two pilots and a second DEA agent, a woman whose gaze ran briefly over Teal and Hawk to settle on Rio. Teal wished she could stretch out across several seats and give in to her fatigue. She fought sleep as the Blackhawk lifted off, but her eyes flew open when Pierce's instructions to the pilot sounded in her headphones.

"Set course to Plainview and radio local emergency services for a landing area as close as possible to their best veterinary hospital."

Teal sat up. "No. We have to go get August first." She struggled to free herself from the harness that held her in the seat.

Pierce tapped commands into the digital tablet he was using to bring up a map of Plainview. "Her testimony isn't worth a damn without the information on those thumb drives to back it up. We'll take care of the dog first."

The last buckle released, and Teal flew across the small space to grab Pierce's collar in both her hands and shake him. "We're talking about a human life. We're talking about August, who has put her life on the line to catch your drug dealer for you."

He stared at her, his eyes lighting with realization, and his mouth drew into a tight, smug smile. "That evidence will put her ex-lover behind bars for a long time. I'm sure you wouldn't mind having her out of the way, would you?"

Teal's hand stung from the slap that connected with Pierce's hard jaw. The fact that she'd finally snapped didn't register in her brain until she was pinned on the floor of the Blackhawk by the other DEA agent, and Pierce's gun was pointed at Hawk, who was halfway out of his seat.

"We've got a landing site and will be on the ground in six minutes," the co-pilot said, turning in his seat at the commotion in the back.

Pierce holstered his gun. "Let's all calm down." He rubbed his cheek. "I guess I deserved that. I was out of line." He signaled the agent to release Teal. "But I'll have Agent McNamara handcuff you to your seat if necessary."

The female agent instantly released Teal and helped her up from the hard floor. She returned to her seat, and Hawk leaned to put his mouth close to her ear.

"The Cobra still pursues. He has not caught up to her yet. We have time."

She frowned at him, but he nodded to reassure her.

"You must trust that I know this."

Teal reluctantly buckled back into her safety harness and accepted the headset Pierce held out to her. It'd been knocked off her head when she was wrestled to the floor, and he waited until she had settled it over her ears before speaking into his. "Captain, how's our fuel?"

"We're still good. When they modified this one, they left the extra fuel tanks."

"Good. We'll drop off the dog and Agent McNamara, then head back for the Caprock coordinates I gave you before we picked up our new passengers."

"Ten-four." The big bird dropped down toward the town that had come into view below. "We'll be on the ground in two minutes. The clinic has been notified to expect you."

Teal opened her mouth to protest but wasn't sure what to say. She wanted to be sure Rio got the best care, but every minute they delayed gave Cobra more time to catch up to August. She looked to Hawk for an answer, but the hand on her knee drew her attention to Agent McNamara. Teal's cheek ached from hitting the metal floor when the agent had efficiently taken her down in the blink of an eye, but McNamara had been gentle when she helped Teal back into her seat.

McNamara's brown eyes held Teal's for a few seconds, then softened as her gaze returned to Rio. "I'll make sure they take good care of her. My wife runs a rescue nonprofit, so we usually have a houseful." She brushed her hand across her pants leg. "I'm surprised you haven't noticed the dog hair on my clothes already."

For the first time in days, Teal felt a little of the weight lift from her shoulders. "Thank you. I really—" Her throat tightened around the next words, and she took a few seconds to swallow her fears. "I really need to find August and see that she's okay."

McNamara nodded, then began releasing the buckles on her harness as the Blackhawk touched down and stood to take Rio from Hawk. "Go get Ms. Reese. I'm sure she'll want to know Rio's getting the best care possible."

CHAPTER NINETEEN

Augt felt for a handhold to her right, the rough rock biting into her raw fingertips. She'd once been an avid climber and cursed the Saturdays that she'd declined invitations from friends to instead spend her weekends digging out from under the ever increasing caseload at the office. She found the small indention and curled her fingers into it. She sucked in a breath and hauled herself upward, searching blindly with the toes of her right foot for the place she'd chipped into the rock with her handpick.

Her hiking boots, too thick for climbing, bumped against her legs as they dangled from her belt, and her left foot slipped. She hung from her handholds for a few seconds, her heart beating wildly, then carefully slid her feet along the wall until she found support for both.

August clenched her teeth and waited for the wave of dizziness to pass. If she could reach the crevice thirty feet above her, she could crawl into it and hide for a while. Even if her pursuer tracked her to the cliff, she doubted he had climbing gear with him. He'd have to backtrack and take a different route into the park. By that time, she'd be among people and could summon Pierce Walker. She rested her forehead against the cliff and silently asked the mountain to forgive her desecration of its face and allow her safe passage.

The hawk's cry startled her, and she realized she'd nearly fallen asleep while still clinging to the mountain. Exhaustion and dehydration were as much her enemy now as the evil pursuing her. She looked over her shoulder as the bird circled again. "Hawk, if that's you looking out for me, then I owe you." Reyes's hit man wouldn't have to bother with her if she blundered like that again and fell to her death.

The cliff face to her left was smooth, without a bump or crevice. She unhooked the small pick from her belt, stretched as high as she could, and carefully began to chip away at the rock. Normally she would take time to drive an anchor and hook her climbing harness to it for safety, but a sense of urgency was growing in her gut.

Cobra paused at the mouth of the wide canyon and scanned the landscape before him. A hot breeze ruffled the tufts of wiry grass that covered the prairie, though it provided no respite from the unrelenting heat. Sweat soaked his undershirt so that it clung to him like a second skin, but he didn't mind. He sucked in the smell of sun-baked earth and his own man scent. Oh, how he relished the hunt.

He studied the ground. She'd long ago stopped leaving obvious hints but wasn't taking time to throw him off her trail either. He squatted to examine the imprints in the dirt. He touched the faint spots that dotted the sand. Sweat, spit, water droplets from her canteen? Whatever the moisture, the sun hadn't completely dried it yet. He was close. She'd paused here to rest—something he didn't have to do. He took the case from his pocket again and started to open it when his eye was drawn to movement to his right. He slid the case back into his pocket and smiled at the figure climbing along the sheer rock wall to his right.

This was turning out to be so much fun that he should cut his fee in half. He laughed. But he wouldn't. He might even charge double for the loss of Tito, considering the time it would take for him to break in a new wingman.

❖

Hawk opened his eyes. He was the most Zen person Teal had ever met. She was exhausted, too, but couldn't imagine sleeping when God knew what was happening to August.

He released his safety harness and put his hand on Pierce's shoulder. "Can this thing go any faster?"

Teal had forgotten about the headset and jumped at the sound of his voice in her ear. "What's wrong?"

We need to hurry," Hawk said. "I can't explain now, but he's found her."

Pierce stared at him for a long moment, then spoke into his headset. "Captain, what's our ETA?"

"Their estimated entry point into the canyons is just ahead."

With a jerk of his head, Pierce directed Teal toward the front of the Blackhawk. "When we get close enough, point out the gorge you took. And, Captain, I want you to fly low and as fast as this bird can go."

The pilot grinned at his co-pilot. "This is going to be fun, but you've got to keep an eye on how narrow this gorge gets. I don't want to stick a rotor blade in one of these cliffs."

❖

August thought she'd imagined the ping and explosion of rock near her hand. Then the crack of the high-powered rifle registered in her tired brain. She closed her eyes. Shit. He'd caught up with her, and she was a sitting duck in a shooting gallery. She looked up. The crevice was still ten feet above her.

She searched the rock face for a new handhold. Where was it, damn it. There. An old one probably chiseled by her or one of her friends. She reached for it, only to have the rock just above her hand explode. She jerked her hand away and closed her eyes against the flying shards of rock so quickly, she nearly fell. Laughter followed the crack of the rifle this time.

"Going somewhere, Ms. Reese?"

August ignored the shouted words and curled her fingers into the small hole, found a new foothold, and propelled her weary body another few feet higher. Rock exploded by her head, sharp slivers slicing into the right side of her face. Blood trickled down her brow to mingle with sweat and dirt. It dripped into her eye, and she blinked rapidly to try to clear it.

"I like you right where you are, Ms. Reese. So, next time you reach up, I'm going to shoot your hand. Then I will shoot a foot. Then I think I will let you hang there until the sun begins to set, and I'll shoot your other foot and make a bet with myself as to how long you can hang by one hand." He laughed again. "Sounds like fun, no?"

So, this was it. She hoped Gus would forgive her for being a coward, but she wasn't going to give him the satisfaction of watching her suffer. Should she just let go and fall? That sounded too painful. Tito's Glock was still tucked in the waist of her jeans. She hoped there was a bullet in the chamber because it would take two hands to cock it if there wasn't. One shot to her head would be less painful than banging against the rocks all the way to the bottom.

August closed her eyes. Could she do it? Would she be brave to steal this dirtbag's moment of sick glory? Or a simple coward?

The cry of the hawk sounded close, just above her, and she opened her eyes. The crevice was only about six feet away. A huge black wolf stood there, looking over the edge at her. She blinked. Black, except for one white paw.

She was probably hallucinating. But as she stared into those golden eyes, she knew she wouldn't give up. She reached for the handhold on her right and suddenly spotted one on her left. Bullets pinged around her, and shards of rock knifed into her skin from both sides. She gasped when pain cut through her right thigh, but she kept going. The crevice was only a few feet away now. The wolf was gone, but howls echoed through the canyon. Almost there.

She snugged her left foot into a hole chiseled deep by a previous climber and pushed until her upper body cleared the edge of the crevice. A roll of low thunder started as she flopped onto the ledge, and a bullet whizzed just past her shoulder. If she'd been a second slower, it would have nailed her in the back. She realized the crevice was actually an opening to the park trail that led to the top of the mountain. The thunder grew louder—so loud she could no longer hear the crack of the rifle, but the rocks around her were still exploding as bullets hit them. Another red-hot stab of pain, this time in her right calf. She reached deep for her last small remnant of strength and crawled forward on her forearms to haul her lower body to safety.

Damn it. Pain burned all the way down her right leg, and that pissed her off. God, she hated Reyes. He'd stolen so much from her and had nearly taken her life. A handgun couldn't possibly be accurate at that distance, but the anger that boiled up fueled one last spurt of adrenaline. She grabbed the Glock and crawled to the edge of the crevice. Maybe she'd get off a lucky shot and nail that son of a bitch. She peered cautiously over the edge, down into the canyon, and gasped. A massive herd of bison was flowing into the canyon, a dark mass against the dry prairie grass. Cobra looked over his shoulder, dropped his rifle, and ran. But the bulky physique of buffalo is deceptive. They can gallop up to forty miles an hour, far faster than a man can run. August watched dispassionately as the herd overtook him.

She collapsed on the hard rock and rolled onto her back. The thunder of their hooves was so loud August could literally feel the vibration in the ground. She closed her eyes against the blinding sun. The thunder was fading, but a chorus of wolf howls and a distant whup of copter blades rang in her ears.

CHAPTER TWENTY

August hummed at the soft kiss then the tickle of tongue against her chapped lips. She kept her eyes closed but couldn't stop the slow smile. "I know that tongue from somewhere," she said. "Come snuggle with me, Rio."

"Rio?"

August opened her eyes at the light slap at her arm and indignant response. "Hey. Don't injure the patient."

"It's okay. You're in a hospital. There are plenty of medical personnel here to patch you up," Teal said, climbing onto the bed and into August's outstretched arms. "Besides, four days is long enough." She indicated some papers on the counter next to the bed. "The doctor has signed your dismissal orders, and someone should be here any minute with a wheelchair so I can spring you."

"Thank God. I thought I'd never get that cute blond nurse out of my room last night."

Teal narrowed her eyes. "That's precisely why I'm taking you home. It felt good to actually sleep in a bed last night rather than in that chair over there, but I'll bet that little minx was in here the minute I left to offer a nice sponge bath or to rub lotion all over your body."

August feigned surprise. "She said the lotion was part of my treatment."

Teal, single eyebrow raised, pushed up to stare down at August. "She better not have had her hands on you."

August laughed again. "Not to worry. Your hands are the only ones I want on me." She pulled Teal back down and kissed her, running her tongue along Teal's lips. Teal took her inside and their tongues danced together. August grasped Teal's hand and guided it between her legs as she ended the kiss. "I could use one of those sponge baths right now." She groaned as Teal cupped her and squeezed.

"How about we get you dressed and home? Then you can have a nice hot shower. I promise to wash every inch of you and take care of every need you have." Teal squeezed again.

August stared into those beautiful brown eyes and thought her heart would burst. "I love you," she whispered. "I thought I loved Christine, but what I feel for you is…so much more."

Teal's eyes shone with affection, and she smoothed her fingertips along August's jaw. "I'm so glad," she said softly. "Because you've stolen my heart, and I need to know it's safe with you."

"Always, baby. I'll guard it with my life."

The door swung open, and the cute blond nurse pushed a wheelchair into the room. "They tell me you're leaving today, so I thought you'd like some help with a bath and dressing." She stopped at the sight of Teal cuddled in the bed with August. "Oh, sorry. I should have knocked."

"No problem," Teal said, rising and climbing out of the bed. "Thanks for the chair. I can help her dress, but we're going to wait on the bath until we're home so I can give her a good scrub in the shower."

The nurse swallowed, her eyes going from Teal to settle on August. "I see." She licked her lips. "Well, your paperwork is done. Do you have the doctor's instructions on how to care for your wounds?"

August pointed to the papers on the counter. "Teal talked to the doctor." She sat up and smiled at Teal. "She has everything I need," she said to the nurse without taking her eyes from Teal.

Teal bent to give her a quick kiss, then lifted a small duffel onto the bed. "Right now, I have the clothes you need to get out of here."

The nurse cleared her throat. "Right. Then I'll leave you to it." She raised her hand in a small wave. "I hope the rest of your recovery goes well."

August slid to the edge of the bed and carefully swung her legs over the side. Cobra's last bullet had only grazed her calf, but his earlier shot had gone through the thick muscle of her thigh, narrowly missing bone. Until it healed more, her right leg was encased in a removable splint to keep her from bending it. She'd be on crutches for several more weeks.

"I found some light jogging pants in your closet," Teal said as she pulled the Velcro closures loose on the splint. "I thought they'd be the most comfortable. You can wear the splint over them."

"Okay. Can we go by to see BJ and Pops before we leave?" August asked. Even though BJ's injuries had required more than one surgery on his shoulder wound, she'd been most worried about the pneumonia that settled in Pops's lungs.

"I thought you'd want to. The doctors say Pops can probably go home in couple of days if he continues to improve at the rate he has. It will likely be another week for BJ." Teal exchanged a bra and polo shirt for the hated hospital gown August stripped off.

"Ha. BJ's probably bribed the doctors to get Pops out of his room so he doesn't have to listen to his complaining." She ran a brush through her hair, then handed it to Teal, who was checking the small closet and drawers to make sure they didn't leave anything behind. Teal had taken the half-dozen gifts of flowers and fruit baskets back to the ranch the night before, so only the small duffel was left.

August stood carefully and rotated on her good leg to sit in the wheelchair, then settled the duffel in her lap and carefully laid her crutches across her injured leg that rested on the chair's leg extension. Man, she couldn't wait to see the ranch. "Let's blow this pop stand."

❖

"What the hell are they doing here?" August stared from the backseat of the truck at the collection of sheriff's cars and black DEA SUVs parked next to the bunkhouse.

"I don't know," Teal said, parking in front of the ranch house. "Let me get you inside and I'll go see."

"Oh, no. I expect they're looking for the thumb drives, but they sure as shit better have a warrant." She opened the door at her back and was trying to figure how to slide out when Teal's arms came around her from behind.

"If you don't wait a second, you're going to end up on your back in the dirt. God, you're stubborn." Teal backed her out and held her upright until her injured leg was free and August could gently lower it to the ground.

"Thanks." August hated being so dependent.

"I love having you helpless," Teal said, kissing her quickly before handing over her crutches. "As soon as we take care of whatever's going on over there, I'm going to clean you up and have my way with you since you can't escape."

August tucked the crutches under her armpits and clutched the front of Teal's shirt to draw her into a long, deep kiss. "I think I'm going to need lots of your kind of physical therapy."

Teal broke their kiss and laughed. "So, let's see if we can clear these people out of here."

Tommy spotted them before they were halfway across the compound and jogged over. "August, you've got to stop them. They're getting ready to dig up Pops's garden. He'll have a fit when he gets home and sees it."

Pierce stood in the middle of a dozen deputies, some holding shovels, and pointed to a map grid as he issued assignments to search every inch of the ranch compound. The deputies stepped back to make way for August after she banged a couple of them on the legs with her crutches.

"I hope you have a search warrant," August told Pierce.

He wheeled to face her. "Glad to see you're home. I was going to call you later. Reyes is in custody. After getting statements from your men about what happened here, we've charged him with conspiracy to commit murder. I need those thumb drives, though, to charge him with everything else and put him away for life. Since we both want that, I didn't think I needed a warrant."

"You do if you think you're going to dig up Pops's garden," Teal said. "He'll be the one in jail for murder if you harm one plant that he's lovingly cultivated."

"Look, Ms. Giovanni—"

"No, you listen, Mr. Walker. If you turn over one shovelful of dirt in that garden, I'll make sure the media knows your first concern was evidence and August's life came second."

August rubbed her hand along Teal's back when she stopped talking, and tears filled her eyes. "Look. Before you dig up my entire ranch, why don't we just ask Rio where she hid the thumb drives?" She turned to Tommy, who stood at Teal's side and looked like he wanted to hit Pierce. "Where's Rio?"

"In the bunkhouse. You want me to get her?"

"If she's up to it."

"Yeah. She's limping around pretty good."

Having recovered her composure, Teal was in a stare-down with Pierce when Tommy returned with Rio at his side. The dog yipped and hobbled to greet August, her tail sweeping back and forth as August attempted to squat, then just sat on the ground to accept a good face licking. "Hey, girl. Did you miss me," she crooned to the dog as she hugged her. "I sure missed you. How's your paw?"

When she held out her hand, Rio carefully placed her leg in August's palm. The hair had been shaved away, and a strip of black, dying flesh ran from the top of her foot to half the length of her leg.

"Steroids took care of the swelling after a couple of days, but the vet said she'll have a deep scar where the venom killed the flesh near the bite. He said it'll be best if we leave it open until the dead flesh sloughs off." Tommy held up one of the cones all dogs dread. "She has to wear this, but I took it off so she could welcome you properly."

They all laughed when Rio glanced at the cone and hid her head under August's arm.

"Sorry, girl. Looks like you're stuck with that like I'm stuck with these crutches for a while." She handed them up to Teal, then held her hands up for Pierce and Tommy to lift her to her feet. Once she was standing, she secured the crutches under her arms again. She was already tiring and wanted to save some energy for a shower and a chance to make love to Teal before she had to swallow another pain pill and give in to a nap. She looked down at Rio. "Remember what Pops gave you to hide?"

Rio tilted her head and gave a sharp bark at the sound of Pops's name.

"Go find, Rio."

Another sharp bark and Rio hobbled toward the barn.

August crutched after her, followed by Tommy, Teal, Pierce, and two deputies holding shovels.

Inside the barn, Rio went into the tack room and used her nose to flip up the top of a wood box, then nosed through an assortment of old leg wraps, first-place ribbons, and other memorabilia from August's teen years of rodeo competition and barrel racing. After a few seconds, she sat back with a box of Pops's favorite cigarillos in her mouth.

August laughed and took the box from Rio and gave it to Teal. "Good girl. We won't tell Pops about your hiding place, but this isn't what I'm looking for." She bent low to talk to the dog. "Pops gave you something else to hide, didn't he?"

Rio's tail swished back and forth in a slow arch.

"Go find, Rio."

The others crowded into the tack room scrambled to get out of Rio's way as she limped out and turned toward the back entrance of the barn's wide corridor. Rio sat down outside the garden shed and waited for the procession of people following to catch up.

August's arms ached, her leg throbbed. She had gone from leading the group to bringing up the rear. She sagged between her crutches when she reached Rio.

"This is ridiculous," Pierce said. "This dog is leading us on a wild-goose chase."

Rio looked up at August and barked.

August pointed to the deputy standing nearest the garden shed. "Open the door for her." She looked down at Rio. "Is it in the shed, girl?"

Rio barked but ignored the open door and hobbled a few feet toward the garden before looking back and barking again for August to follow. She wasn't sure she had the energy, but Rio was better than a padlock. She would accept a "find" command only from August or Pops.

August eyed the distance from the shed to the garden. "I need a moment," she confessed to the people around her.

Teal was at her side in an instant, taking August's left crutch and handing it to Tommy, then substituting her body in its place. August closed her eyes as Teal wrapped an arm around her waist and grasped the wrist of the arm August draped across her shoulders. So much better than a crutch. August shifted against her and absorbed her strength. She was about to tell them she thought she could go on, when Hawk drove up in one of the ranch's golf-cart-sized utility vehicles.

"I thought you might need a lift somewhere," he said.

"Remind me to give you a raise," she muttered as Teal helped her into the passenger seat. When she was settled, August gave Teal's hand a squeeze and spoke to Rio. "Go find, girl."

Once again, Rio tucked her hurt paw up close to her body and hopped off so fast the humans had to jog to keep up. Hawk guided the John Deere Gator alongside them.

"I knew it was in the garden," Pierce said as he jogged beside August.

But Rio veered at the edge of the garden and led them to a pile of rotting wood shavings matted together by a green-and-black substance. They all covered their noses and mouths when the wind shifted.

"Whew, that stinks," one deputy said. "What is it?"

Teal's laugh was muffled by her shirt she'd pulled up to cover her nose. "That's my compost pile. Some of it is rotting vegetables scraps from the kitchen, but it's mostly wood shavings and manure from the chicken coop. Pops and I use it for fertilizer in his garden and the flowerbeds."

One of the deputies peeled off from the group, and August could hear him gagging over by the garden.

"If he's going to upchuck, he should do it over here," Hawk said.

Pierce and the other deputy stared at him, and Hawk shrugged. "It makes good compost," he deadpanned.

August shook her head and laughed, but her eyes were on Rio, who pushed her nose into the stinky pile. "Rio, sit." The dog's odor when she'd found them in the canyon made sense now, but there had to be a ton of bacteria in that compost, and Rio didn't need to be digging in it with an open wound. She pointed to the spot Rio had been nosing. "Start digging there," she told the remaining deputy.

Rio backed away while the deputy, who apparently had a stronger stomach, carefully spread shovels of compost from that spot onto the ground in search of Rio's prize. He froze the fourth time he stuck the shovel into the pile, then wiggled the shovel around before extracting it and dumping the spade's contents at Pierce's feet.

Pierce took a pen from his pocket and flicked away the wood chips that clung to the small tin box, then accepted the handkerchief the deputy offered to pick it up and wipe it clean. He opened the box to find the thumb drives tucked neatly inside. "God bless that old man." Rio barked and Pierce laughed. "And one very smart dog."

"Remember our deal," August warned him. "Steve will be the one to open those. He'll do it in your lab with your folks watching, but a lot of people risked their lives to keep that information safe, and I don't want to lose it like your lab lost the information from the original computers."

Pierce held up his hand. "You have my word. We'll fly back to Dallas this afternoon, and I'll call ahead to have an agent pick Steve up. Are you coming back to Dallas any time soon?"

"Not until you tell me to show up to testify in Reyes's trial. Hopefully, it will be the last time I have to step into a courtroom." August reached for Teal's hand. "Ranching was always my real dream, especially now that I've found someone who shares it."

"I know we don't always see eye to eye." Pierce glanced at Teal. "And I've said a few things I regret." Pierce held out his hand to August. "But I want to thank you for everything you've done. I know you gave up a lot—a partner you'd trusted and a law practice you'd spent years building—and it took real courage to come to me when you realized what Luis and Christine were doing."

"Thanks." August shook his hand. "Don't take this the wrong way, but I hope I have to see you only once more—when we lay out the evidence before the court that will break Reyes's organization."

"For now, you need to rest." Teal settled her hand on August's shoulder and gave Pierce a pointed look, then waved Tommy over. "Can you pick up Rio and hold her in the back of the Gator? Hawk, if you guys will get August and Rio to the house, I'll show our guests to their vehicles."

"Yes, ma'am," Hawk said, waiting as Tommy scooped Rio up and held her in his lap as he sat on the small bed of the Gator.

August smiled and looked up at Teal. "Gotta love a woman who takes charge."

Teal kissed her quickly, then led Pierce and the deputies around the bunkhouse to their cars.

August leaned back in her seat and closed her eyes, appreciating that Hawk drove slowly and skirted as many potholes as possible.

"Tommy, you need to scrape these drives tomorrow," Hawk said.

"That'll have to wait a day or two. I'll ask Teal to call for a load or two of fresh gravel to spread," August said. "Maybe they can deliver that tomorrow, but I want Tommy to drive to Amarillo. The doctor said BJ has to stay a while longer, but Pops can come on home. He asked if Tommy could go pick him up."

Hawk parked as close as he could get to the front-porch steps, then hopped out of the Gator to help August with her crutches. She navigated the stairs carefully, then paused on the porch and waited until Tommy set Rio gently on her feet and straightened. She laid her hand on his shoulder and looked him in the eye.

"Hawk said you saved all of them from drowning. I'm in your debt as much as they are."

Tommy's face flushed red, and he stared down at his boots. "I did what I had to do. Hawk was holding BJ up, and I knew Pops was too old to do it."

She pulled him into a hug and whispered into his ear. "Still, you guys are like family to me. And to Teal, too. Thank you." When she released him, his face was an even deeper red.

"I've got some cows to check on if I'm going to be gone most of tomorrow," he said, backing down the steps and whirling to head off to the barn.

Hawk chuckled. "You know he's got a little case of hero worship where you're concerned, don't you?"

She watched the posse of law-enforcement vehicles drive off and pointed at Hawk. "And you, I owe you a big thanks, too."

"I've known BJ since I was a kid. The only way he was going to drown was if I did first."

"I'm not taking about that. I'm talking about in the canyon. The hawk was you, wasn't it?"

He cocked his head, his expression amused. "You believe those stories BJ tells about skin-walkers? Maybe the heat and exhaustion were playing tricks with your mind."

"I don't think so." She hugged him, too. "Thank you."

"You're welcome."

Teal stopped on the steps, and August held her hand out for her to join them but locked gazes with Hawk.

"I had given up. I was too tired to climb another inch," she said. "Then the cry of the hawk made me look up, and I saw The White Paw standing where I needed to be. I remembered Gus telling me a story about the half-wolf with one white paw that befriended a young rancher lost and injured in those mountains."

Hawk nodded. "He and Julio tried to make a pet out of him, but The White Paw had other ideas. He'd come visit but never stayed long because he had a mate in the canyons."

August looked toward the red mountains of Caprock. "Julio swore he saw him again when old Gus died, but it had to be grief or wishful thinking. That old wolf would have had to be forty years old. Maybe it was one of his offspring. Maybe that's what I saw, too."

"Maybe." They both knew it wasn't an offspring. The truth was in Hawk's eyes before he turned and walked down the steps.

August crutched toward the door Teal held open for her, then stopped to call after Hawk. "I forgot to ask Pierce. What happened to the guy chasing me?"

Hawk turned back to face her. "Cobra? The DEA guys had to almost scrape him off the canyon floor. He'd been trampled." He climbed into the Gator and started it.

Trampled? She was sure she'd wished it, imagined it, dreamed it. "Wait." She hobbled to the edge of the porch. "That's not possible, Hawk. You and I both know the park's bison herd is fenced on the south side of the park. There's no way they could have been in that north canyon."

"Did I say it was bison?" One corner of his mouth lifted in a half smile. "Funny thing, the park rangers searched and couldn't find any break in the fence or buffalo running around in the north part of the park when they searched later. They decided it must have been some rancher's longhorns illegally grazing on state property, and those city boys flying the DEA helicopter just thought they were bison."

August watched him drive toward the bunkhouse. "Pretty hard to confuse a longhorn with a buffalo."

❖

August was trembling with fatigue by the time Teal got her inside and stripped of her splint and clothes. She quickly peeled off her own clothes and shouldered under August's arm to help her hop into the walk-in shower. She tried to ignore the feel of August's skin against hers, but her blood quickened all the same at the intimate contact. August's groan as she leaned back under the warm water was a jolt of sensation that shot straight to Teal's core and left her throbbing.

The two days they'd spent on the run and the past four days August had spent in the hospital seemed like an eternity. But August was injured, so Teal pushed down her need to work shampoo into August's hair, then soap a bath cloth while August tilted her head back to rinse. Teal began with her shoulders, scrubbing gently down her back, then stepping around to soap each of her arms. She bit her lip and fought the urge to linger on August's breasts and turgid nipples. She knelt to wash her left leg, then carefully around the wounds on her right.

"Teal." August's voice was tight and urgent.

Teal stood and held the cloth out. Rather than take it, August grasped Teal's hand and guided it to the one place she hadn't yet touched. Teal closed her eyes when August moaned. "I've missed your touch so much."

"Baby, you're hurt."

"I'm hurting, but not where you think." August wrapped a hand behind Teal's neck and drew her close to capture her mouth. August's tongue and mouth tasted of mint toothpaste, but Teal lingered only a moment before breaking the kiss. "Let's finish this in the bed." Teal gasped when August slid her fingers over her swollen clit.

"I need you now," August said. "I'm so close."

Teal wrapped an arm around August to hold her up and matched her stroke for stroke. Pleasure gathered in her groin. "Can't…hold out…much longer." Orgasm caught her mid-breath and August trembled in her arms, then stiffened.

"Teal, baby, oh God, oh." August slumped against her, and Teal held her up for a few long moments.

"The water's getting cold. We need to get you in bed," Teal said, contradicting her words by tightening her arms around August.

"It's okay. I think I heard sizzling a moment ago. Maybe a little cold water will cool us off."

"I don't ever want what's between us to cool." Teal clutched August tighter.

August's laugh rumbled through her chest. "Are you kidding? You thought this sweltering heat was just Texas weather? This heat wave is us, baby. And that's never going to change."

THE END

About the Author

D. Jackson Leigh grew up barefoot and happy, swimming in farm ponds and riding rude ponies in rural south Georgia. Her passion for writing led her to a career in journalism and North Carolina where she edits news at night and writes lesbian romance stories with a bit of Southern humor by day.

She has published nine novels and one collection of short stories with Bold Strokes Books, winning three Golden Crown Literary Society awards in paranormal, romance, and fantasy categories. She also was a finalist in the romance category of the 2014 Lambda Literary Society Awards.

Friend her at facebook.com/d.jackson.leigh, follow her on twitter @djacksonleigh, and check her out at djacksonleigh.com.

Books Available from Bold Strokes Books

18 Months by Samantha Boyette. Alissa Reeves has only had two girlfriends and they've both gone missing. Now it's up to her to find out why. (978-1-62639-804-7)

Arrested Hearts by Holly Stratimore. A reckless cop who hates her life and a health nut who is afraid to die might be a perfect combination for love. (978-1-62639-809-2)

Capturing Jessica by Jane Hardee. Hyperrealist sculptor Michael tries desperately to conceal the love she holds for best friend, Jess, unaware Jess's feelings for her are changing. (978-1-62639-836-8)

Counting to Zero by AJ Quinn. NSA agent Emma Thorpe and computer hacker Paxton James must learn to trust each other as they work to stop a threat clock that's rapidly counting down to zero. (978-1-62639-783-5)

Courageous Love by KC Richardson. Two women fight a devastating disease, and their own demons, while trying to fall in love. (978-1-62639-797-2)

One More Reason to Leave Orlando by Missouri Vaun. Nash Wiley thought a threesome sounded exotic and exciting, but as it turns out the reality of sleeping with two women at the same time is just really complicated. (978-1-62639-703-3E)

Pathogen by Jessica L. Webb. Can Dr. Kate Morrison navigate a deadly virus and the threat of bioterrorism, as well as her new relationship with Sergeant Andy Wyles and her own troubled past? (978-1-62639-833-7)

Rainbow Gap by Lee Lynch. Jaudon Vickers and Berry Garland, polar opposites, dream and love in this tale of lesbian lives set in Central Florida against the tapestry of societal change and the Vietnam War. (978-1-62639-799-6)

Steel and Promise by Alexa Black. Lady Nivrai's cruel desires and modified body make most of the galaxy fear her, but courtesan Cailyn Derys soon discovers the real monsters are the ones without the claws. (978-1-62639-805-4)

Swelter by D. Jackson Leigh. Teal Giovanni's mistake shines an unwanted spotlight on a small Texas ranch where August Reese is secluded until she can testify against a powerful drug kingpin. (978-1-62639-795-8)

Without Justice by Carsen Taite. Cade Kelly and Emily Sinclair must battle each other in the pursuit of justice, but can they fight their undeniable attraction outside the walls of the courtroom? (978-1-62639-560-2)

21 Questions by Mason Dixon. To find love, start by asking the right questions. (978-1-62639-724-8)

A Palette for Love by Charlotte Greene. When newly minted Ph.D. Chloé Devereaux returns to New Orleans, she doesn't expect her new job, and her powerful employer—Amelia Winters—to be so appealing. (978-1-62639-758-3)

By the Dark of Her Eyes by Cameron MacElvee. When Brenna Taylor inherits a decrepit property haunted by tormented ghosts, Alejandra Santana must not only restore Brenna's house and property but also save her soul. (978-1-62639-834-4)

Cash Braddock by Ashley Bartlett. Cash Braddock just wants to hang with her cat, fall in love, and deal drugs. What's the problem with that? (978-1-62639-706-4)

Death by Cocktail Straw by Missouri Vaun. She just wanted to meet girls, but an outing at the local lesbian bar goes comically off the rails, landing Nash Wiley and her best pal in the ER. (978-1-62639-702-6)

Gravity by Juliann Rich. How can Ellie Engebretsen, Olympic ski jumping hopeful with her eye on the gold, soar through the air when all she feels like doing is falling hard for Kate Moreau, her greatest competitor and the girl of her dreams? (978-1-62639-483-4)

Lone Ranger by VK Powell. Reporter Emma Ferguson stirs up a thirty-year-old mystery that threatens Park Ranger Carter West's family and jeopardizes any hope for a relationship between the two women. (978-1-62639-767-5)

Love on Call by Radclyffe. Ex-Army medic Glenn Archer and recent LA transplant Mariana Mateo fight their mutual desire in the face of past losses as they work together in the Rivers Community Hospital ER. (978-1-62639-843-6)

Never Enough by Robyn Nyx. Can two women put aside their pasts to find love before it's too late? (978-1-62639-629-6)

Two Souls by Kathleen Knowles. Can love blossom in the wake of tragedy? (978-1-62639-641-8)

Camp Rewind by Meghan O'Brien. A summer camp for grown-ups becomes the site of an unlikely romance between a shy, introverted divorcee and one of the Internet's most infamous cultural critics—who attends undercover. (978-1-62639-793-4)

Cross Purposes by Gina L. Dartt. In pursuit of a lost Acadian treasure, three women must not only work out the clues, but also the complicated tangle of emotion and attraction developing between them. (978-1-62639-713-2)

Imperfect Truth by C.A. Popovich. Can an imperfect truth stand in the way of love? (978-1-62639-787-3)

Life in Death by M. Ullrich. Sometimes the devastating end is your only chance for a new beginning. (978-1-62639-773-6)

Love on Liberty by MJ Williamz. Hearts collide when politics clash. (978-1-62639-639-5)

Serious Potential by Maggie Cummings. Pro golfer Tracy Allen plans to forget her ex during a visit to Bay West, a lesbian condo community in NYC, but when she meets Dr. Jennifer Betsy, she gets more than she bargained for. (978-1-62639-633-3)

Smoldering Desires by C.E. Knipes. Evan McGarrity has found the man of his dreams in Sebastian Tantalos. When an old boyfriend from Sebastian's past enters the picture, Evan must fight for the man he loves. (978-1-62639-714-9)

Taste by Kris Bryant. Accomplished chef Taryn has walked away from her promising career in the city's top restaurant to devote her life to her five-year-old daughter and is content until Ki Blake comes along. (978-1-62639-718-7)

The Second Wave by Jean Copeland. Can star-crossed lovers have a second chance after decades apart, or does the love of a lifetime only happen once? (978-1-62639-830-6)

Valley of Fire by Missouri Vaun. Taken captive in a desert outpost after their small aircraft is hijacked, Ava and her captivating passenger discover things about each other and themselves that will change them both forever. (978-1-62639-496-4)